AN UNCHARTED DREAM

ADVENTUROUS HEARTS
BOOK THREE

ABBEY DOWNEY

WILD HEART
BOOKS

Cover design by: Carpe Librum Book Design

ISBN: 978-1-963212-33-4

To the girls who, like me, dreamed of being Indiana Jones one day. Maybe you didn't get that adventure in the jungle, desert, or ancient temple, but your life can still be filled with exploration and meaning.

CHAPTER 1

JANUARY 1910
MILWAUKEE, WI

*L*eonora Thornton closed the doors of the Milwaukee Public Library behind her, shutting out the cold winter air and sounds from the busy street. She paused just inside, giving herself a moment to soak in her favorite place. There was nothing as wonderful as stepping into a library, with the smell of books permeating the air and the potential of discovering some wonderful new knowledge waiting on every shelf.

Looking upward at the domed rotunda that towered above the lobby, Leonora frowned. Could she call herself an adventurer if her favorite thing was the library? Shouldn't it be discovering a new place, trying exotic food, or mastering a difficult skill?

Rather than stand right in the middle of the lobby thinking about the qualities of an explorer that she seemed to lack, Leonora gathered herself and strode across the marble floor to a coat room, which was tucked into an alcove created by massive marble columns. On the way, she waved to the librarian directing guests. "Good evening, Miss Draper. It looks like a nice turnout tonight."

Miss Draper was one of Leonora's favorites among the library staff. The diminutive older woman clasped both hands together in front of her plain gray skirt while smiling at Leonora. "I think so. I'm glad people are interested in this explorer's lecture. We never know for sure if a topic will be of interest to patrons or not. Are you here to attend, as well?"

"Yes, and some of the club members are meeting me."

Miss Draper was interrupted by a couple asking where to go, so Leonora continued into the coat room. As she removed her heavy wool coat and hung it on a hook, her hand grazed the pocket, a papery crinkle reminding her of the letter she'd slid inside when Mother handed it to her as she left the house. She had a few minutes before the lecture was scheduled to begin, so she reached into the pocket and tugged the letter out. It bore no address, only her name written across the front in unfamiliar handwriting. Mother hadn't known who it was from when Leonora asked. She'd only said it was sitting on the front step when she came home from a ladies' meeting at the church.

Leonora tore open the envelope and slid out the single page. More of the same neat, flowing script filled it. She skimmed the contents, then went back to read it a second time when the startling words refused to settle in her mind.

Dear Miss Thornton,

As someone who followed your father's illustrious career in world exploration, I send you my deepest condolences on the tragedy of his death. Even though it has been five years now since that terrible day, you should know that many men were inspired by his bravery, intelligence, and commitment to his work.

It truly is a shame that no one has taken the time to further investigate the reports of what happened that night in Peru. I had hoped you, as the most enterprising of his offspring, might take up the cause and discover the truth, which I believe has been hidden for nefarious reasons.

However, I'm sure that a young woman has different priorities than a man like your father, who dedicated himself to exploring the world and making historic discoveries. Certainly, you must be setting your mind toward marriage and children, rather than even considering something so perilous as a journey into the wild jungle. Your father always hoped one of his children would continue his work, should anything happen to him, but isn't that something all fathers want, regardless of how unrealistic it might be?

All that to say, you have every reason to be very proud of your father and the sacrifices he made for the sake of furthering our understanding of history. Even if the accident that caused his loss was contrived, he was a good man and remains an example all explorers should strive to emulate.

Signed,

An Observer

Leonora glanced over her shoulder at the coatroom and through the open door into the busy lobby, as if the anonymous author of the letter might be watching her read it right then. Emotions raced through her—pride in the legacy her dear papa had left for his fellow explorers, but also confusion.

The reports about Papa's death on a river in Peru had been quite clear. Father had been a faithful member of the Explorers Club, attending events at their headquarters in New York City as often as he was able, as many of the scattered members did. Because of that and their financial backing for the expedition, the club had sent representatives to gather information from the crew and locals and then gave Mother a copy of their findings. In the night, the crew's boat had hit an obstacle under the muddy water. Papa and a crew member, Hugh Randall, who were keeping watch together, had been thrown from the boat and lost to the river. No one had questioned those reports in the five years since. Why would someone come forward now hinting that there might be more to the story?

And why did the author seem disappointed in Leonora for not questioning what they'd been told? She'd only been twenty at the time and deep in her college studies. She'd dropped her classes and returned home to be with her mother after word came of the accident, but she'd never had cause to doubt what had happened to him.

Shuffling feet and approaching voices broke into Leonora's thoughts. She stuffed the letter back into the pocket and spun around as two of her friends, twin sisters Charlotte and Alice Bauer, stepped into the coatroom. The sisters were deep in conversation, with Charlotte's hands flying around in animated gestures while Alice remained more reserved. Their matching blond hair was the extent of their similarities. Where Alice stood tall and slim, her brown eyes taking things in before she spoke, Charlotte's blue eyes usually flashed with a quick wit that made her seem more impressive than her diminutive stature would indicate.

Alice spotted Leonora first, flapping one hand at her sister to stop the endless flow of opinions. "Good evening, Leonora. Look, we almost made it to an event before you for the first time ever."

Charlotte huffed as she removed her velvet cape. "Our consistent lateness isn't my fault. You don't remind me to get ready soon enough, and then we don't leave the house on time."

Leonora smothered the laugh the sisters' antics almost brought out of her. "I'm quite proud of you both. Let's hurry so we can find seats with a good view of the stage."

Despite the strange letter and the questions it raised, she enjoyed the company of these women...and everyone in the Exploration Society, for that matter. The evening's outing for members of her club to attend the lecture was just what she needed to keep her thoughts from spiraling.

Leading the way toward the lecture room, Leonora couldn't help glancing toward the lobby door. She would feel better once Marcus arrived. She could use the calming presence of her best friend. He was one of the few constants in her life since Papa's death and all the changes that had come along with her older siblings starting their own families. Through everything, Marcus was steadfast.

Inside the lecture room, Charlotte and Alice chose a row and went in single file, pushing down the folding seats of two wooden chairs far enough in to leave space for Leonora and Marcus at the end. Over the next ten minutes, several of the other club members arrived—their secretary, Effie Alder, and one of the few male members, Edwin Howard. Once Marcus got there, that would likely be all of the Exploration Society members who would attend. Her entire club wasn't big enough to fill half of the row of seats on a good day, but numbers weren't the most important thing.

Leonora prided herself on having begun the Exploration Society after learning it wasn't only her lack of field experience that would keep her from joining the Explorers Club as her father had. The prestigious organization was also only open to men. If her father had known that, he no doubt would have withdrawn his membership. Papa had always encouraged her dreams of going on expeditions like he did, supporting her hopes of discovering significant sites and digging up artifacts that could change their knowledge of history while spreading the truth of the gospel in the process. He'd called her desire a noble goal.

His belief that anyone could participate in discovery was what led her to start this club. It might be small, but it included anyone who wanted to join, no matter their gender, race, or level of experience. Papa would have loved it.

But did her members? After three years of running the club, Leonora was beginning to sense that they wouldn't be happy much longer with lectures and hikes and the occasional camping trip or museum visit. Enough time had been spent on organizing the new group. They wanted to move toward achieving the purpose she'd sold them on when they joined— exploration, discovery, and connecting with new cultures and experiences.

The grandiose words sounded wonderful in her mind, but the prospect of living them out kept Leonora awake at night. As much as she longed to live up to Papa's legacy, she'd never brought herself to so much as step foot outside Wisconsin except for when she and Mother took her sister, Cassia, to Chicago to complete her trousseau before her wedding. Despite all the plans Leonora had dreamed up over the years, Papa's death had forced her to confront the reality of the risks that were inherent to such expeditions. Hiking and camping were one thing. Leaving everything she knew for months on end and possibly risking her life and those of her crew were quite another.

The time was coming soon when the club would have to do more. But when it did, would Leonora be strong enough to lead them into the unknown?

~

A spray of chilly raindrops pelted Marcus Turner's face, giving him yet another reason to hurry down Grand Avenue. The first reason was the expectation of seeing Leonora's joyful expression when he walked into the lecture. Few things would drive Marcus to hurry toward a presentation on a faraway place he had no interest in, but the prospect of pleasing Leonora Thornton did the trick.

Thankfully, the sprawling public library building came into

view before the sky opened up and drenched him completely. Marcus hadn't paid enough attention to the weather when he decided to walk the five blocks from the bank to the meeting, or he might have caught an electric streetcar instead. The habit of saving money wherever possible had been formed out of necessity, though, so he would likely have chosen to walk, anyway.

Inside the hushed lobby, Marcus wiped raindrops off his glasses before glancing at his pocket watch. Five minutes until the start time. He went straight to the coatroom to hang up his overcoat, dodging several people who were coming out of the open doorway as he headed in. But the hooks around the room were already crowded with coats and wraps, leaving no space open.

No matter. Marcus was familiar enough with the library that he knew there was more than one place to hang coats. He made his way down a narrow hallway at the far end of the lobby, toward the back of the lecture room. There was another coat rack there, and sure enough, only two garments hung there.

After removing his overcoat and arranging it on a wooden hanger, Marcus smoothed his hair and straightened the vest and jacket that had gotten a bit rumpled while he hunched over loan applications at the bank that day. Once he felt presentable, Marcus glanced at his watch again. Two minutes to find Leonora.

He let out a slow breath and turned to head back toward the lobby. However, a booming voice echoing from around the corner brought him to a halt. "I most certainly will not give in to these types of demands, madam. You didn't complete the work I asked for. Therefore, I'm not beholden to pay you a cent."

Peeking around the corner, Marcus found the source of the angry words. A lanky, almost gaunt man about fifteen years Marcus's senior towered over a ragged older woman. The man wore a sneer along with his tattered brown suit and the red handkerchief tucked into his collar.

"Please, I need that money. And I tried to do what you asked —truly, I did. I can't help that I didn't do it as well as you wanted. Please, pay me for the time I spent trying." The woman's slumped shoulders and pitiful voice signaled she was likely about to burst into tears.

But the man crossed his arms over his chest, looking entirely unmoved. "I think not. I've secured another source that suits my needs better. Now I need to go, or I'll be late. Please remove yourself from this institution before you cause a scene."

The woman let out a sound that was nearly a wail. Even if he didn't know what was going on between the two, Marcus couldn't let the man berate that poor woman. He took a step out into the side hall.

But then he stopped. It wasn't his place to interfere. What if that man had a legitimate reason to be upset?

Still, cruelty in the face of her obvious distress wasn't necessary. Marcus started toward them again, but he was too late. A librarian stepped through the door at the end of the hall and gestured the man through, to the area behind the lecture hall stage. After a whispered conversation with him, the librarian turned to the woman and gently tugged her toward a different door that led outside through the back of the building.

"Wait, Miss Draper," Marcus called to the librarian, finally breaking out of his indecision and hurrying in their direction. "I saw a bit of what was going on. Can I help in any way?"

Miss Draper turned toward him while pulling the back door shut behind the other woman. "I'm certain you can't. It was a minor dispute, that's all. You should get into the lecture hall before you miss the opening. Miss Thornton is already waiting."

Everything within Marcus screamed to do something about what seemed to be more of an injustice than a minor dispute.

But she was right. The lecture was about to begin. Plus, Miss Draper was a kind woman and seemed to know more about the situation than Marcus did. She wouldn't have sent the other lady away if something was wrong.

Doing his best to put the matter behind him, Marcus made his way back to the lecture hall and paused in the doorway, scanning the room for the one person he always wanted to see most, his spirits lifting when he caught a glimpse of wispy golden curls caught up in a loose pompadour. There was Leonora, with some of the club members seated on her right while the seat on her left was open—saved for him, he felt confident in assuming.

As he approached, Marcus got a better look at her, the mere sight like a breath of fresh spring air after a long winter. The Thorntons didn't have a great deal of money, but with four women in the family, they had plenty of clothing to swap, so he was sometimes surprised by her wearing a new dress. Tonight, she'd donned a gauzy black gown that had flowers and stripes embroidered in black across the top, flowing straight from her waist into a simpler skirt with the pattern repeated on a flounce at the hem. Now and then, one of the tiny gems sewn onto the top would catch the light from the ceiling fixtures, almost matching the sparkle in her eyes.

She was by far the most beautiful woman in the room.

But then, he'd known that from the first moment he'd seen her in her father's study—a gangly girl who already, at the age of seven, had the most enchanting hazel eyes. He could still feel the way the world had frozen around him as their fathers' voices faded into the background. All the information about Mr. Thornton's extensive map collection, which nine-year-old Marcus had been quite excited about on the way over, went unheeded as he stared at the perfect vision before him.

Until she caught him gawking, that was, and arched one delicate eyebrow, lips pursed. But she hadn't been able to hold the faux haughtiness long, dissolving into giggles before Marcus could even begin to blush. She had immediately latched onto Marcus, prattling on about anything and everything that came to her mind while their fathers pored over the old maps. And they'd been friends ever since.

A smile came more easily to his lips than it had all week, and when Leonora turned her attention from the Bauers and noticed Marcus taking the seat next to her, the way her face brightened made everything and everyone else fade away. They might as well have been sitting in an empty room. Her hazel eyes crinkled around the corners, thanks to the cheerful grin she sent his way while one slim, graceful hand rose to smooth back tendrils of hair from her forehead. Marcus could finally release the breath he'd held most of the way there. He wasn't late. He hadn't disappointed her.

He might take second place to her desire to explore the world, but at least for tonight, his presence was enough to make her smile.

"Good evening, Leonora. You look lovely."

She beamed. "Thank you. I'm so glad you made it. The librarian who organized this lecture told me this Mr. Flemming is a marvelous speaker. And I'm desperate to learn if his experience intersects with what Papa was working on. He's been to South America, after all, and from the description of his lecture, he might have been to southern Peru, just where Papa was when..."

Marcus's stomach clenched when Leonora's voice trailed off. She hadn't been the same since her beloved father died. She still talked about exploration and all the places she wanted to travel to, and Marcus fully believed that when the opportunity arose, she would go. But she'd quit pursuing a degree in anthropology and instead devoted her time to her mother and siblings, as well as to ministries at her church, even teaching a class for immigrants wanting to learn English. All good things, of course. But clearly, the tragedy had left a bigger impact on her than she wanted anyone to know.

Had it changed her dedication to remaining single? For most of the years Marcus knew her before her father's death, Leonora had staunchly declared she wouldn't consider any courtship until she'd been on several expeditions. Her siblings had often teased her about it, but Marcus had always tried to avoid the subject. Once Leonora set her mind to something, she followed through. He had no hope of changing her opinion, no matter how badly he might have wanted to all these years.

The room began to quiet as one of the librarians walked out onto the low stage and crossed to the podium in the middle. She waited for the final conversations to die down before addressing the room with a gracious smile. "Welcome, seekers of knowledge and those interested in discovering more about our vast world. I'm so very honored to present to you Mr. Vernon Flemming, renowned world explorer and our guest speaker for tonight."

While the polite applause filled the room, Marcus closed his eyes for a moment to keep from letting irritation show on his face. Such grandiose pretension wasn't something he preferred, although he encountered enough of it at Mother's society events that he should be more capable of controlling himself by now. Acting superior to others was a common trait amongst her social group, but it always hit him the wrong way.

He opened his eyes in time to see the lauded explorer enter from behind the stage. But the sight before him did nothing to help clear Marcus's frustration because it was none other than the angry man from the hallway. Now he wished more than ever that he'd confronted the man about his behavior. A renowned explorer shouldn't go around shouting at women or refusing to pay for whatever service she'd tried to render.

The man on the stage accepted the librarian's introduction with a dramatic bow. "Thank you, madam." Then he turned to the crowd. "I'm honored to stand in front of you tonight and share about the wonders I've witnessed on my travels, as well as the exciting venture I'm planning next."

Marcus had expected coarse, cruel words like the ones he'd overheard. Instead, Mr. Flemming spoke with a cultured, smooth voice that had almost every person in the room captivated in moments. It reminded Marcus far too much of another man he'd known once, one whose personality could turn in an instant. The horrible similarity left him almost breathless— because sometimes the people who appeared most reputable and trustworthy were the ones who most needed to be watched out for.

CHAPTER 2

"*L*adies and gentlemen, some of you may have heard of Vitcos, the lost capital of the Incan empire. Well, I'm here to show you not only proof of its existence but also to tell my own story of discovery, one that will confirm in your mind that we are one expedition away from finding it."

Leonora had to stop herself from scooting forward to the edge of her seat. This was exactly what she'd hoped the explorer would be covering in his lecture. It was the same mission her papa had been pursuing on his last journey to southern Peru—the search for the last Incan capital, which had been lost to time and the encroaching jungle. Would she one day be strong enough to follow in Papa's footsteps—perhaps even to complete his goal and find the city?

As a younger girl, it had seemed inevitable to Leonora that she would. But now, after her life had taken a turn for the mundane, she often doubted that God intended for her to accomplish anything at all, much less something so historically significant.

Mr. Flemming listed some of his qualifications, including several expeditions to Africa and South America that Leonora longed to learn more about. Then he waved at the waiting librarian, who rushed to turn off some of the lights and then to start the magic lantern projector that sat on a stand in front of the stage, aimed at a section of blank wall to the left. The machine began to whir, and the first image appeared on the wall, a section of a map that looked ever so familiar to Leonora. She couldn't help gasping, "The Urubamba River."

She glanced at Marcus, knowing he would understand the significance of that location, the river on which her father had been lost. But instead of seeking to comfort her, he was scowling at the explorer on the stage. Leonora followed his gaze to find Mr. Flemming looking right at her. Most likely, the light emanating from the sides of the projector illuminated only a few faces, and hers was one of them. He had no reason to pick her out of the crowd otherwise. But once she realized Mr. Flemming was watching her, she couldn't stop peeking back at him regularly to see if he still was.

Doing her best to focus on the lecture, Leonora returned her attention to the images being projected onto the wall. After the map, there were several photographs of dense jungle with rocks poking through here and there that could very well have been formed by human hands, but the quality of the photography made it difficult to tell.

The explorer launched into an explanation of what the audience was seeing. "These photographs were given to me by an acquaintance, who stumbled across the ruins while returning from a long and arduous exploration. He recorded everything meticulously, intending to return, but unfortunately decided not to venture back to the wilds of the Peruvian jungle. Luckily for me, though, he passed on all his research, including a very detailed map revealing the locations of several potential Incan cities."

At first, it seemed odd for an explorer to simply abandon his work if there were sites he knew could be found again and explored. But Leonora knew as well as anyone that sometimes life didn't go the way one expected, and those sudden turns could easily derail everything one had hoped to accomplish. Who knew what might have occurred in that man's life to change the course of his plans?

Mr. Flemming continued, pointing out features in the photographs that made a convincing argument in favor of the site being worth an archeological expedition. He spoke with the conviction and passion of a man who knew what he was doing, who had seen and experienced things Leonora could only dream of. When the lights were once again turned on, the fascinated expressions around her proved that Leonora wasn't the only one now swayed to belief by Mr. Flemming's compelling lecture.

As the librarian ended the event and the explorer left the stage by way of a set of stairs on the side so he could talk with attendees, the audience began rising from their seats. But instead of following most of the crowd from the hall, Leonora held back in the aisle. Her friends formed a tight circle with her, gushing over the details of the lecture, but she was distracted by tracking Mr. Flemming's progress as he made his way through the guests vying for his attention.

Marcus cupped Leonora's elbow in his hand and leaned close to her ear. "Why don't we find a quieter spot to discuss the lecture? The lobby is sure to be less crowded."

There was quite a crush of people in the aisle waiting to talk to Mr. Flemming. But Leonora hesitated. If she was honest, she would admit that she hoped the explorer would somehow notice her amongst the other guests and come speak to her. That was silly, of course. He didn't know her from anyone, and there were so many people wanting his attention. She started to agree with Marcus's suggestion.

Then, before she quite knew how it happened, Mr. Flemming walked through the group of men standing nearby and stopped right in front of Leonora. His gaze swept her companions, then returned to her. "It's a pleasure to see so many interested ladies in the crowd tonight. May I have the honor of learning your names?"

His deep voice resonated in Leonora's chest. What amazing wonders those pale gray eyes must have seen on his travels. Leonora nodded, struck enough by his confident, worldly demeanor that she forgot for a moment that she had to speak in order to make introductions. "Oh, uh, yes. This is Miss Alice Bauer, Miss Charlotte Bauer, Mrs. Effie Adler, and Mr. Edwin Howard." Gesturing to her side, Leonora took a half step to include Marcus. "This is Marcus Turner. And I'm Leonora Thornton. We're all members of the Milwaukee Exploration Society."

One bushy eyebrow had quirked upward when Mr. Flemming heard her name. "How delightful to meet you all. Miss Thornton, you say? Are you related to Henry Thornton?"

Leonora's heart fluttered. "Yes. He was my father."

A wide smile split Mr. Flemming's thin face. "What luck. It's such an unexpected delight to meet Henry Thornton's daughter. His work in Peru inspired my interest in the area. While I would have loved to meet the man himself, meeting you is the next best thing."

A swell of pride rose in Leonora's chest, though it was accompanied by discomfort. The questions raised by that dratted letter swirled in Leonora's mind, obscuring her usual joy in discussing her father's renown. "Thank you, Mr. Flemming. This was an excellent presentation. We were all quite taken with the information about your upcoming expedition."

A choked cough from behind her almost made Leonora turn to check on Marcus, but then Mr. Flemming swept one hand theatrically to his side. "I'm glad to hear it. Raising enough funds and putting together a team qualified to uncover a site that's likely large and significant is an overwhelming task at times. But it's worth every penny if we can add to our understanding of history—that's what I always say."

Now a soft snort came from Marcus's direction. Leonora glanced over her shoulder at him. Had he found something funny about that impassioned statement? But Marcus didn't look at all amused. In fact, with his lips pinched tight and eyebrows drawn together, he looked almost...angry.

Before she could unravel the mystery of why, Charlotte leaned forward across Mr. Howard to address Mr. Flemming. "I was so curious during your lecture that I must ask—what distinguishes manmade stone from something natural? How would anyone know from just looking at it that those rocks in your photographs are signs of human activity?"

"Uh, well, of course there's the..." Mr. Flemming frowned and rubbed his chin. Why the hesitation, when he'd expressed himself with absolute clarity on stage? Finally, he cleared his throat and began again. "There are always signs. It's a matter of practice to spot them, that's all. Takes years of experience."

"Now, that's not what I've learned. It only takes looking for tool marks, straight edges, and angles that don't form naturally, that sort of thing." Marcus's deep voice from behind Leonora was calm and steady, but there was an edge to it that Leonora couldn't miss. Did the others hear it too? Or did she just know him well enough to catch details like that?

Mr. Flemming once again pulled her attention away from Marcus. "I apologize for cutting this conversation short, Miss Thornton, but more guests are waiting to speak to me. I hate to waste this fortuitous meeting, though. Would we be able to speak again sometime? I'd love to tell you more about this site that is a common passion between us."

Nodding before he even finished speaking, Leonora attempted to respond without her delight spilling out. "Yes, of course, that could be arranged. You would be most welcome to join the Exploration Society for a ski outing next weekend, if you'll be in town that long."

Mr. Flemming took her hand in both of his. His skin was clammy and his touch not at all appealing, but she would not disgrace her father by pulling away and seeming rude. The explorer leaned toward her with that wide grin again. "It would be an honor, to be sure."

After looking her over for far too long, Mr. Flemming released Leonora's hand and pulled a pencil and calling card from his jacket pocket. He wrote out something on the back of the card and handed it to Leonora. "Please send word of the arrangements to the Hammond Hotel. I look forward to seeing you again, Miss Thornton."

It took Leonora a moment to make out the address for the hotel that he'd written in scrawling, messy handwriting. By the time she'd looked back up, he'd whirled away to greet another group of attendees waiting nearby. Leonora slid her hand along the folds of her skirt to wipe off the dampness that remained from his touch. Her elbow brushed Marcus's arm when she scrubbed a little too hard, reminding her of his steadfast presence. Where Mr. Flemming left her feeling unsettled, Marcus brought peace to her world.

But what had made Marcus so irritated during the lecture? How would he respond if she told him about the letter in her coat pocket?

❧

*T*his was *not* what Marcus had hoped for in the evening. First, the scene in the hall. Then as Mr. Flemming spouted his arrogant posturing from the stage, his gaze rested on Leonora far more often than it needed to. In fact, it was enough to be downright inappropriate. Improper. Unacceptable. Why he'd picked her out of the crowd, Marcus could only guess. Although, he probably would have done the same.

And now Marcus couldn't dispel his unease. Mr. Flemming was too much like another man who had brought disaster to Marcus's family—full of pride in himself despite his limited accomplishments. Flemming clearly possessed the same selfish, exploitive tendencies. Throughout the lecture, his crew had hardly been mentioned while he claimed the glory. The fact that almost everything this explorer might have done was the result of teamwork never crossed his mind.

Why had Mr. Flemming focused his attention on Leonora? Marcus would not stand for such a swindler to hurt her.

Still wrapped up in worry, Marcus followed the others to the coatroom. He held Leonora's coat by the shoulders to help her shrug it on while they said goodbye to their friends. Once they'd departed, he led Leonora to the back hallway so he could get his own coat before accompanying her to the streetcar stop that would take her home, as he often did after club meetings or outings.

As they walked down the much quieter back hall, Marcus couldn't keep his words inside any longer. They'd been burning in the back of his throat, demanding to be released. "Leonora, what were you thinking asking that charlatan to go skiing with the club? I can't believe you could have taken any of his nonsense seriously."

The shock that widened her eyes hit Marcus square in the face, sharp enough to sting like icy snow hitting him on a cold wind. He hadn't intended to use such a harsh tone. "Please don't speak to me like that, Marcus. I don't know why you're so angry, but asking an accomplished explorer to join us isn't nonsense. He does seem a bit arrogant, but he's been places we haven't. What's wrong with wanting to learn more from someone who has so much experience and a solid lead for his next expedition?"

Coming to an abrupt halt in the middle of the hall, Marcus turned to face her. He tried to speak more calmly, even with the tightness in his chest building. "But does he? How do you know those photographs are real? Or that he didn't steal them from that explorer he mentioned? He couldn't even tell us basic ways to distinguish man-made stone structures. I don't trust him."

The gray and green mixed in Leonora's hazel eyes turned stormy. "What makes you think he's being untruthful? I didn't see anything amiss. The library wouldn't have invited him to speak if he was, as you put it, a charlatan."

She wouldn't feel that way if she knew all that Marcus knew. He couldn't reveal his past experiences to her, but perhaps she would understand if he explained what he'd seen earlier. Marcus gestured toward the other hall that split off near where they were standing. "He's not a good man. Before the lecture, I saw him mistreating a woman in the hallway, just down there."

"Mistreating a woman? What do you mean?"

"She was begging him to pay her for some sort of work she'd done, and he refused. With a great deal of cruelty. It was a terrible scene to witness, and you wouldn't trust him, either, if you had."

Leonora drew back a bit, her brow furrowed as if she was trying to solve a puzzle. "That seems out of character, don't you think? He was so polite and polished. Perhaps he was nervous about speaking, or worried about it not going well. His next expedition depends on funds raised from his speaking engagements, and he said himself that it's a weighty task. That kind of pressure can make a person respond harshly. I don't condone it, of course, but we can't judge his authenticity based on one moment. We don't even know the whole story."

Marcus crossed his arms. If only he was more eloquent so perhaps he could say something that would make her see how serious this was. "Please take my word for it that that man isn't genuine. I'm trying to protect you and the club, Leonora."

"I'll take your concern into account. But I've already asked him to go skiing with us. I can't uninvite him now."

Laughter drifting down the hall from the lobby reminded Marcus that the evening was growing quite late, and the library would soon close. He started walking toward the coat rack again, relieved when Leonora followed. Marcus gathered his thoughts while removing his coat from the hanger and sliding it up his arms. He hated being at odds with Leonora. Perhaps he had misinterpreted what he'd seen before the lecture. Couldn't there be other reasons for it than the conclusion he'd jumped to—that Mr. Flemming was the same sort of con man who had destroyed Marcus's family?

Glancing at Leonora while he settled his hat in place and adjusted his glasses, Marcus was troubled by the tiny groove still marring her forehead. It was most likely unremarkable to anyone else, but he'd noticed everything about Leonora Thornton since he was nine years old, when their fathers bonded over a shared love of cartography. Over the years, he'd learned every mannerism, every habit, every strength she possessed, and even her one or two weaknesses. And knowing he was the reason for that wrinkle that indicated she was still upset caused every muscle in his body to clench.

Before they returned to the lobby where others would be leaving for the night, he rested his hands on her upper arms. Just for a moment. "Of course, you can't uninvite him. You would never be that rude. Maybe he won't be so unpleasant once we're outside in the elements, doing something active. Maybe the overconfidence is a persona he puts on for the stage."

Instantly relaxing, Leonora giggled. "When you put it that way, I can just imagine him pulling that smooth arrogance off like a mask."

The glow in her eyes set everything back to rights in Marcus's world. Well, almost everything. His demanding family and unwanted responsibilities were something that simply couldn't be fixed. But having Leonora at his side made those things infinitely more tolerable.

When he held out his arm and Leonora wrapped hers around it without hesitation, Marcus's heart swelled painfully. Maybe he couldn't go on the adventures she intended to have one day. Maybe the promises he'd made to his family made it impossible for him to give in to the deeper-than-friendship feelings that often threatened to spill over. But he *could* be a good friend to her.

Even if that was all he ever got to be.

CHAPTER 3

*A*rriving home after getting Leonora safely on board the streetcar, Marcus steeled himself with a few deep breaths before opening the door to the imposing house where he lived with his mother and older brother, Eli. Quite frankly, Marcus hated the house. Pale brick covered the three-story structure, which was adorned with far too many stone columns, some of them even clustered in groups of three or four. Two porches and a balcony existed only to make the house appear more impressive from the street. His family never used them for anything.

The one thing Marcus liked about the exterior was how the bricks framing all the tall windows had been curved to form arches at the top. That softened the structure somewhat. But as soon as he walked inside, any beauty was forgotten. It was cold, dark, cluttered, and far too large for the three of them. The house had been constructed entirely to impress others, with no consideration for the comfort of the family living there.

But Mother loved living in a house that her society friends envied. And spoiled Eli wouldn't know what to do with himself in a modest home like the Thorntons maintained while refusing to help carry the weight of managing such a home. So Marcus continued devoting himself to his work, earning money that would keep them in the style Mother and Eli demanded no matter how miserable it made him.

Inside the echoing entry, Marcus handed off his coat and hat to the butler, Walter, thanking the aging man with a smile. Walter had been hired by Marcus's father, and thus, he was treasured, almost a part of the family. He was also the only member of the staff left except for a girl Mother paid to clean several times a week and the cook who came in daily.

If only Father was still alive, he would have set Mother and Eli to rights years ago. Instead, Marcus was forced to be the voice of reason in the Turner family. Even though none of them liked that arrangement.

Marcus paused on the study threshold. Eli sat at the large desk in the room, his head bent as he scratched an ink pen across a piece of paper. His blond hair was neatly combed, but that was where the resemblance between Marcus and his brother ended. Where Marcus was average height and stockier, Eli was tall and thin, looking a great deal like their father. He usually shied away from anything that resembled work, however, preferring instead to spend his time with friends at his club, so seeing him stationed at the desk was strange. Marcus cleared his throat and rapped his knuckles against the doorframe.

Eli's head shot up, red splotches appearing on his cheeks. "Oh, it's you, Marcus. Why are you sneaking about? I'm busy."

Trying not to let Eli's harsh tone bother him, Marcus stepped into the study and crossed to stand in front of the desk. "I just arrived home and thought I'd see what you're doing. If there's some kind of family business that needs attention, I can handle it tonight."

Eli shoved the papers on the desk into a stack and rose, nearly upsetting the chair in his hurry. "No, this is work for the head of the family, not the younger son. You're off galivanting around the countryside with that silly club so often that you wouldn't know enough about the situation to help, anyway."

While Marcus sputtered an argument, Eli pushed past him and strode out the door. Marcus stood frozen in place for a moment, trying to guess what on earth his brother's angry words could have meant. In the past three months, since it turned too cold to do many excursions, Marcus had only gone to work, had an occasional supper with the Thorntons, and attended two club meetings. Otherwise, he was always available to his family. What situation had Eli been referencing?

Marcus ate supper alone and tried to read in the library until bedtime without receiving any answers. By nine o'clock, his only option was clear—he'd have to visit Mother and see if she knew what was going on.

The lack of desire to hear her go on about the fancy gowns her friends wore recently, or the new automobile the neighbors bought, or anything else he'd told her time and again they couldn't afford made Marcus put off the visit for as long as possible. But as the only one in the family with a job that required waking early in the morning, he would have to get some sleep that night. So he finally forced himself to mount the stairs and stop in front of the door to Mother's suite, where she preferred to spend every possible moment of her time at home.

When he knocked, her soft voice beckoned him in. Marcus entered her parlor, which was decorated in shades of yellow and cream, brighter and more soothing than the rest of the house. Mother sat in her favorite plush chair with a lamp as close as possible on the table next to her so she could see the embroidery she was working on. But she didn't glance up from the handiwork until Marcus was seated in one of the tufted chairs opposite her.

Myra Turner had been a beautiful woman in her day. There were still hints of it in the wide eyes, the graceful sweep of her hair, her perfectly full lips. But time and tragedy had not been kind. Her skin was more creased every time Marcus saw her. Sadness weighed down every feature on her face, even when she tried to hide it from society with a tight smile. Everyone seemed to attribute it to the tragic early death of her husband. But Marcus knew that wasn't the only reason. Perhaps not even the biggest reason.

No, Mother's own mistakes had caused her far more grief than Father's death.

When she finally set aside her sewing hoop and folded her hands in her lap, Mother's faded green eyes looked over Marcus appraisingly. "What brings you to visit tonight? It's been quite some time since you've stopped by. I think the last time we spent any time together was at the Christmas ball, wasn't it?"

Marcus nodded. Instead of celebrating the holiday with a cozy family gathering, Mother preferred to throw a lavish ball right before Christmas, one that used to nearly bankrupt them every year until she'd learned to put on a show of wealth while being economical in reality. Marcus attended for her sake, then spent Christmas Day going to the service at church and stopping by to drop off small gifts for the Thorntons.

Mother tilted her head. "Then what is it now? Have I unwittingly overspent again?"

Marcus winced. He hated that so much of their relationship revolved around money or the lack thereof. He reached out to take her hand, the skin fragile under his touch, like paper that had turned brittle. "No, and I'm sorry I've had to bring that news so many times that you assume it's my purpose. Eli was acting strange when I got home. I thought you might know what he's up to."

Pulling her hand away, Mother pursed her lips while smoothing back nonexistent loose hairs. "I don't like to meddle in his affairs, Marcus. Eli is the head of this family. He's entitled to his privacy."

It was all Marcus could do to keep from slamming his fist down on the table next to his chair. "Mother, Eli doesn't support this family. He doesn't handle creditors or paying bills. He's a figurehead, placed there to keep up the appearance that everything is fine. If there's something going on related to this house or our livelihood, I'm the one who should know about it."

Mother's chin snapped up, her eyes flashing. He'd done it now. She'd never tell him anything if she was indignant. "Marcus Samuel Turner. You do not speak about your brother that way."

Marcus hung his head, but it had nothing to do with the reprimand. How could she not see what a heel Eli was and how much of a burden he placed on their family when he should be helping them rebuild as Marcus was? But she'd never been able to look past social expectations, and society didn't know that Eli no longer had a large inheritance to manage. There would be a great deal of gossip about their family if he were to go out and find a menial job. The fact that Marcus had done just that already brought Mother enough censure from the more traditional members of Milwaukee's upper crust. She would never stand for Eli adding to it, even if he'd ever expressed a desire to help.

But revealing any more anger wouldn't further his cause, so Marcus pulled himself together with a few deep breaths and looked up again, trying to soften his expression. "I apologize, Mother."

Her thin lips tilted up at the corners. "Thank you. I will let you in on a little secret, though, since you came to visit me."

Bracing himself for society gossip he cared nothing about, Marcus regretted knocking on her door more than ever.

Mother's eyes twinkled, completely in her element now that she got to reveal someone's private business. "The situation Eli spoke of isn't at all what you're thinking. He's planning to propose, Marcus. Isn't that wonderful?"

Marcus blinked several times, trying to understand the words he thought she'd said. "Propose? To whom?"

A tinkling laugh fell from Mother's lips, and Marcus caught a glimpse of that once-legendary beauty again. "Why, Ada May Schuller, of course. They've danced at every ball for the last three months. He's quite taken with her. And she with him, I'm certain."

His mind scrambled to place which young woman this Miss Schuller might be, but he paid little attention during the balls he attended grudgingly. He was always too busy wishing Leonora was there so he could dance with her instead of another simpering socialite who thought he had a fortune she could marry into.

Mother leaned forward in her chair with a conspiratorial lift of one eyebrow. "See? Eli will fix our problems, after all. Miss Schuller comes from quite a well-to-do family. She'll bring money from her father's company, and we'll be back to living the lifestyle we should have been all along. All he has to do is keep our shameful secret long enough to secure her hand."

As Mother picked up her sewing again, now humming happily, Marcus's heart dropped. This poor young woman would be duped into joining their fragmented, almost destitute family. She wouldn't see the truth of their life until it was too late, while Eli and Mother would use her for her father's money without a qualm. Guilt turned into nausea in his stomach. Was there any way he could stop it from happening without destroying the little that was left of his family?

~

*A*fter parting ways with Marcus and completing an uneventful streetcar ride, Leonora stepped through the front door of the narrow two-story house where she lived with her mother, her brother, Felix, and his family. It didn't take long to realize her sister, Cassia, had also come to visit. She almost tripped over eight-year-old Oscar, Cassia's middle son, who sat propped against the wall in the hall with a copy of *The Call of the Wild* held close in front of his face. Leonora had to smile. It was probably the calmest spot he could find to read while the others created chaos.

Before she could hang her coat in the hall closet, the distinct voices of the rest of her many nephews grew loud enough to wake the dead, as Papa would have said. She had seven nephews, to be exact, between both of her siblings. Thumps and bangs coming from the drawing room told her without the need to look through the open door that the older boys were wrestling or pretend sword fighting.

In the midst of all the commotion, sweet little four-year-old Eleanor sang her heart out while someone—another of the boys, no doubt—pounded his fists on the keys of Mother's piano. The only girl among so many brothers and male cousins, Eleanor could hold her own but always did so in the most angelic and feminine of ways.

The sounds of her happy family members put Leonora at ease as she walked through the house. With her family, Leonora didn't have to worry about being braver or stronger than she felt. She didn't have to wonder what they thought because they would tell her without hesitation. And she didn't have to step out of the secure life she'd somehow fallen into in order to prove she was good enough to be Henry Thornton's daughter. Within these walls, she could simply exist and enjoy the wildness her family created around her while remaining ensconced in safety.

That easiness was threatened by the letter still stashed in her coat pocket, however. Before he'd started making claims about Mr. Flemming, she'd nearly convinced herself to tell Marcus about it. But how could she bring it up when he was in such a critical mood? He was likely to immediately tell her it was a prank. She didn't like keeping things from him, though, and she longed to hear his perspective on the possibility that the Explorers Club might have missed something. Maybe with some time, she could uncover information about where the letter might have come from, something that could ensure it wasn't a prank. Then she would tell him.

Returning to the drawing room doorway, Leonora took a moment to discern the boys' game of the day. There were indeed wooden swords, but there were also Mother's decorative cushions spread across the floor. The boys were holding swords aloft while jumping from cushion to cushion, taking great care not to let any bit of a foot slide off onto the plush carpet. Every now and then, one boy would stop to swing his weapon in front of him like a machete.

Jungle explorers, it seemed.

Henry and Julius noticed Leonora in the doorway and grinned, waving their weapons and shouting her name.

Leonora saluted the crew. "Hello, brave explorers. What discoveries have you made today?"

In a tangle of words, three of the boys rushed to explain their game to her at the same time. Leonora caught enough to laugh and applaud their creativity. "Carry on, gentlemen!"

She left the boys to their game and followed the rest of the voices across the hall to the parlor, where Mother sat with Cassia on the sofa. Next to each other, the two women looked remarkably similar, with the same blond hair that Leonora had, combined with green eyes, rather than Leonora's hazel ones. The biggest difference between the two women was the age that had begun to show in lines around Mother's eyes and mouth.

Across from them, Felix's wife, Arabella, had pulled five-year-old Cornelius into her lap and taken over the piano, presumably to save it from destruction by pounding. With her arms stretched around her youngest son, Arabella accompanied Eleanor in the most charming rendition of "Let Me Call You Sweetheart."

As the last note sung in her trembling, soft little voice trailed off, Eleanor noticed Leonora standing in the doorway. "Aunt Nori!"

The child launched herself forward. Thankfully, Leonora's quick reflexes enabled her to extend her arms and catch the wild ball of lace, tangled blond curls, and energy before Eleanor hit the floor. "Hello, my darling. What a lovely song you were singing."

Eleanor beamed while she dragged Leonora to sit in a chair and climbed straight into her lap. Mother smiled in their direction as Arabella joined them, all but forcing Cornelius to remain on her lap. Most likely, punishment for mistreating the piano. Despite the effort it took to keep the boy still, Leonora's sister-in-law looked as composed as ever, not a pleat on her simple blue gingham dress or a hair from her golden-brown pompadour out of place.

In her familiar gentle manner, Mother immediately included them all in the conversation she and Cassia had been having. "Leonora, your sister pointed out it's been several weeks since we've had Marcus over for a meal. Will you invite him this Sunday? I can't begin to understand why his mother and brother prefer to dine alone on weekends rather than as a family."

Cassia clicked her tongue in a disapproving way. "Doesn't it sound terrible? To eat all by yourself in an empty room. Why on earth would they enjoy that?"

Leonora bit her lower lip to keep from responding. With the exception of the somber year after Papa died, the Thornton home had always been filled with boisterous, joyful noise and activity. Even before her siblings had children, Leonora's parents loved to invite people into their home, so there had always been friends coming and going. As the youngest, Leonora had never gotten a moment alone growing up. She'd often envied Marcus his independence, the ability to have time to himself whenever he wanted. But she could see how it might get lonely if it was always that way.

Realizing the women were waiting for her to respond, Leonora straightened as much as she could with Eleanor curled in her lap and nodded. "I'll send a note to ask him later this week. But I'm sure you don't need to wait for his answer. He never turns down a meal here."

Cassia wiggled her eyebrows at Leonora, an all-knowing smirk twisting her lips. "And we know why that is, don't we?"

Mother smiled indulgently, and Arabella snickered, but Eleanor looked up into Leonora's face with her forehead scrunched in thought. "Why, Aunt Nori? I want to know why."

Thankfully, Arabella tutted at her daughter, saving Leonora from answering. "Now, Eleanor, you shouldn't interrupt adult conversation. Why don't you go see what the boys are doing? Cornelius, take her along to find the others."

The two children left, Eleanor sending one last confused look into the room before disappearing. Cassia laughed, a light, tinkling sound that she'd practiced endlessly while trying to win her husband, Paul. "Oh, Leonora. Don't think that was enough to distract us from this conversation. The relationship you claim you don't have with Marcus is my favorite topic."

Rising, Leonora marched to the sideboard and poured herself a glass of water from a pitcher Mother kept there, taking a moment to calm her frustration over the frequently discussed imaginary relationship while she drank a few sips. For years, her sister had refused to listen to the truth and accept that Leonora and Marcus were only friends with no romantic intentions whatsoever.

Once she had control of herself, Leonora turned back to Cassia, finding all three women inspecting her. "As I tell you every time, there's no relationship to speculate over, unless it's a lifelong friendship. There's nothing more."

Mother didn't always include herself in Cassia's constant efforts to convince Leonora that Marcus was in love with her, but this time, she spoke up too. "The way he looks at you says otherwise. We all see it, dear. What would be so bad about admitting it to yourself?"

It wasn't as if Leonora hadn't pondered this before. She'd asked herself quite a few times over the years why she was so reluctant to believe Marcus might feel differently about their relationship than she did. Perhaps it was because no matter how much he supported her love of adventure, shy, serious, sweet Marcus hated her excursions. He disliked both hot and cold weather. He bemoaned the existence of every insect on the planet. He was dedicated to his safe office job at the bank.

But even if things were different and he loved adventuring at her side, there was a more substantial, undeniable truth she could never forget for long. "He's never spoken a word regarding deeper feelings, Mother. If he wanted something more than friendship, he would say so. He's happy with the way things are, and so am I."

Usually, that was enough to stop the line of questioning before Cassia went any further. But today she seemed inclined to push her opinion on the matter. "You've been part of each other's lives for so long, he's probably afraid to say anything for fear of changing things. He knows as well as anyone that this family doesn't have any secrets. If you turned him down, we'd all know within an hour, and that might make visits with us awkward. You'll have to encourage him, Leonora. Give him some hints that his advances won't be rebuffed. I think you'll be surprised at what happens."

Oh, for heaven's sake. Leonora shot her sister a pointed glare. "I will not throw myself at Marcus, Cassia. Our friendship is fine how it is. We're both happy with it."

For the first time, Arabella joined in. "We want to see you settled down, that's all. The three of us found happy marriages, and we know what a blessing they are. You should have the same. But very few men would be able to look past your close relationship with Marcus. If you can't even convince us he's only a friend, what must all the eligible men think?"

Leonora glanced at her sister-in-law in surprise. "If a man can't take my word for it, then he isn't the one for me, anyway. Now, I'm going to my room to clean up before supper. I'll see you all in a bit. And I expect the conversation to remain far away from gossip about me and Marcus."

She marched out of the room and up the stairs, barely getting her bedroom door closed behind her before tears began to well in her eyes. She was happy. Usually. As a girl, she'd thought marriage and exploration weren't things that could be combined. It had worked for her parents because her mother had stayed in Milwaukee. She'd handled raising her children and managing the household with ease when Papa had been away. But no man would want to stay home and do those womanly tasks while his wife traipsed around the world.

There had been a time that followed that, though, when Leonora realized marriage and her dreams didn't have to be mutually exclusive. She'd imagined she and Marcus would fall in love and marry. Then they could go about exploring the world together. But she'd been honest with her family. He'd never spoken a single word that made her think he had romantic intentions or that he'd welcome them from her. And having him in her life was too important for her to risk destroying their friendship by pursuing something that was unlikely to work, anyway.

So she'd long ago set aside that dream and turned her mind to fulfilling her father's legacy. While she did wish for a husband and children of her own to join the cousins she could still hear downstairs, the reality was that her friendship with Marcus wasn't what would run off any potential suitors. Her goal of exploring the world and building a thriving club would dissuade any men before they even knew Marcus existed.

No, her life would remain on the course she'd set after Papa's death. She would build her club. She would conquer her fear and go on expeditions. She would make great discoveries and spread the gospel, just as Papa had done.

And that would be enough.

CHAPTER 4

*T*he morning of the ski outing dawned clear and crisp, a disappointment to Marcus. He'd hoped for an unexpected storm to cancel the event. Or even a warm spell that would have melted the thick snow currently blanketing the world in white and made it impossible to ski. As much as he loved being with Leonora and enjoyed the company of the others in the club, he had a bad feeling that Mr. Flemming would indeed join them and ruin what could have been a nice day.

On his way to meet the others at the park where they would practice skiing on the bluffs overlooking Lake Michigan, Marcus met up with Mr. Howard to stop by a local ski club and pick up the skis and poles they'd arranged to borrow for the day. During the following streetcar ride that took them southeast out of town, Mr. Howard remained quiet, his attention focused on the newspaper he'd brought along.

But Marcus had no inclination to read the business reports or investment updates Mr. Howard was perusing. It had been a long, busy week at the bank, and he'd had enough of boring business talk and the constant pressure to make more money by whatever means necessary.

In his youth, Marcus had wanted excitement, similar to Leonora. But his dreams had always focused not on discovery, but on recording—specifically, the process of surveying. Along with his father, he'd fallen in love with cartography and thought he would be able to spend all his time as an adult drawing detailed maps of the world around him.

During the first few years he worked at the bank, Marcus hadn't had the time or heart to pursue any other interests. In recent years, though, he'd secretly begun collecting equipment related to his youthful yearning, almost as if he could make it become reality by having the tools he would need around him. He read library books about surveying techniques and began practicing whenever possible, developing what he thought were decent enough skills in estimating measurements and calculating triangulations.

But while it entertained him to do pretend calculations in his head, he did sometimes wish he could tell the Exploration Society members about his deep-seated interest in the topic. Practicing taking measurements at home, where the city setting made everything far too easy and predictable, had long since grown dull. What he wouldn't give to be able to survey the wild landscape while on one of their outings.

But he was not inclined to reveal such a subject to anyone who might scoff at it as his brother did. The memory of Mother's horror and Eli's censure upon discovering his hobby was enough to give Marcus a headache by the time the streetcar stopped at the entrance to the park.

Despite the cold, the weak winter sunshine was enough to bring quite a few people out to enjoy the park, most of them walking along the ice-strewn lakeshore or sledding down the steep hill near the entrance. At over two hundred acres, it was one of the largest parks in the area, and that meant there were plenty of wild areas hidden away where the club could practice in rougher conditions than a manicured path.

Marcus and Mr. Howard, each carrying a pile of skis and poles, made their way to the trailhead where the others would be waiting. As they rounded a clump of evergreen trees, Marcus's heart dropped. As he'd feared, Vernon Flemming was not only present but also standing far too close to Leonora while the others milled about. Marcus almost turned around and left her to the consequences of her actions. Unfortunately, he was the only one among them who had experience skiing, and thus, he was essential to the excursion. He had never been able to back down from something that was his responsibility.

Plus, his heart wouldn't allow him to leave Leonora unprotected with Mr. Flemming, no matter how frustrating the situation was bound to become.

Mr. Howard had already taken his half of the equipment over and begun distributing items. So Marcus tugged his knit winter hat down farther over his ears with one hand while balancing the pile of skis and poles in both arms and approached the group with confident steps that definitely didn't mirror his emotions.

Leonora, dressed in a thick black skirt with a long sweater buttoned to her neck, listened intently to whatever tall tale Mr. Flemming was spinning. A few feet away, Mr. Howard was attempting to help Mrs. Adler and her husband with their skis, but it appeared he wasn't having much success. Charlotte and Alice Bauer stood close by, Miss Charlotte rocking between her toes and heels with uncontainable excitement, while her sister clasped her hands in front of her, more subdued.

When she noticed Marcus was also there, Miss Charlotte rushed in his direction, speaking loudly enough to gain the attention of the entire party. "Mr. Turner, Mr. Flemming feels we ought to get started right away. He says he feels a storm brewing. Apparently, his intuition on weather is never wrong."

Marcus adjusted his glasses while trying to contain his derision. If Mr. Flemming's intuition was so good, he should know his opinion wasn't needed. But Marcus forced a tight smile as he dropped his hand. "I suppose we shouldn't delay, then. Have you all gotten your skis tightened?"

The group quieted as Marcus helped the Adlers get their rattan ski bindings secured. Then he checked the Bauer twins' skis and Mr. Howard's.

Leonora grinned when he finally stood in front of her, a teasing light in her eyes. "I think you'll find I'm outfitted perfectly."

As he glanced up at her from the crouch he had to drop into to tug on the ski bindings, it was on the tip of Marcus's tongue to state that she was always perfect. He bit the words back just in time. How careless of him to almost reveal his true, unrequited feelings for Leonora in front of all their friends. He had to be more cautious than that if he was to avoid being soundly rejected in public.

Once Marcus had gotten all the equipment in order, he stood, prepared to give a brief lesson for those new to skiing. However, Mr. Flemming began speaking before Marcus could utter a word. "Ladies and gentlemen, I'm honored to have been invited to join you today. I've spent more than a few hours on skis such as this, traversing wild lands of beauty beyond imagination. You'll find this to be a most useful skill in your own future explorations. Now, let's be off!"

Jumping in front of Mr. Flemming before the man could lead the society members to certain injury, Marcus bit the inside of his cheek, trying to maintain a polite demeanor. "Many of our members are new to skiing, Mr. Flemming. I'd like to be sure everyone has a basic understanding of how to do it first. Please give us a few moments."

Mr. Flemming aimed a hard stare at Marcus as if

attempting to punish him for interrupting. "And you're qualified to teach them?"

Marcus drew himself up straight. "I've skied quite a few times with my mother and her friends, including Mrs. Allis and Mrs. Pabst, who I'm sure you've heard of. They had the finest instructors, so I think you'll find I'm more than qualified."

While throwing around the names of his mother's society acquaintances didn't usually appeal to Marcus, Mr. Flemming's condescending attitude brought out a desire to show him he wasn't superior to anyone here. So he held his ground, allowing Mr. Flemming to consider what it might mean to know someone who rubbed shoulders with families that were so influential in Milwaukee.

Tilting his head, Mr. Flemming stepped aside. He then tapped his foot while Marcus helped Mr. Howard get his skis lined up. He took a moment to correct the way Miss Charlotte was trying to use her sturdy ski pole. Then he had everyone shuffle into the open area in front of the trailhead, using their poles to help push themselves forward. They spent some time slowly traversing the snowy clearing, which was nicely secluded from the busier areas of the park by clumps of trees.

Once Marcus was convinced they would be able to ski with some amount of competence, he stood back and gestured to Leonora to take over. She and Mr. Flemming took the lead, guiding the group onto a familiar trail, one that the society members liked to hike in nicer weather and had snowshoed recently.

It was an easy enough trip for Marcus, who had spent too many hours learning this skill with his mother, albeit on much flatter terrain. Her upper-class friends liked to think they were quite bold and daring, but in reality, even their so-called adventures were cultured and controlled. Thankfully, those in this group who had never attempted to ski caught on quickly, leaving Marcus free to enjoy the outing.

But as Mr. Flemming doted on Leonora while they shuffled along the trail, a sour taste rose in Marcus's throat. He might be confident that Leonora didn't intend to marry until she'd begun her career as an explorer, but that didn't mean he was comfortable with a man he didn't trust sniffing around her. What if she got swept up in his charms and gave up everything she'd dreamed of doing, just to learn she'd shackled herself to a man who wasn't worthy of her?

Attempting to adjust his glasses so they wouldn't get fogged up from his breath, Marcus shook off the powerful longing that always came with thoughts of the future. He was hardly worthy either. His life was dedicated to ensuring his mother and brother didn't lose what little they had left. He couldn't go on expeditions with her. Then there was an entire part of his life he was beholden to keep a secret, even from her. What kind of man would pursue a romantic relationship when he couldn't even tell his sweetheart about the most significant thing that had happened in his past, the event that changed the course of his choices forever?

Marcus looked up from his pondering just in time to avoid walking straight into Miss Alice, who had stopped in front of him. With Mr. Flemming in the lead, the group had reached a creek in a ravine, which was wide enough to pose some amount of difficulty in crossing. Thankfully, the group stopped at the edge of the bank. Marcus wanted to assess the thickness of the ice and decide for himself if it was safe to attempt skiing across.

Leonora had dropped back until she was only ahead of Marcus. He thought she would follow him to the front when he passed, given her preference for forming her own opinion in situations that might require a decision. But he found himself next to Mr. Flemming instead, while Leonora remained a bit apart at the back of the group.

As Marcus approached the bank, Mr. Flemming began speaking. "Now, a water crossing is an opportunity for disaster.

You must take great care to consider various factors when deciding if the crossing is safe or not."

What hogwash. Had the man ever been on a walk in the woods, much less an expedition? As the others listened intently, Marcus crouched next to the ice to assess it from ground level. When it looked solid all the way across, he took several steps out and tested its strength, tapping his ski pole and listening for any cracking or hollow sounds that might indicate weakness.

While Marcus checked the ice and then returned to solid ground, Flemming kept talking. A familiar heat built in Marcus's chest. One thing he couldn't stand for was a man taking advantage of others, using deception to get what he wanted. And he was growing more certain all the time that Vernon Flemming was doing exactly that. If it wasn't for Leonora, Marcus might have ousted the man from their group himself. Since he refused to embarrass her that way, he would wait, watching for an answer to the question that currently loomed in his thoughts. What could Flemming's end game be?

～

*L*eonora stood behind the society members with her eyes squeezed shut so tight that she saw stars behind the lids. But no matter how hard she tried to think of good reasons why she needed to do this, she wouldn't be able to cross the creek. Whether the surface was frozen or not, all she could see was crashing water underneath breaking through and carrying her to her death.

She had to convince the group to go another way.

With shaking hands, Leonora wiped sweat from her forehead despite the chill in the air, hoping there was a reasonable amount of color in her face given the energy they'd been expending for the past hour. No one could see how terrified she was. No one could ever know that the mere thought of going out on any amount of water was enough to paralyze her. It was the reason she couldn't take the leap into actually going on an expedition. If she couldn't even cross a frozen creek, how would she traverse an ocean or a rushing jungle river?

Forcing her feet to move closer to the creek while every inch of her body screamed in resistance, Leonora made her way to stand beside Marcus and Mr. Flemming. The explorer was just finishing addressing her group when she brought herself into the present enough to hear him. "And as Mr. Turner here will confirm, the creek should be passable. Wouldn't you say, Mr. Turner?"

Marcus's face was fixed in the sort of scowl she'd only ever seen when he was telling her about one of his spoiled brother's exploits. He cast a sideways glance at Mr. Flemming before turning to the rest of them, his gaze finding hers. "Yes, the creek is passable. But only for another hour or so. It's beginning to warm up too much to count on the ice holding."

An opening. Leonora jumped on it immediately. "Then we should go another way. It would be foolish to cross without being sure we can get back over. There's no reason we need to continue on this specific path, anyway."

Marcus nodded, his scowl softening. "I agree. If I remember right from one of our hikes, there's a lovely view of the lake at the top of this bluff. We could go that way and still get plenty of skiing experience."

Mr. Flemming's face flushed red at their arguments against his conclusion. Leonora prayed he wasn't the sort of man who would cause a scene. It wasn't as if they had a destination to reach, after all. What reason would he have to argue with the safest course of action?

"You'll all have to push yourselves to take risks at some point, Miss Thornton. If you're going to participate in expeditions, you'll encounter times when there's not another way to reach a destination besides the dangerous one." Mr. Flemming's voice was nonchalant but may have carried an undertone of tension.

Still, she wasn't about to miss the opportunity to keep them away from the creek. "Be that as it may, there's no reason to take unnecessary risks while we're out on a practice excursion. And I'd like to see that view Marcus mentioned. I don't remember it from the last time. This way, everyone."

Now that a water crossing was no longer part of the journey, Leonora gladly reclaimed her spot at the front of the group, leading the way up the hill. Her knees and ankles ached from the unusual way the skis forced her to move, but learning new skills always exhilarated her enough that she could ignore quite a bit of discomfort. As long as there wasn't water to contend with.

At the top of the hill, the others explored while Marcus joined her in enjoying what was indeed a lovely view of Lake Michigan stretching out endlessly below. The light covering of fresh snow that had fallen overnight glistened in the chilled sunlight as if diamonds were strewn over everything. Marcus stood close enough that his sleeve brushed hers. If only they didn't need such heavy outer garments so she could feel the warmth of his skin.

Ridiculous notions like that had been crossing her mind more and more frequently, making her feel silly enough that she shook her head to get her thoughts back in line. Marcus turned and gazed down at her with a quizzical look in his eyes, so Leonora drew her back up straighter and looked out from the hill again. "You were right about coming up here. I'd forgotten it was so beautiful."

"I'll never forget the way the setting sun turned your hair to gold when we stood up here at that picnic last summer." At his unexpected statement, Leonora's eyes shot up to meet Marcus's, but he averted his gaze, pink tinging his cheeks. His throat worked as he swallowed. "I mean—"

"Miss Thornton, we need you over here!"

The shout from Mr. Howard cut off Marcus's words. Leonora's heart dropped like a stone in her chest at the interruption. He'd never said such a lovely thing to her before. What could it mean?

But she put away the questions piling up in her mind for the moment, fully intending to examine them in much more detail later. She and Marcus skied down the side of the hill a few dozen yards to where Mr. Howard and the Bauer twins clustered close together next to a sparse pine tree. The Adlers and Mr. Flemming were making their way over to see what the fuss was about, as well. Leonora craned her neck to see what they were staring at so intently. "What is it? Is someone injured?"

Alice stepped out of the way while her sister spoke. "No, nothing like that. We found animal tracks."

Unmindful of the snow dampening her skirt, Leonora knelt to look closer. She traced the outline of a cloven print with one finger. "We studied wild animal identification last year. Does anyone want to guess what made these?"

The gathered society members leaned over Leonora to see the tracks. Mrs. Adler was the first to hazard a guess. "Deer? They look very much like hooves."

Leonora beamed up at her. "Exactly right. These belong to a rather large white-tailed deer. It's a shame we didn't get to see the creature itself."

The group discussed the tracks for a few more minutes. Mr. Howard skied off in the direction of the tracks but returned after only a few moments. "They disappear into the undergrowth. It's too thick to follow on skis."

That was a bit disheartening, but Leonora rallied the group. "This has been good practice, but I for one am quite tired. Let's head back. We can try to identify bird calls on the way."

That roused the group enough to begin the trek back with

cheerful discussions about the various birds they thought they heard. Leonora hung back to make the return journey next to Marcus. Without needing to say so, they both slowed their steps to let the others get a lead on them.

Marcus tilted his head toward Leonora. "Did you get enough of traveling with Mr. Flemming already?"

She might have been offended at the criticism dripping from his words except that he was completely correct. "I know you've noticed his flaws, Marcus. You were looking for them like an eagle hunting a mouse in an overgrown field, so it's hardly a surprise that you found some."

"I suppose I do expect the worst from him. But can you blame me? He's brash and arrogant. I'm concerned that he's not telling us everything. Maybe he's not even the successful explorer he claims to be."

Leonora prodded his side with her elbow, hoping to keep the conversation from turning sour. "I agree that he's a bit much to handle in large quantities. But don't you think as Christians, we ought to show him kindness despite his personality flaws?"

Marcus's lips turned up in a fond smile, and Leonora barely restrained the urge to skip. How she might accomplish that on skis was a mystery, anyway. But the soft expression only lasted a moment before Marcus's brow furrowed in the way it did when he was trying to talk the group out of an especially dangerous outing idea like the rock climbing Mr. Brighton suggested last year. "Being kind doesn't mean we have to trust someone who isn't worthy of it. Are you certain having him involved with the society is a good idea, Leonora?"

She did her best not to bristle at the question. Marcus always had her best interests at heart. But he also tended to underestimate her ability to make wise choices. "He's pompous, Marcus, but he's been on expeditions to places we've only dreamed of. What can be so bad about learning from his experience?"

One of Marcus's hands rose to rub the back of his neck, his blunt fingers rasping across the skin. He had surprisingly strong hands for a man who sat at a desk all day. "Have you checked into his claims? That he's done the things he says? It would only take one letter to the Explorers Club in New York to learn if he's being honest about his experience."

He was questioning her wisdom again. Leonora's fingers twitched inside the mittens Cassia had knitted for her two Christmases ago, longing to clench into fists. "Why would he lie to us about going on those trips? He has photographs, for goodness' sake."

Wrapping his fingers around her forearm, Marcus stopped Leonora while the others continued moving farther away, pulling her around to face him. "Please don't be angry with me. Sometimes you're simply too trusting. I'm only trying to protect you."

It was on the tip of Leonora's tongue to lash out, to yell that she didn't need his protection. Papa had raised her to be self-sufficient and industrious. She trusted people because she saw the good in them, whereas Marcus tended to assume there was bad.

But the words died before she could utter them when she saw the intensity in Marcus's eyes while he adjusted his glasses. His forehead wrinkled, and his lips were drawn tight. As if he forgot he'd just done it, he reached up and pushed his glasses into place again. Her heart softened. He meant what he said. He was simply worried about her and their friends.

But while that concern was endearing, what would it take for her to convince him that she was as capable of making good choices as he was?

CHAPTER 5

*M*arcus noticed the exact moment Leonora stopped herself from arguing with him, despite her obvious desire to do so.

She snapped her parted lips shut and jerked back, her body angling away from him. For a moment, he couldn't draw a deep enough breath. He hated to hurt her, but he could *not* allow her to start asking questions about why he doubted Mr. Flemming in the first place. She couldn't know his family's shameful secret, but it was the only thing Marcus had ever kept from her.

Besides how deep his feelings for her ran.

Swallowing hard, he turned to follow the rest of their companions. It was safer for his secrets if he and Leonora stayed with the group. Leonora trotted—the best one could on long, awkward skis, anyway—to catch up to him, but she didn't speak anymore. He could feel her watching him, though. She might not push for reasons why he was skeptical of Mr. Flemming now, but she wouldn't let it go forever. He had better be ready with an answer when she finally asked, because she wasn't a woman who could leave anything alone once it roused her curiosity.

Mr. Flemming was once again regaling the rest of the club members with tales of his exploits when Marcus and Leonora caught up to them. Back at the streetcar stop, they all removed their borrowed skis and waited. Once the streetcar arrived, clanging its bell incessantly to inform anyone nearby of its presence, the group filed aboard and settled into seats close together. It was a rather subdued trip back into Milwaukee. The club members were probably tired. Skiing was a different sort of exertion when one wasn't used to it, utilizing muscles that everyday activity didn't often strain.

But Marcus was quiet because he was eavesdropping. Out of the corner of his eye, he watched Leonora and Mr. Flemming discuss the day for a bit before the man glanced around the streetcar, lowering his voice enough that Marcus had to strain to discern his words over the noise of the vehicle, even from his spot in front of the seat they shared. He kept his face buried in the newspaper he'd borrowed from Mr. Howard in hopes the two wouldn't notice he could still hear them.

"Miss Thornton, I'm impressed with the knowledge and capability of your group. And yourself, especially. You would make your father proud, I'm certain."

Marcus pressed his lips tight together to keep from scoffing out loud. He managed not to look up to see how Leonora reacted, but she always took delight in people praising her father. "That's a lovely compliment. Thank you, Mr. Flemming." Pleasure mingled with the hesitation in her voice.

The creaking of the seat indicated the man shifted, probably leaning closer to Leonora. "It's more than a compliment. I plan to return to Peru again this spring to complete the work I began on my last journey. I think it would benefit you to get some real exploration experience, on a larger scale than amusing trips around your hometown. And in return, your connections could do wonders for the funding of my expedition, which is the purpose of my current lecture tour. What do you think, Miss Thornton? Will you join my crew?"

Marcus grunted with the effort it took not to shout out a resounding *no* on her behalf. He must have made some noise, however, because when he turned slightly to glance back, both Mr. Flemming and Leonora were staring at him, the former with his lips curled up and Leonora with her chin pointed in the air. She expected Marcus to insert his opinion again. And he wanted to, quite desperately.

But in this moment, with Leonora's very life at stake if she went on a badly planned expedition, Marcus couldn't risk her strengthening her resolve and agreeing simply to spite him.

So he cleared his throat as if that's what he'd done a moment before. "Excuse me. The cold air must have gotten to me."

Leonora crossed her arms. She knew him far too well to fall for such a foolish excuse.

But Mr. Flemming tilted his head. "When you get home, have your staff prepare a very hot cup of tea with a generous amount of honey." He'd assumed that annoyingly wise tone again. "That should clear it right up."

The man spoke as if he was imparting deep wisdom, as if the use of honey for a sore throat wasn't already known by... well, everyone. But for Leonora's sake, Marcus offered a smile that hopefully wasn't too strained. "Thank you for that advice. I'll be fine, I'm sure."

Mr. Flemming regarded Marcus for several moments while Marcus met his gaze, unwilling to break the stare first. The way the man spoke about Marcus having staff and his reference to Leonora's connections being financially beneficial for his expedition revealed the heart of his purpose in Milwaukee. He was looking for money, plain and simple. And while most explorers had to raise funds for their trips, Marcus could feel the greed seething behind Mr. Flemming's words. He wanted more than to raise enough to finance an expedition. Marcus would bet on it.

Eventually, Leonora spoke through the tension. "Mr. Flemming, I do appreciate your offer. You'll have to give me some time to consider it and speak with my family, though. In the meantime, could you provide me with more details about the itinerary and costs?"

Turning his attention away from Marcus, Mr. Flemming slipped back into the more charming façade he used when interacting with the women. "Certainly. And it's quite wise not to rush the decision. A trip like this naturally involves a significant amount of risk, no matter how well planned or executed."

Marcus let the drone of Mr. Flemming's rambling about his plans for the expedition fade into the background. He was proud of Leonora for choosing to consider the offer rather than jumping in headlong as she was wont to do. Could he nudge her in the right direction? If he could set aside his derision for Mr. Flemming and remain close by her side while the man was in town, perhaps he could plant subtle seeds of truth in her mind, clues that would help her realize Mr. Flemming couldn't be anything but a fraud.

Leonora had invited the club members to return to her house after the outing to warm up and enjoy each other's company a bit longer. They disembarked at the closest streetcar stop to the Thorntons' home and walked there. Once they were all settled in the parlor with coffee and hot chocolate Mrs. Thornton had kindly prepared, Leonora looked around the group. "Now, let's all take a turn and share our favorite part of the day. Mine was learning something new. I'm impressed with how well we all caught on to skiing."

The Bauer twins switched back and forth, talking about how much they enjoyed the sparkling snow and the view of the lake. Mr. Howard brought up the deer trail and added that the weather had been better than he expected.

Leonora looked between Marcus and Mr. Flemming, the last two who hadn't added anything. Marcus's throat went dry. With her expectant gaze on him, suddenly, all he could remember was how the color of Leonora's scarf made her hazel eyes appear deeper green than usual. Which was hardly an appropriate observation to point out in front of the group.

Unfortunately, his hesitation gave Mr. Flemming an opening. Rather than speaking from his seat like all the rest, the man rose and moved to stand right next to Leonora's chair, towering over her in a way that must have been uncomfortable for her. If not for the room full of people, Marcus might have said something along those lines.

Raising one hand to his chest like a stage actor, Mr. Flemming spoke in a voice that boomed too loudly through the cozy room. "Miss Thornton, members of the Milwaukee Exploration Society, I was honored to be your guest today. The crisp air invigorated me. The exertion revitalized me." His tone lowered to a more intimate level as he glanced down at Leonora and rested his hand on her shoulder. "And the company was unparalleled."

Dropping his hand, he looked up again and met each club member's gaze—except for Marcus's. "But seeing the way this group approached a challenge with excitement and willingness to face any obstacle that arose—well, that was inspiring, my friends. And that's why I extended an invitation for Miss Thornton—and all of your club, by extension—to join my next expedition to Peru. It could be a valuable experience for any who choose to join us, especially if we uncover the lost Incan city, as I expect we will."

Murmurs flew around the room. Marcus could only look at Leonora, whose shocked expression mirrored the uncomfortable tingle that raced across Marcus's skin. What happened to giving her more details and time to consider it?

Mr. Flemming held up both hands in the air to quiet the group before continuing. "Now, it's a far more dangerous trip than you're used to, and there will be a great deal of hard work involved. Since most of you aren't specifically skilled in archaeology or related fields, you'll be doing much of the manual labor—removing jungle growth, hauling dirt, or helping relocate the camp when necessary. I want each of you to carefully consider the level of involvement you're comfortable with. Voyages like this are costly. There are supplies and equipment to buy, transportation and accommodations to arrange, along with guides and translators to hire. Even if you don't want to join the crew, each of you can help raise money for the rest of us to go."

Leonora jumped up from her chair, clapping her hands and cutting off whatever else Mr. Flemming might have been hoping to say. "Let's thank Mr. Flemming for joining us today and for extending that...unexpected invitation."

Polite applause went on for a few seconds while the club members glanced at each other as if trying to decide what to think. Before Mr. Flemming could get another word in, Leonora began gathering cups, causing the others to start rising from their seats. The club members departed as a group, with Mr. Flemming among them, finally leaving Marcus alone with Leonora.

∼

*A*s soon as the door closed behind the last guest, Leonora returned to the parlor and dropped into Papa's oversized leather chair, letting her head fall against the worn back.

Marcus claimed her mother's usual chair, which was the closest seat to Leonora. He ran a hand through his hair as if he felt as dazed and bewildered as Leonora did. "What just happened?"

Leonora sighed. "I believe that situation got away from me a bit. You heard our conversation on the train." It wasn't a question. She hadn't missed that he'd nearly choked with the effort of restraining himself, despite his claim of a sore throat to cover it up.

He didn't try to deny it now. "You had the perfect response, firm but not impolite. It's not your fault he didn't follow through on his word to give you time."

Warmth spread through Leonora. It was silly to be so pleased that Marcus approved of her simple request to consider the invitation, but she was, nonetheless. "Why on earth would he go and make that grand speech, then? And to focus so heavily on asking us to help him raise money..."

Marcus only shrugged. Even if he didn't say it out loud, he would no doubt agree that Mr. Flemming's behavior was uncouth, at best. But he seemed determined not to begin the same argument they'd had earlier again.

With agitation growing in her chest, Leonora rose and paced in front of the fireplace, the warm blaze helping to ease the chill that still clung to her fingers and toes. "Should we tell the club not to support him, though? Simply because he went about it rather rudely? I'm not sure that's the Christian thing to do."

Emotions played across Marcus's face. He could often be very closed off, hiding his feelings deep inside. But she loved that when it was the two of them, he tended to lose that hiddenness to an extent. She was the one person he opened up to, and she tried hard not to take that for granted.

After a thoughtful pause, Marcus leaned forward, resting

his elbows on his knees. "What do you think *is* the Christian response to a man who went back on his word, then?"

Pursing her lips, Leonora fought back frustration. Now was not a time when she wanted to figure out the right answer for herself. She was trying to ask for his help. "If I knew, I would have said so."

When Marcus didn't respond, silence filled the room, broken only by the clock on the mantel ticking away and the fire popping and cracking. Finally, Leonora gave up. She turned to pace across the room, pretending to study an embroidered sampler Cassia had made when they were younger. None of Leonora's needlework was framed and hanging anywhere, which made an accurate statement about her level of interest in sewing. And any ladylike hobbies, for that matter. While she could get along well enough if needed, she'd never actually cared about the skills required to run a household. Despite the fear that had wracked her for the last few years, she had only ever longed to explore and discover.

That truth secured the decision in her mind, even without Marcus's advice. If she wanted to follow in Papa's footsteps, she would have to take chances. She'd been putting off taking any real risks since his death. It was high time she *did* something. Maybe this was the push from God she'd been waiting for, the clear sign that she should step out in faith and go.

She spun to face Marcus, and at finding him watching her with a warm, direct gaze, heat rushed up her neck. She squared her shoulders and pushed her chin upward to project a confidence she didn't feel. "I want to go on the expedition. And I feel we ought to help Mr. Flemming raise the necessary funds. It's only right to help pay for my expenses and those of any other club members who want to go."

Would Marcus argue? Would he once again insinuate that Mr. Flemming was a fraud? Leonora refused to explain herself further. She had every right to make this choice for herself.

This might be her best opportunity to go on an expedition, and it just so happened to be to the very place she wanted to go most. That had to be God arranging things for her. And she couldn't use Marcus's doubts as a reason to refuse to follow God's lead.

Although moving forward with the decision without Marcus's support would be one of the most difficult things she'd ever had to do.

Unexpectedly, Marcus stood and walked over to stand in front of her. He placed a hand on each of her shoulders, his warm touch over the fabric of her shirtwaist sending strange tingles across her skin. His head dipped so he could look straight into her eyes. "Leonora, you're the bravest woman I've ever met. If you want to do this..." He paused, his eyes flicking away for a second before returning to hers. "I'll support you the best I can. I'll help raise money. But I have too many responsibilities here. I can't pick up and travel for months at a time."

His words should have been comforting. He was offering to help her, rather than arguing against her decision as she'd expected. But she hadn't considered that he wouldn't be able to join her on the expedition. Of course, she should have realized that. He had a job to do. He wasn't free to travel on a whim as she was.

But the idea of going without him extinguished a great deal of her excitement for the journey.

Still, she had good reasons for going. It wasn't entirely because of the letter she hadn't told Marcus about, which was currently stashed in a drawer in her room. She wasn't taking the veiled insults in it to heart, of course.

Without her meaning for it to, her hand slid into the pocket of her skirt, where a new letter was currently hidden, one Mother said had been delivered while they were gone that day. She should tell Marcus, even if the letters weren't her reason for wanting to go. Shouldn't she?

Caught in indecision, she jumped when Marcus reached out to tilt her chin up with his index finger, bringing her attention back to the conversation. "Leonora? Are you sure you want to do this? I can't be there to help you if anything goes wrong."

He sounded almost...anguished. The thought of him worrying while she was away spurred her into action. She forced a smile, ignoring the heaviness in her heart at knowing she had to do this without him. "Nothing will go wrong, Marcus. I can do this. Remember, Papa used to take me out when he was training for expeditions all the time. He might not have thought I was ready to lead an expedition of my own, but surely, I can handle being part of an experienced crew. Just promise me you'll help us raise the money and get prepared, and that's all I need from you."

She'd hoped the words would release him from feeling responsible for her, but for some reason, his eyes dimmed as she spoke. He pressed his lips tight together, then nodded once. "Of course. I'm always here to help you." Dropping his hands, Marcus stepped back. "I should be going. I'll see you Monday evening?"

She nodded, glad he would be there to help with the English class she taught every other week for new immigrants, but unable to form any other response while the wall that had risen between them threatened to crush her.

Marcus smiled, but it was his business smile, the one he used at the bank but never with her. "Then good night, Leonora."

He disappeared into the hall, but Leonora could only stand frozen, unable to see him out. What had gone wrong? Why had distance grown between them so suddenly?

Eventually, Leonora moved to the sofa and slid the new letter from her pocket. She tore it open and read every word with slow deliberation. This time, it was shorter and much more direct. It seemed the writer was rather put out with her.

Dear Miss Thornton,

I'd thought my encouragement might have been enough to prod you into action, but I see you still hesitate to take on the responsibility of discovering what happened to your father. Perhaps I was right and you are more concerned with finding a husband than with tragic events that happened so far away. It must be easy for you to put it out of your mind.

However, consider this—the situation didn't only affect you, but also your mother, your siblings and their children, Hugh Randall's wife, and his children, who are still so young to have to live without their father.

If the truth isn't important to you, don't you think it might be to some of them?

It might seem odd to you that a stranger would be so concerned with this matter. It rankles me to see an injustice go unpunished. The Explorers Club didn't investigate fully, and you, as the most qualified and capable person affected by the tragedy, might be the only one who can set it to rights.

Sincerely as ever,

An Observer

Refolding the letter and hiding it away again, lightheadedness washed over Leonora. The accusations in the letter were surreal. How was she the only one who could repair a possible injustice?

But a part of her heart perked up, as bothered by the possibility of injustice as this stranger was. As he said, she was the one who should determine if the investigation had been complete and accurate. And now she had the perfect opportunity to do so. The best way to get answers was to go see the site of the accident for herself, to talk with the local guides Papa's crew had used and listen to people who might have witnessed something. She was done relying on the Explorers Club, which had disappointed her in too many ways.

Even Marcus, a constant supportive presence in her life since she was seven, couldn't be there to help her with this. But God was guiding her steps and surely had a hand in placing this opportunity in front of her. She refused to shirk that calling.

CHAPTER 6

*M*arcus strode into Leonora's church on Monday after work with a quiver in his stomach that set every nerve in his body on edge.

Helping teach English to Polish and German immigrants was not the problem. While he wasn't the best teacher, he was good at organizing class material for those who did instruct the attendees, and he liked feeling that he was helping people who had worked so hard to build a new life for themselves, much as he'd had to do for his family.

No, it was working side by side with Leonora without revealing how he felt about her choice to go on the foolhardy expedition that had him hesitating outside the door to the room the church had set aside for the classes. The issue had weighed on him all night and during his hours at the bank, and it was making him regret his commitment to help her now.

But he'd made a promise that he would see Leonora there, and he refused to be a man who didn't keep his word. Marcus pushed the door open and entered the room, finding it occupied by a few families and a handful of men, along with two other teachers. Straightening his spine, Marcus greeted people as warmly as he could manage while they settled into their seats. But he wasn't so occupied as to be able to miss the moment when Leonora walked in with a small child on each side of her, both of them clinging to her hands. She glanced over, offering him a hesitant, uncertain smile. Perhaps he hadn't hidden his reaction to her decision as well as he'd hoped.

What was he to do, though? He couldn't leave his job or his family to go halfway around the world to protect Leonora from her own bad decisions. The only option available to him was to proceed with her plan, to be supportive enough now that she might listen to reason before going on what he feared would be an ill-fated trip.

Once all the attendees were seated, Leonora moved to the front and waited as quiet spread across the group. Marcus joined her, mentally preparing for his usual portion of the program. Several years ago, Leonora had convinced Marcus that joining the volunteers who helped local immigrants learn English was a good way to practice telling others about the Lord. Since then, Leonora had grown into an excellent teacher. Knowing that she hoped to one day combine missionary work with her exploration, Marcus loved to watch her flourish in this area.

But while Marcus tried to live the way the Bible taught, he wasn't at all comfortable with telling people about his faith. How could he be, when he frequently doubted it himself? God seemed like a far-off overseer, someone who handed out blessings to others but didn't often send them Marcus's way. No, Marcus wasn't there out of any desire to convert others, but because refusing to help Leonora achieve something she wanted was impossible for him.

That was exactly why he was planning to pack his true feelings about Vernon Flemming down deep inside and wait for the moment when Leonora would realize for herself what a fraud the man was. He just hoped she would see it before it was too late.

Standing at Leonora's side in front of the group, Marcus cleared his throat. "Let's begin with prayer. Please bow your heads."

Praying aloud was a struggle for Marcus, so he usually spent an hour or so on Sunday evenings practicing a prayer that might sound like he was coming up with it in the moment. As the room grew even quieter and the few children calmed most of their squirming, he drew a deep breath and began, hoping he appeared confident. "Lord, we thank You for our family and friends, and for the lesson Miss Thornton is about to teach. Help these students learn well tonight. Amen."

Before he moved toward the side of the room so Leonora could begin the lesson, she reached out and rested light fingertips on his shoulder. When Marcus met her gaze, which held nothing but approval, the weight of worry over how his prayer might have sounded lifted from his shoulders. His lungs relaxed, and he was able to draw a full, cleansing breath while he stepped aside and Leonora began addressing the group.

"Welcome, everyone. Adults, you'll begin tonight by reviewing the list of words from last week. Children, I have a special story for you. Come gather around."

Marcus and the other volunteers began helping the adults review a list of homonyms. Meanwhile, Leonora sat on the floor with the children and enthralled them with her dramatic telling of a Bible story, then asked them questions about what the passage meant, easily translating the concepts into simple English words that even the youngest children could understand. And that was one of the reasons Marcus would never ask her to stay in Milwaukee just to be with him. Leonora longed to share the gospel with those who hadn't heard it, and it would be a shame to waste her talent for doing so. She was meant to do much greater things than Marcus could ever hope to attain.

On Tuesday of that week, Leonora sent word to the club members that Mr. Flemming was giving another lecture, this time at Marquette University. She requested the presence of as many members as possible in order to help make the event a successful fundraiser.

Once again, Marcus considered excusing himself. He did have a meeting with an important potential client at the bank scheduled toward the end of the day, and that would make the perfect excuse. But his mother had thwarted that with an unexpected invitation to the same lecture from one of her closer society friends, Mrs. Millian.

By eight o'clock that evening, Marcus found himself escorting his mother into an impressive lecture hall on the Marquette campus. He had to admit that no matter how much he might not want to be there, it was a good thing that he was able to be. It was difficult enough to protect Leonora from Mr. Flemming, but Marcus absolutely would not allow his mother to be deceived again. She'd fallen for the same kind of tricks Vernon Flemming liked to use once before. It was Marcus's responsibility to see that she never repeated that mistake.

Once they made their way through the people lingering in the lobby and entered the hall, Marcus caught sight of Leonora at the other end, helping Mr. and Mrs. Adler settle into seats at the front of the room. The gown she wore was made of gray lace, lined with white underneath and accented by a wide band of flowing gray satin at the bottom. The delicate shade complemented her fair coloring in a way that drew many more eyes than just Marcus's.

"Marcus, darling, you don't have to stay by my side all night."

Marcus tugged his attention from the beautiful vision across the room to his mother, who had turned from greeting Mrs. Millian. The two women had seated themselves while he remained standing, a testament to how easily distracted he was whenever Leonora was in sight.

He lowered himself into the chair next to his mother and attempted not to crane his neck to catch another glimpse of Leonora. While Mrs. Millian spoke to a woman on the other side of her, Mother fidgeted with the beaded fringe on a gown he was certain he hadn't seen her wear before. His chest constricted with the weight of knowing every cent he earned went toward keeping the family from social ruin, while Mother and Eli gave no thought whatsoever to the cost of their purchases. Or how much harder Marcus would have to work to make up for their excesses.

But now was not the time or place to upset her with talk of their tight budget. He patted her arm in an effort to stop her fiddling. "It's all right, Mother. I don't mind spending an evening with you."

She arched one eyebrow and tipped her head toward Leonora. "Then perhaps you should pay attention to the person you've escorted here instead of the young lady across the room."

Myra Turner might often put on the guise of being oblivious, and she'd certainly made her share of mistakes when it came to judging people's character. But she wasn't ignorant about Marcus's persistent feelings for his lifelong friend. While she'd always disapproved of both his father's association with the Thorntons and now Marcus's, she didn't usually make a scene over it. Still, he did owe her his attention, and daydreaming about Leonora from a distance didn't do any good. "No, she's busy tonight. I'm fine right here."

"And how exactly did you and Miss Thornton come to know this explorer?" Mother asked with genuine interest.

Marcus recounted the facts of their connection to him, trying to keep his feelings for the man to himself.

Mother eyed the room thoughtfully. "He must be quite an

intriguing speaker to get all these members of society to come and learn about his adventures. Usually, these lectures aren't so well attended."

His attention had been so focused on Mother and Leonora that Marcus hadn't paid much attention to who was present. He took his own look around and found that Mother was right. This was not the normal crowd for a lecture on the exploration of Peruvian jungles.

The room quieted as a man opened the program and introduced Mr. Flemming. But as the evening moved forward, Marcus watched the faces of those who had come to hear the man speak. They were charmed. Enthralled, even. Something about Mr. Flemming's manner made people trust him, even when they shouldn't. And Marcus knew from experience that that was the most dangerous kind of man there was.

～

It wasn't worth trying to lie to herself. Leonora was relieved that Marcus was somewhere in the crowd. She'd only caught a glimpse of him by the doors with Mrs. Turner, but there were more people present than Leonora would have imagined, making it difficult to pick out anyone in particular. Somehow, Mr. Flemming had drawn an unusually large and well-to-do audience. Lectures on provocative subjects —advancements in human flight, the ethics of Charles Darwin's studies, or even campaign speeches by local Socialist mayoral candidate Emil Seidel—often brought out upper-class patrons. But a simple presentation on exploration in Peru wasn't generally the same crowd.

He couldn't be as bad as Marcus seemed to think if all these people were so interested in hearing him speak. Could he? It was certainly true that the explorer was far more personable on stage than in individual conversation. But that didn't mean he was fraudulent.

Leonora leaned back in her seat and tried to focus on taking in both his presentation and the way the crowd responded to him. It would help the Exploration Society's efforts to find investors for the expedition if they understood Mr. Flemming's strengths and weaknesses. They could compensate for any deficiencies in his social skills. Usually, Leonora loved a good lecture and could listen in rapt attention for hours on end. But Mr. Flemming was repeating much of the same information and stories from the first lecture.

By the time she'd drawn up a mental list of several event ideas and a handful of names of people in the room who might entertain an investment request from the club, the lecture was drawing to a close and guests began moving to the refreshment tables in the lobby. Leonora jumped up and addressed the club members she'd been sitting with. "If you don't mind, please socialize with anyone you know to be charitable and generous, or exceptionally interested in world exploration. Report to me if you think someone might welcome a request for support."

The club members wandered off to do as instructed. She should do the same, but Leonora found herself instead searching the room for Mrs. Turner or Marcus. There. Mrs. Turner's heavily beaded mustard-yellow gown flashed an announcement of her presence near the doors.

But before she could take more than two steps, a familiar voice called her name. Turning, she found Cassia and her husband, Paul, beckoning for Leonora to join them.

While attempting to unclench her jaw, she made her way around departing attendees until she reached her sister. Cassia enveloped Leonora in a loose hug, and stoic Paul nodded his greeting. Leonora looked all around them, finding no evidence that any of her nephews had been there. "What on earth convinced you to go to a lecture about Peru, Cassia? And where are the boys?"

Before answering, Cassia threaded her arm through Paul's and leaned close to his ear. "Darling, won't you go get me something sweet before all the refreshments are picked over? Thank you, my dear."

Without a word, Paul tipped his hat to them before walking away.

Cassia waited until he disappeared into the crowd before turning back to face Leonora. "The boys are staying overnight at your house with Felix and Arabella. And I'm here because, quite frankly, Mother and I are worried about you."

Leonora drew back. That was the last reason she might have expected her sister to give for coming to the sort of event she'd always deemed tedious to the point of tears. "Worried about what?"

Cassia waved a careless hand toward the front of the room. "The entire idea of this expedition you're so set on, not to mention Mr. Flemming. I needed to see the man for myself before I could confidently entrust your safety to him."

Heat burned up Leonora's neck. Since having children of their own, her older siblings had spent less time treating Leonora like a child herself, but their youthful habit still emerged on occasion. And it never ceased to frustrate her. "I don't need you to investigate the man for me, Cassia. I'm capable of taking care of myself."

Cassia sighed heavily, as if Leonora's independence was an inconvenience for her. "Of course, Peru is of interest to you because it was Papa's passion. But what Mother and I want to understand is, why now? Is it because this explorer is giving you an opportunity, or is there some other reason?"

Leonora shrugged, keeping her gaze glued to anything but her sister's face. She couldn't *not* feel Cassia's pointed stare, though.

A few long moments passed while tension built in Leonora's chest. She hated the way Cassia had always known when she wasn't being completely honest. "Fine," she burst out. "I want to look into Papa's death."

Now it was Cassia's turn to draw back, her forehead furrowed. "But we all know what happened. There was quite a bit of detail in the report, considering the language barrier and the difficulty in getting officials to investigate jungle accidents. What could you possibly want to look into?"

Leonora dropped into one of the empty seats behind her, considering how much she wanted to tell Cassia. She wouldn't lie to her sister, but she also wasn't ready to reveal the letters to anyone. Settling on a truth she felt comfortable divulging, Leonora leaned forward. "I sometimes feel as if everyone else has moved forward with their lives, while I'm stuck in the same place I was in when Papa died. You and Felix have your families to keep you busy. Mother has filled her time with volunteer work and friends. I'm happy for everyone, but maybe it's time for me to move on too."

Cassia chewed on her bottom lip while nodding. "I see what you mean. But like Mother, you've filled your time with worthwhile causes. You lead your club, teach classes for immigrants, spend time with your family. Why do you need to leave the country to move forward?"

For once, Cassia was truly listening, rather than playing the part of a know-it-all older sister. Leonora's heart lifted. "It's been my dream for so long. And now it's as if God placed Mr. Flemming in my path for a reason. How can I allow the opportunity to pass me by without trying to see if it's what I'm meant to do?"

Cassia's shoulders sagged, and Leonora knew she'd won. "I still have concerns, but I can't deny that it's always seemed like you were born to follow in Papa's footsteps. I'll tell Mother that you know what you're doing. But don't make me a liar for saying so, Leonora."

Paul returned then, with several sweet options in hand. He offered the first choice to Cassia—smart man—then held out the remaining cookies to Leonora. His expression was cautious, as if he was trying to decide what he'd walked back into. "Did you ladies have a nice chat while I was gone?"

Relieved to have Cassia's approval for once, Leonora chuckled. "Yes, Paul. We found some common ground, so you needn't worry about a chilly family meal on Sunday."

With a nod of agreement, Cassia released a genuine smile. "Quite right. At least, not about the expedition. There's plenty of time for us to find something else to argue about before Sunday, right, Leonora?"

All three of them laughed, although there was a measure of truth to Cassia's words. But Leonora did appreciate that any time they fought, she and Cassia could always repair their relationship without too much fuss. Neither tended to hold a grudge. She would hate for a petty disagreement to put a lasting wedge between them.

When Cassia and Paul decided it was time to leave, Leonora walked to the door with them, bidding them good night. She glanced around the dwindling crowd in the lobby, heaviness settling over her. Marcus must have slipped out. She tried to shake off her silly reaction. She saw him often enough. Missing him this one time shouldn't make her melancholy. She was sure to get a chance to talk to him at the same Sunday lunch she'd just talked about with her sister, if not before.

Despite her efforts to talk herself into more steady, controlled feelings, when she finally caught sight of Marcus across the lobby, a warm rush pushed everything else aside. He stood next to his mother while she spoke to Mr. Flemming with a broad smile and enthusiastic gestures. While Leonora had always known Marcus was handsome, something about the way he stood there struck her anew. His blue eyes were so inviting, even with his glasses obscuring them a bit from this distance, and she couldn't help admiring how broad his shoulders looked in the suit he'd chosen for the evening.

Leonora gave in to the sudden rush of nerves and allowed herself a moment to smooth her skirt and run her hand over her hair to assure herself the silk flower she'd woven in wasn't coming loose. Was Arabella's new evening gown she'd worn too pretentious for a lecture? It had seemed understated enough when she put it on.

But honestly, it wasn't as if Marcus would notice, anyway. He was not only a man and thus usually unconcerned with fashion, but he would *not* look at her and see anything other than his old friend. She was the woman who had always been there for him, not a mysterious, enchanting creature he might moon over.

But she would miss the chance to talk to Marcus if she fussed over her appearance much longer. Leonora turned with what she hoped was a relaxed smile and made her way across the room at a stately pace. Marcus noticed her approach first, and his lips parted while warmth filled his eyes.

Mr. Flemming saw her next, finishing a rather lengthy sentence before pausing to greet her. "Ah, Miss Thornton. What a lovely evening we've had, wouldn't you agree?"

Tilting her head in greeting, Leonora shot a fleeting glance toward Marcus, trying to keep her attention on the others. "It certainly has been. Good evening, Mrs. Turner. It's good to see you again."

Mrs. Turner nodded in Leonora's direction, then immediately turned back to Mr. Flemming. Marcus's mother had never been warm toward Leonora, so her quick dismissal wasn't unexpected. Still, it was never pleasant to realize that her company didn't even warrant the woman's interest, much less any eagerness.

While the other two continued their conversation, which sounded like a great deal of proud posturing, Leonora shuffled a step closer to Marcus. His gaze alighted on her for a moment before shifting away, leaving Leonora wondering if whatever had been bothering him on Saturday night after the ski trip was still on his mind. Was he angry because she'd decided to go on the expedition without him? Or perhaps because she was placing her trust in Mr. Flemming despite Marcus's warnings about the man?

As much as she hated having an argument distance her from Cassia, the mere idea of that happening with Marcus was even worse. It was enough to turn her blood cold, to make her feel as if she might be ill right there in front of all those influential people.

But how could she keep that from happening to their relationship while still staying true to what she wanted—no, needed—to do in order to follow the path God had put her on?

CHAPTER 7

*M*arcus did his best not to stare at Leonora, but he kept finding his gaze sliding toward her as she stood at his side. That gown was more beautiful up close than it had been from across the room, and Leonora all but sparkled under the glow of the electric lights. He wanted nothing more than to whisk her to a secluded corner so he could have her attention all to himself.

His mind might be trying to put some distance between them, but his heart certainly didn't agree.

On his other side, Mother and Mr. Flemming were going on about their respective society acquaintances, one-upping each other at every turn. He didn't care to join that conversation. It sounded like a nightmare come to life.

So he tilted his head toward Leonora. "I saw the club members making rounds and talking with the guests. I suppose they've all been convinced to join in this fundraising venture." Marcus winced. That sounded peevish and bitter. Feelings he might be experiencing, yes, but Leonora didn't have to know how deep his derision for this situation ran. That would only put more distance between them, which was a wholly unacceptable possibility.

Her jaw tightened as she clenched her teeth together before speaking. "No one was dragged into this against their will, Marcus. Those who attended tonight want to help. They see value in taking a necessary risk for the sake of furthering our understanding of the world."

Marcus's fingers twitched at her tart retort. He usually appreciated that she never let his surly behavior go unaddressed. It made him a better man. In most situations, at least. Tonight, he'd rather sulk without censure.

Marcus turned so his shoulders blocked them from Mother and Mr. Flemming and lowered his voice. "I just hate to see so many of our friends being told that this man is trustworthy. I know you have doubts about him, Leonora. I've seen you when you're completely convinced that something is right, and the way you're acting now proves to me that you aren't sure about your current path."

Leonora stepped closer, tipping her face up to practically hiss at Marcus. "At least I'm trying to follow the path I'm supposed to go on. I'm taking a risk in order to do what I'm meant to do. What are you doing while sitting in that bank all day besides growing more frustrated with your life?"

Marcus drew back. The words stung, to be sure. But she wasn't wrong.

Leonora swallowed hard and squeezed her eyes shut for a moment. Then she rested the fingers of one hand on his forearm. "Marcus, I'm sorry. That wasn't kind, and you didn't ask for my judgment on your life. Please forgive me."

Her apology brought a thickness to his throat. It pained him to think of it, but what if she had hidden reasons for doing what she was doing, as he did? He expected her to let him make the right choices for his life without understanding why, so shouldn't he extend the same trust to her?

"Of course. I'm sorry for questioning your choices." He softened his expression and his tone in an attempt to communicate what he couldn't say out loud. "I'm worried, but I'll try not to let that cause me to treat you as if you aren't a strong, capable woman. You are, without a doubt, the most..."

Gazing down into her beautiful face, Marcus trailed off. He couldn't say what he wanted to. She was preparing to leave, to finally pursue her dreams. He'd waited this long for her to explore enough of the world that she would feel ready to open herself up to romantic possibilities. He could keep waiting. His heart ached when he thought of her going on this expedition, though. But was it because he had reason to doubt Vernon Flemming? Or because she was going with or without Marcus?

While they stared at each other with Marcus's unspoken words hanging in the air, silence had fallen behind them. Marcus swiveled around to find Mother watching with raised eyebrows that signaled her disapproval. Mr. Flemming considered Marcus and Leonora with narrowed eyes, looking as if he was learning something new about them, but what that might be, Marcus could only guess. He prayed it wasn't something the man would use to hurt Leonora.

Marcus faced the pair, trying to erase any signs of dislike from his face. Hopefully, the two of them hadn't overheard Marcus's whispered conversation with Leonora. "Mr. Flemming, I hope you've taken note of how hard Miss Thornton has worked tonight on your behalf."

Before the explorer could respond, Marcus's mother cut in with a sharp tone. "Do you mean to tell me that this young woman is...employed by you, Mr. Flemming?" She looked so aghast at the idea that Marcus almost barked out a laugh.

While Leonora was clearly trying to keep from lashing out in response, Marcus saw an opportunity to try to make up for his own actions and prove he could support Leonora's choices.

"No, not exactly employed by him, Mother. She's part of Mr. Flemming's next expedition. It's wonderful that she has the opportunity to participate, isn't it?"

Mr. Flemming slid into the opening Marcus unintentionally created. "Mrs. Turner, I would never employ a young woman. But I'm quite good at seeing when someone around me has a helpful talent. Take you, for example. You're a respected, well-connected woman. Perhaps you would agree to help me meet those in Milwaukee society who might be interested in supporting our quest for discovery?"

Mother simpered, taken in by Mr. Flemming's flattery as easily as Marcus would have expected. At least the man hadn't asked her for money. Not yet, anyway. Marcus would have to talk with her as soon as possible and remind her of what had happened ten years ago, of why he had to work so hard at the bank to keep their family from losing everything. She would rail and complain, but in the end, it would be worth the pain he might have to endure if he could protect her from herself this time.

Because while he wouldn't come right out and throw it in her face, the reason she didn't have money to give to Mr. Flemming was that she'd already foolishly thrown it away on a man who had been even more manipulative and dishonest.

Marcus brought his attention back to the conversation in time to hear Mr. Flemming ask if he could call on Mother later that week. She agreed, tittering like a girl with a crush, which made Marcus feel a bit ill and desperate for some fresh air. "Mother, it's getting late. We should be going now. Good evening, Mr. Flemming."

As Marcus turned away from the pair while they said good-bye, his gaze caught on Leonora, whose mouth hung open at Mother's girlish behavior. He held out his arm for Leonora to take and turned her toward the doors, then leaned in close to whisper, "You might want to fix your expression before Mother has more reason to snub you than the fact that your family isn't rich."

Replacing her slack jaw with a grin, Leonora leaned against Marcus and let him lead the way from the building. Amusement danced in her eyes, assuring him the comment about her family's financial status wasn't offensive to her. The two of them had spoken about his mother's terrible attitude toward Leonora many times in the past, but Marcus still worried that it would bother her.

Outside, Leonora pulled her arm from Marcus's, preparing to let him join his mother in the hired carriage while she walked home, which Marcus hated. "Leonora, are you sure you won't allow us to drive you? It's not that far out of our way."

Shouldering past them on her way toward their vehicle, Mother sniffed. "It most certainly is out of our way. I'm tired, Marcus. Please get in so we can go home."

Marcus returned his attention to Leonora with a sigh. "I'm sorry about her. Again."

Sweet as ever despite the way his mother's behavior must sting, Leonora responded with a gentle smile. "Never mind that, Marcus. You're kind to me and that's all that matters."

Marcus reached out to wrap his hand around hers, squeezing her fingers before nodding and heading toward the carriage. But he didn't hear a word of Mother's constant commentary on all the important people she'd seen that night as they traveled the dark streets.

Was his kindness toward Leonora all that mattered, though? He didn't even do that well, as proven by his behavior that evening. But more worrisome than that, was he doing her a disservice by being her friend when nothing more could come of their relationship?

Leonora deserved a man who would give her the adventures she longed for. Marcus couldn't be that man—at least, not for the foreseeable future. Was his presence in her life keeping her from finding the love her heart longed for?

Or was there a way Marcus could become that man? He glanced at his mother, nodding as if he heard her words. If Eli did convince a rich woman to marry him, Marcus wouldn't have to continue reining in his family and working at the bank forever. Perhaps he could finally hand off care of Mother to Eli and follow the path he wanted, rather than the one he'd been forced into.

∼

Several weeks after the lecture, Leonora stood at the front of the room at the library where the Exploration Society usually held their meetings. She thumped her gavel against the podium, bringing the board meeting to order. The conversation quieted, Marcus, Mrs. Adler, Charlotte, and Alexander Brighton watching her in expectation.

It was nice to have Mr. Brighton back with them. Other than Mrs. Adler's husband occasionally joining an outing, Marcus and Mr. Howard were usually the only male members who participated when Mr. Brighton was away on his frequent business trips. Her goal had been to create a co-educational club, but she had to admit that the membership currently leaned heavily toward females.

Fixing a bright smile on her face, Leonora straightened her notes while speaking. "Good evening, everyone. Most of our time tonight will be spent deciding how the club can best support Mr. Flemming's fundraising efforts and how we can prepare any members who choose to join the expedition."

Charlotte raised her hand. "Alice and I agree that we should go camping soon. If the weather allows, of course. What better practice is there than that?"

Leonora glanced toward Mrs. Adler, who was taking note of

the suggestion. "Thank you, Charlotte. That's an excellent idea, and we'll talk about the details in a few moments. What other preparation ideas should we spend time on?"

Over the next hour, the group made plans for a few more long hikes to increase endurance, an overnight camping excursion, and a simple food preparation demonstration using nonperishable items, which Leonora thought was quite a clever idea from Mrs. Adler.

When Leonora was about ready to conclude the meeting, rather anxious that they hadn't thought of any fresh ways to approach fundraising, Marcus finally spoke up for the first time. "Have you considered partnering with other clubs and organizations in town to raise money? The state museum might be willing to work with us. Or the Milwaukee Historical Society. We went on that tour of the native mounds last year, and their members were quite interested in working with us on projects, if you remember."

Leonora's heart warmed. No matter how frustrated Marcus might have been about her decision to join Mr. Flemming, he was still her friend and had jumped right in to champion her efforts. He was a better man than he ever gave himself credit for. "Very good ideas, Marcus. I'm glad you thought of that. I'd nearly forgotten about that trip, but they were looking for ways we could work together, weren't they?"

There was a bit more discussion amongst the board members about how they might approach other groups, but Leonora was rather distracted by considering the various ways Marcus had supported her plans in the weeks since the lecture. He had helped her begin making lists of equipment they would need, and he'd set up a ledger for her to use to track the funds they gathered. More than that, he hadn't spoken a word against Mr. Flemming or criticized Leonora's choice to go on the expedition.

A flutter in her stomach accompanied those thoughts. Thank goodness for Mrs. Adler's thorough notetaking so Leonora could go back later and see what she'd missed while admiring how good a friend Marcus was. If only that flutter would stop making her feel as if there could possibly be more behind his actions than friendship.

Once it was clear there was no more business to discuss, Leonora moved to end the meeting. Mr. Brighton seconded her motion right as the shuffle of feet at the back of the room caused them all to turn and look in that direction. A handsome, broad-shouldered young man stood in the doorway. His head dipped, making his words barely audible. "Sorry for interrupting. I'm here to walk Miss Bauer home."

Everyone turned to look at Charlotte, who smiled through a deep blush. "We're almost done, Ernst. Give me a few minutes."

Ernst clutched a fancy confectioner's box and a decorated envelope, drawing a smile from Leonora as well. She'd forgotten it was Valentine's Day. Good for Ernst for coming prepared to sweep Charlotte off her feet. "Mr. Brighton seconded the motion to end the meeting. I'll see you all at the club meeting next week. Have a lovely evening."

Before Leonora hardly finished speaking, Charlotte jumped to her feet and rushed to the door, where she met Ernst with more blushing and smiling and murmured thanks for the gifts. Mr. Brighton and Mrs. Adler joined the couple on the way to get their coats, leaving only Marcus, who was once again going to walk Leonora home.

"What has you smiling that way?"

She met his amused gaze and shrugged at the sappy grin she couldn't seem to erase from her face. "Wasn't that sweet? A beau bringing his girl Valentine's gifts. She better hold on to that one."

Marcus watched her for a long moment without responding. What had she said that warranted such thorough consideration? Before she could figure it out, he tilted his head toward the door. "Are you ready to go? There's a stop I need to make on the way."

They stopped in the coatroom to pull on their warm layers, although the weather was starting to improve from the frigid winter temperatures they'd been experiencing. Marcus offered Leonora his arm as they left the library, and she took it, reveling in the companionable silence as they walked through the still evening air.

But rather than stopping at the bank as she'd supposed he might need to, Marcus paused in front of a row of small shops two blocks from Leonora's house. He reached out to open the door to Harvey's Confectionary, a delightful little place that had installed a soda fountain last year. Leonora didn't move, instead raising her eyebrows at Marcus. "You have business at the drugstore?"

His lips quirked in a lopsided grin. "I never said it was a business stop. It's Valentine's Day. Wouldn't you like to celebrate?"

A myriad of emotions raced through Leonora all at once, swirling around in her chest. Delight, uncertainty, thrill, confusion. Just in time to avoid blocking other patrons trying to get through the open door, her feelings settled into anticipation. She'd never spent time with a man like this before. Sure, she was with Marcus on many occasions, but there was always a purpose—club meetings and events, the times he accompanied her home out of politeness, meals with her family. An evening out publicly in each other's company felt quite different.

It felt like something couples did.

Oh, but that thought was dangerous. Leonora cleared it immediately from her mind. Friends could also go to a soda fountain together. They could celebrate a holiday. Even if it was one usually connected with romance.

Squaring her shoulders, she nodded. "This is a wonderful surprise, Marcus. Thank you."

Inside the store, Marcus led the way to the right, where a long marble counter extended the length of the narrow building. Patrons occupied most of the cast-iron stools in front of the counter. Behind the bar, wood and glass cabinets ran from the floor to the ceiling, all filled with various flavored syrup dispensers, glasses, and other necessary items. In the center of the cabinets was the soda fountain, designed with a sturdy marble base and a large mirror in an ornate wooden frame mounted on top. Gleaming handles lined the front, each marked with the type of soda it would dispense when pulled.

The other side of the shop held a smaller counter where a young attendant sold confections, which on this day was quite busy. At the end of the room sat a hulking orchestrion, a wood cabinet housing a multitude of pipes, pumps, keys, and drums that simulated the sounds of different instruments. The resulting music sounded like an entire orchestra was right there in the shop. Beautiful Tiffany lamps dropped from the pressed tin ceiling high above, giving everything in the shop an opulent glow.

Marcus waited by two empty stools until Leonora seated herself, then he took the other. "What's your favorite? I don't think we've ever had a soda together."

It was hard to believe that in all their years of friendship, they hadn't done something so simple together, but he was right. "Oh, I love root beer. I always think on the way here that I'll try something new this time, but I end up choosing my old favorite instead."

Without offering any criticism of her comfortable choice, Marcus ordered a root beer for her and a Cherry Smash for himself. Then he returned his attention to her. "There's no shame in enjoying what you know you like. It does surprise me, though, knowing how much you love adventure and new experiences."

Indeed, that was how everyone saw her, but could she still claim to love those things when fear so easily kept her trapped in her current safe life? She used to be someone who thrived on change and excitement. But perhaps the expedition was God's way of pushing her right out of her cage. "Isn't it funny that we can still learn new things about each other after being friends for so long?"

Without answering, Marcus stared at Leonora, his eyes turning intense and sparking with heat and what seemed to be a little worry. The shift in his mood charged the air between them. Gone was the light camaraderie she'd felt walking into the shop with her best friend. In its place was something much stronger—and much more unsettling.

Rather than face whatever might be hanging between them, Leonora rushed to say the first thing that came to mind. "How do you feel about the plans we made tonight for the expedition?"

When Marcus's jaw tightened, she flinched. That had not been the best change of subject. He'd been helpful about the expedition, yes, but they'd both avoided discussing how either of them felt about it. The damage was done now, though, and at least the strange mood had dissipated with her faux pas.

Marcus shrugged as the soda jerk set a tall glass in front of each of them. Leonora took a small sip of the fizzy, spicy drink and let it ease down her throat. Marcus didn't taste his soda right away but twirled his straw in it while he spoke. "You know my stance on the entire trip. But I do feel better knowing those of you who choose to go are taking steps to prepare as much as you can."

On impulse, Leonora reached out to cover Marcus's free hand with hers. "You won't reconsider going with us?"

The words hung in the air between them, and her breathing

turned shallow. She wanted nothing more in that moment than for him to agree to go with her. It felt as if the only thing holding her back from fully committing herself to the expedition and the adventure that awaited was the fact that Marcus wouldn't be there to share it with her. And now that she'd realized it, she wasn't sure she could stand to go without him.

CHAPTER 8

*M*arcus had been mulling over a similar question since Mr. Flemming's last lecture, the night he realized Eli's engagement—if it happened—might free Marcus from the responsibilities he'd been forced to carry since he was seventeen.

But his version of the question had never been *would* he consider it. He'd been trying to think of ways to go with Leonora since the moment she first expressed her intention to follow in her father's footsteps.

No, the question for him hinged on *could* he consider it. And finally, for the first time in his adult life, he saw a way that maybe he could.

But was this the right time to tell Leonora? Eli claimed he was going to propose to Miss Schuller very soon. Mother said their courtship was going well and the young woman seemed quite partial to Eli. Marcus still worried about whether or not she knew what she was getting into, but he had to believe that the family of a young lady who was as beautiful and rich as Miss Schuller was said to be would take care to evaluate any man who called on her. They must approve of Eli, for reasons Marcus couldn't quite understand.

Marcus took a drink of his soda, letting the burst of tart sweetness fade from his mouth a little before leaning closer to Leonora. "Since you asked, I'm hoping that I'll soon get a little leeway to travel and might be able to join the expedition, after all. I've decided to go ahead and prepare with you and the club in case the opportunity comes to fruition."

The way her face lit up and her entire body seemed to come alive in response was worth all the disapproval Marcus was sure to experience from his family. Disregarding the public setting, Leonora launched herself off the stool and threw her arms around Marcus's neck, her words muffled by his shoulder. "You have no idea how glad I am. Oh, Marcus, it was going to be so difficult going without you."

Time slowed as he wrapped his arms around Leonora's back, his fingers savoring the warmth of her skin even through layers of clothing. She fit so perfectly against him, and her breath on his neck sent shivers up and down his spine.

All too soon, she seemed to realize where they were and released her hold on him, settling back onto her stool with a flush creeping up her neck. Not wanting to embarrass her more, Marcus refused to acknowledge the embrace, even though it was sure to play in his mind over and over for the rest of his life. "I'm glad you're excited to have me along. I thought you might think safe, boring Marcus would be a detriment to your expectations for the trip."

She guzzled her soda as if parched, then licked her lips before replying. "Actually, your instinct for safety is one of the reasons I'm most excited to have you along."

The words were spoken with slow deliberation, setting off alarm bells in Marcus's mind. His lungs constricted as if her statement had slapped him in the face. She wasn't excited to have his company. She needed him there to act as the voice of reason. "Well, I suppose I can oblige and fulfill my usual role as the spoilsport in the group."

"Oh, no, that's not it at all, Marcus. I promise, no one sees you that way. It's...something else."

She appeared so earnest with her eyes widening as she spoke and her lips parting while she waited for his response that he couldn't help but believe her. "Then why worry about safety? Isn't Mr. Flemming capable of making arrangements that minimize risk?"

"It's...the boat." Leonora blurted out the words while her fingers twisted a button on her coat so far around that it might well pop right off at any moment. For some reason, she was distressed about whatever boat she was referring to.

Marcus leaned forward, abandoning his soda to rest his elbows on his knees so his face was in line with hers. "What boat? I'm not sure what we're talking about, but I want to understand why it has you looking so pale."

Her eyes finally rose to meet his, and Marcus read in them an emotion he'd never seen in Leonora—fear. Genuine fear. "It's the boat part of the trip. Or the water, to be specific. Since Papa died, I can't enter the water. My body simply won't allow me to. When I'm faced with a large amount of it, I freeze up and can't catch my breath. Of course, I can bathe, sit by a fountain, or enjoy a rainstorm. But I can't swim, and I'm certain I can't get on a boat. I couldn't even cross the frozen river when we went skiing with the club."

One of her hands rose to scrub across her face, and a deep breath whooshed out of her as if saying the words had allowed her to finally release it completely. Then she seemed to pull herself together and looked at him again. "But please, don't tell anyone else about this. It's difficult enough for a woman to be accepted as an explorer. If anyone knew that a simple body of water incapacitates me...I couldn't stand the inevitable ridicule, Marcus."

In any other situation, he might have argued that no one would fault her for having a fear. It didn't seem to be holding her back, since she planned to go on the expedition even knowing there would be an entire ocean crossing to get to Peru. But there was such dismay in her eyes that all he could do was offer his support. "I wouldn't dream of it. But how will it help to have me there? We'll still have to be on boats and cross rivers and who knows what else."

A sweet smile played around Leonora's lips, brightening her eyes. "You make me feel safe just by being near, Marcus. Having my dearest friend there—someone who knows about my fear now and can help me manage my reactions—will make all the difference. I'm sure of it."

If he'd been standing, Marcus might have stumbled backward. The force of Leonora's trust hit him square in the chest like a punch. It didn't even hurt as much as usual to have her categorize him as simply a friend. Her claim that she felt safe in his presence warmed Marcus inside and out. Their gazes held as he considered those words over and over, rolling them through his mind, loving the way they made him feel.

But soon enough, he realized they were doing more than staring. He'd started to move toward her, his subconscious mind deciding this was the moment for a kiss. Which it wasn't. She'd just declared that his friendship meant safety to her. He couldn't betray her by adding something new and potentially damaging to their relationship now.

But still, his shoulders continued to lean forward, his heart thumping harder with every inch he moved. Was she moving too? Had she shifted as if to meet him halfway?

Marcus forced himself to pause before he got so close he couldn't see her entire expression. Trust and confidence warred with confusion and uncertainty on her face. No, he couldn't change their friendship before this trip, when she needed him to be present and strong for her. Because if he revealed his feelings and she didn't return them...the last thing he would be was strong.

Closing his eyes to block out the vision of her pink lips and the flush on her cheeks, Marcus forced himself—with an effort he usually only expended at the YMCA gymnasium—to retreat and sit upright again. Only when he was sure there was a space of at least two feet between them did he open his eyes, almost afraid to see what Leonora's expression would hold.

But when he finally got the courage to look at her, she revealed nothing. Her expression was blank as if she hadn't noticed him moving closer and almost kissing her. Maybe she hadn't. Had the romantic moment only been in his mind? Had he imagined the pull between them?

Marcus took a long swig of his soda, letting the burn of the carbonation searing his throat bring tears to his eyes. He blinked them away before they fully formed, but the sting was enough to bring him back to reality. Whether she'd noticed or not, Leonora did not look like a woman who was disappointed because she hadn't been kissed. Which meant if he had been careless enough to do so, she likely wouldn't have welcomed it.

If he was to even consider going on this trip, he needed to get his wild impulses under control, or he would ruin their friendship and possibly lose Leonora forever.

～

*M*arcus had been about to kiss her.

Leonora had tried very hard for an entire week after Valentine's Day to convince herself otherwise, but it simply wasn't possible. He'd been leaning toward her, his eyes closed, his lips aiming for hers. She couldn't come up with a single explanation to support any other conclusion.

So why hadn't he?

The way he'd pulled back and immediately arranged

himself to look as if nothing had happened caused an ache in Leonora's chest that couldn't be soothed. She would have welcomed his kiss. She'd tried to appear that way, to encourage him.

Had she failed somehow, and that's why he retreated?

A loud wail dragged Leonora's thoughts from the almost kiss back to supper with her family—the *entire* family. Eleanor was crying because Cornelius had apparently pinched her and then taken her jam-smeared bread while she was distracted. Felix and Arabella were both engaged in attempting to remedy the situation while Cassia and Paul made a valiant effort to get all their boys to sit and eat without flinging food at each other by using their forks as miniature catapults. They'd made quite a mess of the linen tablecloth already, but what an ingenious way to throw food without leaving evidence on their hands.

Mother sat at the head of the table, two fingers rubbing her right temple. Leonora was too far away to remind Mother it had been her idea to invite all of them over for supper more often, but that wouldn't have helped, anyway.

Finally, the chaos died down a bit. All the children were convinced to return to their meals, and the adults did the same. Small side conversations had resumed when Arabella leaned over her plate to look down the table at Leonora. "How is the planning going for your expedition?"

Every adult eye in the room swung to her at the same time, forcing Leonora to muster a bit of false confidence. "Quite well. We'll do some practice trips soon, camping and hiking, mostly. And we are getting some interest from local businessmen and philanthropists who might be potential investors."

Felix rubbed his hand over his chin. "Huh. I thought the whole thing would have fallen apart by now."

Arabella's swat at his arm was probably meant to be furtive, but Julius caught the action and queried in a plaintive voice, "Mama, why did you hit Papa?"

Chuckles rose from around the table, but the burn of Felix's lack of faith remained in Leonora's heart. What was she doing, thinking her little group of hikers could go on a full-fledged jungle expedition in just a few months?

Papa hadn't thought she was ready to even join him on an expedition, so how could she get others prepared for the certain challenges and dangers they would face?

That question still hung heavy over Leonora when supper concluded, and Paul and Felix disappeared into the study while the women settled in the parlor. The children went anywhere they liked, given freedom to wander by their mothers. But Leonora hung back, still hovering in the dining room entrance when a knock sounded at the front door. As the only one in the hallway to hear it, she went to see who might be calling at such a late hour.

She pulled the door open and nearly stopped breathing for a moment as she came face to face with the object of her thoughts and dreams for the last week. "Marcus? What are you doing here tonight?"

If it was possible, he looked more handsome than usual, the chilly evening air combined with what had most likely been his walk over from the bank giving his skin a glow. His hair was mussed, just the way she liked it. "Mother invited the young woman Eli's been calling on to bring her family for supper. I have a hunch he might even propose to her tonight."

Leonora stepped back, holding the door open wide so he could enter the warm house. "Shouldn't you be there for that occasion?"

The minute she asked the question, she knew the answer. Marcus's lips twisted in a grimace. "And listen to him extol the wonders of himself all evening? I'd rather not if I can help it. So I found an excuse. I hope this isn't an inconvenient time?"

A corner of Leonora's heart warmed at knowing Marcus felt confident enough to use her as a reason to escape a miserable family event. "Of course not. Everyone is here, though. You'll get drawn into the study with Felix and Paul if you're not careful."

He hung his coat on a hook and held up a file folder that she'd been too preoccupied with his unexpected arrival to notice. "Felix was my excuse to come over, anyway. He needed some documents from the bank, so I determined this to be the perfect opportunity to deliver them myself."

"Oh, yes. Bank papers. Of course."

Leonora heard the odd cadence in her tone but couldn't stop it. It had been foolish to assume he was there to see her. To be honest, he rarely showed up where she was without a good reason—an invitation to eat with them, a club function, a social event he was escorting her to with the club members. Had he ever come to the house specifically to see her, to spend time with her?

Thankfully, Marcus didn't seem to notice the way her heart had dropped to the floor. He tapped the folder against his leg and offered her a nod. "I'll see myself to the study, then."

He turned to walk into the hall, but Leonora reached out and touched his arm, causing him to stop and glance over his shoulder at her. He shuffled from one foot to the other, tilting his head the longer she stood there, but she wasn't sure what reason she had to keep him. Finally, she blurted, "Do you think the expedition is doomed to fail?"

She winced at her own outburst, but Marcus returned his entire attention to her, pivoting around to face her with his forehead creased as if he was concerned over the question. "Not at all. Why would you ask that?"

Twisting a button on her plain white shirtwaist, Leonora shrugged, hoping to appear less invested in his answer than she was. "Felix said something at dinner to that effect. It made me wonder if that's a widely held opinion."

Unable to meet his eyes, Leonora was still completely aware

of Marcus's movements as he reached out to set the folder on the hall table, then stepped closer and rested both hands on her shoulders. "Look at me, Leonora."

His voice had dropped, the depth of it releasing a swirl of energy that raced through her body. Between that and his warm touch, she wasn't capable of refusing. Her gaze found his, and she was instantly lost in the sapphire depths of his eyes.

When he spoke again, it was in a tone that allowed no argument—firm, but still thick with kindness. "The expedition is not going to fail. You know I don't trust Vernon Flemming, but I trust *you*. I've seen you make things happen that no one else ever could have. Leonora, you are the piece that will make the expedition a success, whether you make historic discoveries or not. Don't listen to anyone who says otherwise."

Leonora wasn't sure how long it took her to draw a full breath, but she could have stood there lost in Marcus's intense gaze and wonderful words for an eternity. How did he so often say just the right thing, the exact words she needed to hear at that moment? Bringing her hands up, Leonora let them cover his. "Thank you, Marcus. I needed that encouragement."

Marcus's fingers curled to catch hers and squeezed them. Leonora's heart picked up its pace until she was certain he must be able to hear it thumping. But all too soon, another argument between the children broke into the moment, shattering it as if they'd thrown a ball through the picture window in the parlor.

Releasing her hands, Marcus stepped backward and grabbed the folder from the table. "I do need to get this to Felix since I'm here. Will you be all right? I can stay and talk for a bit afterward if you want."

The offer was tempting, simply because she loved having him with her. But if he stayed, the only proper thing to do would be to sit in the parlor and visit with her family, not alone. And right now, that prospect didn't satisfy her at all. "No, I'm fine. You spend some time with Paul and Felix and return home when you need to. I'll see you at the club's hike on Saturday, won't I?"

He responded with a quick nod, then backed several more steps down the hall, his gaze never leaving hers. Eventually, though, Felix stuck his head out of the drawing room, calling down the hallway to see if Arabella needed his help. He caught sight of Marcus and ushered him into the room, pulling Marcus's attention away from Leonora and leaving her alone in the hall.

Rather than join the ladies in the parlor, Leonora found herself desperate for some time alone. So she retreated to her room to pace for the rest of the evening while trying to figure out what Marcus's enigmatic expressions were trying to say.

CHAPTER 9

*M*arcus glared at the morning sun streaming through the tall windows of the breakfast room the next morning, making it appear as if it might be warmer outdoors than it most likely was. Late February was hardly the time for bright sun and chirping birds. It made one think of spring, which was still farther away than anyone wanted to admit. All the brightness only served to stir up a longing that would go unfulfilled for quite some time.

Or Marcus's foul mood might have been the problem, rather than the weather.

Lifting the porcelain cup that sat next to his breakfast plate, Marcus took a long sip of hot coffee. He'd tried to avoid being pulled into his brother's gathering the night before. After spending as long as he could justify at the Thornton home talking business with Paul and Felix, Marcus had been hopeful he would get a chance to see Leonora again, even if just to bid her goodnight. But Mrs. Thornton had let him know that Leonora took to her room quite early.

Was that his fault? She hadn't seemed like her usual self

when she'd answered the door. The way she'd looked to him for encouragement that the expedition wasn't doomed...that uncertain, searching expression had sent his already wayward thoughts into turmoil. He'd wanted more than anything to pull her into his arms and reassure her with more than words that she was the strongest, most capable person he knew. He'd meant what he told her. Nothing she planned would ever be a failure.

But he couldn't get his near mistake at the confectionary out of his mind. He'd almost kissed Leonora. In the middle of a busy public place. His resolve to let her meet a man who could give her everything she wanted in life was weakening by the day. Especially now that it appeared Eli was actually taking steps to involve himself in the family's financial situation.

Despite Marcus's best effort to sneak in unnoticed the night before, Mother had been walking through the kitchen right as Marcus crept up the back staircase. She'd insisted he join her, Eli, and the Schuller family. Miss Schuller and her parents were quite nice. Her father seemed to be a good man, though rather dull. Her mother was taken with Marcus's mother, obviously delighted at the rise in social standing their family would receive through the match.

But, as Marcus had predicted, Eli spent a large portion of the hour Marcus had endured in the parlor making himself look like the most important, well-respected, well-known member of society who ever lived. The Schullers had appeared not to mind Eli's posturing, so perhaps everyone involved would be satisfied with the union, after all.

Which was good, since there was now an official engagement. Eli had indeed proposed to Miss Schuller while on a walk through the park earlier in the evening. The young lady had accepted, and both Marcus's mother and the Schullers seemed pleased.

For the first time in ten years, Marcus felt as if he could make a decision for himself without leaving his family to flounder.

But while he'd dreamed for so long of doing just that, the reality of his newfound freedom was more frightening than he'd ever imagined.

Picking up his fork, Marcus dug into the fried eggs on his plate while contemplating how different his life seemed this morning. Ever since the moment he'd been called upon to support Mother and Eli, Marcus had had his steps laid out. He'd always understood numbers, so he found a job at the bank because it was more secure and steady than what he would have preferred to do. While he'd picked up surveying as a hobby in the last few years, he'd never allowed himself to dream of doing it all the time, of leaving the boring, predictable bank behind.

Could he do so now? Was he brave enough to take a risk like that? Could he even travel with Leonora, given this new freedom?

Footsteps alerted Marcus that he would soon have company, so he set aside thoughts of how his life might change now that he no longer needed to be the sole provider for Mother and Eli's desired lifestyle. He would consider all his new options later.

Eli entered the room with a curt nod in Marcus's direction. Marcus returned it and set about trying to finish his meal so he could escape without needing to talk to his brother for long. But Eli sat down only moments later with a plate piled high. He didn't waste any time. "Now that I'm to be married, I hope you understand that I'll be taking over managing the finances."

Marcus nodded again, busying himself with a gulp of coffee in place of a response.

Eli shoved a bite of sausage into his mouth, continuing

before he swallowed it, which muffled his words. "Good. That means you can stop telling us what to do with our money now. I'll handle everything from here on out."

Despite the fact that Marcus was well aware of his brother's tendencies, the harsh dismissal stung. It wasn't as if Marcus had ever enjoyed holding the reins to the family's finances. He hated being the one who had to convince Mother and Eli that they couldn't spend money the same way they used to. But someone had to do it, or they would have been destitute in a month, out on the street while Mother's family home was sold to pay their debts and society scoffed at their downfall.

But neither of them had ever bothered to thank Marcus for either his wise handling of the finances or how he'd given up his dreams to support them. And while he'd learned not to expect gratitude, it hurt every time they made it seem as if he was a power-hungry tyrant. As it turned out, being relieved of that duty with such little regard for all he'd sacrificed hurt in the same way.

Marcus was about to abandon his breakfast and leave when Eli leaned back in his chair, resting his hands over the heavily embroidered vest he wore. "Did you finish your business with Felix Thornton last night? I would have thought you'd have errand boys for such tasks at that prestigious bank."

"We do, but he's a friend, and the documents were time-sensitive. I wanted to be sure no mistakes or miscommunication occurred." At least, that was the excuse he'd given last night, which Eli clearly hadn't paid any attention to.

"Mother mentioned she went with you to a lecture given by that explorer Miss Thornton is going to travel with, didn't she?"

Glancing at his brother, a knot formed in Marcus's stomach. Eli was very deliberately breaking small bites off a piece of toast, his tone all too knowing, while he refused to meet Marcus's gaze. What was he getting at? "Yes, a few weeks ago."

"And I suppose you're considering going on that foolish voyage?"

Heat swamped Marcus. Eli never listened this well or took such an interest in Marcus's activities. Something was behind this. "It's not foolish, and yes, I am considering it."

Eli finally looked straight at Marcus, abandoning his food to lean forward with his elbows on the table. "You're not using our money to finance this, I hope? I know what a weak spot that woman is for you."

Ah, there it was. Eli was concerned that Marcus would drain the little they had in their bank account to pay for the expedition. "No, Eli. I'm not using the money I earn for this family to finance the trip. Mr. Flemming and Miss Thornton are finding investors to supply the needed capital. Thank you so much for your interest, though."

Rising, Marcus drained the last of his coffee, then plunked the cup down hard. On his way out, Marcus gave Eli a hard stare. "You're free to do whatever you want with the finances now. The ledger is in the study. Help yourself. But I'm going to open my own account at the bank today, so be aware you'll have to live rather frugally until your marriage to Miss Schuller is complete."

Ready to wash his hands of the whole thing, Marcus left his brother with his jaw hanging open and retreated through the back of the house so he wouldn't run into Mother. He couldn't handle any more family that morning. Outside, it was as cold as he'd imagined, despite the sun, but the burn in his chest kept Marcus from feeling it during his brisk walk to the bank.

His brother was easily the most hurtful person Marcus had ever known, but the encounter had upset him in another way as well. The gleam in his brother's eyes when he'd brought up the family's money and learned that Marcus wasn't giving it away—that look was all too familiar. He'd seen it in the eyes of the man who'd nearly ruined the Turners. And, even worse, he'd seen it in the eyes of Vernon Flemming when he learned who Marcus's family was. It was greed, plain and simple.

And Eli's greed was another reminder that Mr. Flemming was not a trustworthy man. He had some kind of angle, some plan that would result in him becoming wealthier while others suffered. While Marcus had been unsuccessful in convincing Leonora of that, there was one thing he could do to ensure she wasn't the one who got hurt. His mind was now completely made up.

He had to go on the expedition.

~

"*I*s there anything as lovely as the smell of a museum?"

Leonora grinned at Charlotte Bauer's delighted sentiment. "A library filled with old books, perhaps?"

Charlotte nodded in eager agreement while casting her gaze around the expansive lobby. Most of the members of the Exploration Society had convened at the Milwaukee Public Museum, which comprised the other half of the building that held the library. While the museum was a place Leonora normally loved, she would almost have preferred a few quiet hours of reading next door on this particular day. But they'd been extended a very kind invitation by the curators of the museum to view a new group of Incan artifacts that had recently been acquired and only just arrived. Leonora couldn't refuse such an opportunity, for herself or her friends.

Between the Bauer sisters' heads, Leonora caught a glimpse of Marcus entering the museum, and her heart warred with itself over whether to be thrilled at his arrival or to pull her feelings back under control. Ever since Valentine's Day—which had somehow only been three weeks ago—it seemed she couldn't think of Marcus as the friend he'd always been. But she'd been reminding herself every time she saw him that it wasn't as if he'd actually kissed her. They'd simply leaned close together, as they had on many occasions over the years.

But if that was true, why did it seem so different, so monumental?

Her favorite museum curator, Matthew Marion, approached the group, spreading his arms wide to encompass them all in his greeting. "Good afternoon, fine friends from the Exploration Society! Are you ready to experience the joy of discovery?"

Leonora couldn't help but smile, even with the turmoil in her heart. Mr. Marion was the most delightful fellow. About the same age as her parents, his often messy white hair and somewhat tousled clothing always reminded her of Papa, who had been too busy with his endless curiosity to worry about his appearance. And Mr. Marion's warm smiles and enthusiasm for the work of the museum only further endeared him to her.

As the group members gathered close together, Charlotte spoke up. "Isn't Mr. Flemming supposed to join us?"

Along with all the others, Leonora glanced around, finding the explorer hadn't arrived yet.

Marcus refused to meet her eyes, instead addressing the curator. "I suppose he can catch up if he decides to join us, after all. I'd hate to waste your time, Mr. Marion, or that of those in our group who arrived when they said they would."

A nugget of discomfort lodged in Leonora's throat. Marcus sounded more than irritated by Mr. Flemming's impolite lateness. It seemed as if he was trying to make a point about Mr. Flemming. As if Leonora wasn't already completely aware of Marcus's opinion of the man and needed it pointed out again.

As if she wasn't capable of seeing what kind of man the explorer was.

Not sure how else to handle the now tense situation, Leonora nodded toward the curator, and Mr. Marion took several steps backward, gesturing for the group to follow him. "We'll get started, then, and I'll leave word with the docents to escort Mr. Flemming to the back when he arrives."

Leonora finally caught Marcus's eye, but he glanced away immediately. What on earth was going through his mind right now? She used to think she could read all his moods, down to his very thoughts. But it was increasingly difficult for her to figure him out these days.

And Leonora hated that feeling of distance between them.

Mr. Marion led the group through an unobtrusive door at the far end of the lobby. They wound through several hallways and down a wide stairway before reaching a large, well-lit room that was partly tall shelves stacked high with boxes and partly a staging area. Long, heavy tables lined the front part of the room, several covered with an array of artifacts from the museum's collection, while the two Mr. Marion led them toward were empty.

As the club members gathered around the two tables, Leonora maneuvered herself into a spot next to Marcus. It wasn't unusual for them to be together during club activities, but Marcus startled a bit when he noticed her at his side. No matter. Leonora was where she always wanted to be, and she wasn't going to let his strange mood dissuade her from being there.

While everyone pulled on lightweight cotton gloves, Mr. Marion asked Mr. Howard to join him, and together they pried a heavy lid off the first of several large crates that were sitting on the floor between the tables. "This acquisition comes to us from a reliable source in Peru, an antiquities hunter we've worked with several times. He says they're from outside the city of Huancayo, which is in the southern part of the country and quite near several Incan sites."

The two men set the crate lid off to one side, and Mr. Howard returned to his spot while Mr. Marion rustled through the straw that cushioned the artifacts inside the crate, speaking as, with slow, steady hands, he pulled out a package wrapped in brown paper. "Our head curator trusts this source, and so we bought this collection unseen. You're among the first non-natives to ever set eyes on these items."

Leonora's heart thumped hard in her chest, the thrill of discovery building. As much as she wanted to find out more about what happened to Papa on the expedition to Peru, this was the drive behind her lifelong desire to follow in his footsteps. One of the items in those crates could change their understanding of history. What if she was able to play a part in a world-altering discovery like that?

Leaning forward across Marcus, she stared intently at the item as Mr. Marion unwrapped it. Glimpses of cream in between the layers of darker paper were the first indications of what it might be. Round. Squat. There was a handle. No, two handles.

Mere inches away from her, Marcus reached out and rested his hand on her shoulder. Leonora's breath had caught in her lungs, and she let it out in a rush. A glance upward revealed that he was looking at her with a fond expression, one she could read much easier than his mood in the lobby. She returned his smile and focused again on the now-unwrapped object, this time relaxing a bit. There would be opportunities to examine it more closely. She didn't need to climb over the table to see it.

The other club members seemed as interested as Leonora was, all of them peering at the object and murmuring together. Mr. Marion moved around the group, letting each person touch what they could now identify as a ceramic jar. When the curator finally reached Leonora and Marcus, he allowed her to take the jar and hold it in her gloved hands.

Marcus leaned down to examine it as Leonora held it. She remembered all at once that they were there to learn about

Incan artifacts, so she addressed the group. "Would anyone like to share what distinctive features you can observe on this jar?"

"The red paint is immediately noticeable. It's a human-like figure, a warrior in armor, even though the face is that of a bird and it has wings," Mr. Howard pointed out.

Charlotte nearly danced in place with excitement as she chimed in. "The two spouts rising from each side to join in the middle, which I at first thought were handles."

Leonora nodded. "And they could have functioned that way, as well as for pouring."

While the others went on about the jar, Marcus bent down more, immersed in examining the artifact Leonora held while his nearness distracted her from it. She would barely have to move to brush her hand through his golden hair. A mere twitch of her fingers would have been enough to push up his glasses for him.

But then Marcus suddenly straightened, a scowl marring his features and bringing Leonora back to the matter at hand. "I'm not an expert, but this doesn't appear to be Incan. What do you make of it, Mr. Marion?"

While Mr. Marion rushed to take the jar back and spun it around slowly, examining every inch, a new voice rang out from the door. "Of course it is, Mr. Turner. I can see from here that it's ancient Peruvian pottery, and the Inca painted on most of their work."

Mr. Flemming stood there looking as self-assured as ever, despite his late entrance. But he wasn't finished. He strode across the room and gave the jar a cursory glance while addressing Mr. Marion. "Plus, this museum is a world-class institution. They wouldn't acquire something without knowing its origin." He held out a hand to Mr. Marion. "Vernon Flemming, world explorer. I've seen ceramics just like this *in situ* in Peru with my own eyes."

Shocked silence expanded through the room. Leonora was

close enough to see Marcus's jaw tense when Mr. Marion began nodding, red blotches spotting the curator's cheeks. "So nice to meet you, Mr. Flemming. Of course, we wouldn't purchase items without trusting our source. It must be Incan, Mr. Turner."

CHAPTER 10

$\mathcal{I}$t was all Marcus could do to hold his temper in check. Who did Vernon Flemming think he was, walking in and immediately discounting Marcus's knowledge, not to mention insinuating himself in a conversation where he wasn't needed? The man was a menace.

Marcus was tired of standing back and allowing Mr. Flemming to spout nonsense while everyone around him agreed blindly. "Look closer. You might have seen similar work in the Incan ruins you've been to, but not a piece like this."

Mr. Flemming finally turned and gave Marcus his attention, standing with a wide stance and crossed arms, as if he thought he could stare Marcus down. He better get used to being wrong, though, because Marcus was not going to allow the museum to incorrectly identify their new acquisitions. His life was changing, and he was ready to change the way he responded to men who used others for their own gain as well.

Flexing his jaw, Mr. Flemming scowled. "How would you know, Mr. Turner? Have you had any field experience? Uncovered any historical treasures of your own?"

The sarcasm in Mr. Flemming's voice chafed at Marcus, but

he pushed his chin up and remained strong. "I have not, as you well know. And I wouldn't claim to know everything about South American ceramics. But what I do know is that the Inca, at almost all points in time, preferred multiple paint colors. And they never portrayed humans alone like this, instead using geometric patterns to cover most of the object, even if the motif included human or animal figures."

Every eye in the room locked on Marcus, and every stare burning. Without meaning to, he let his gaze stray to Leonora, who was close by his side. Her lips were parted and her hazel eyes were wide as she stared at him. He shrugged in response to the question that emanated from all of them, including Leonora. "I've been studying for our trip. I started with artifacts we might encounter. The library has an excellent collection of recent archaeology journals."

When Mr. Marion positioned the jar in the center of the nearest empty table, a collective sigh of relief spread through the room. "Well, for now, how about you all help me unwrap the rest, and we'll begin cataloging what we have? Confirmation of the origin can be dealt with later when staff members complete the paperwork."

Mr. Flemming finally stepped away from Marcus and found a spot at the opposite table while the others gathered around the crates, lifting bundles out with the utmost care. Quiet side conversations started up, chasing away the remnants of uncomfortable silence.

Leonora's arm brushed Marcus's as they worked side by side without looking at each other. "I'm very impressed with your knowledge, Marcus. You'll have to show me what journals you've found most helpful so I can catch up."

He couldn't resist a glance in her direction, the sweet smile that lifted her lips also lifting his spirits. "Anytime. I can borrow them from the library and bring them to the next club meeting to share if you'd like."

Their gazes held for a long moment, both of their hands going still. But Marcus was all too aware of the people surrounding them, so long before he would have liked, he turned his attention back to the object he held.

Across the table from them, Mrs. Adler asked Mr. Brighton if he would be able to attend the camping trip they were organizing as practice before the expedition. Mr. Brighton smiled as he set a jagged piece from a jar similar to the first one in the middle of the table. "I am. I heard you and your husband won't be accompanying us on the expedition. Is that correct?"

Mrs. Adler launched a long-winded explanation of how her daughter was due to give birth to their first grandchild during the time of the expedition and how torn she was between wanting to be with the club and staying at home with her daughter.

Once she concluded, Mr. Brighton murmured his approval. "That's not at all something you could miss. So by my count, five club members are going on the voyage. Do I have that right, Miss Thornton?"

Leonora nodded. "Yes. You and me, Mr. Howard, and the Bauers."

"And me."

Marcus hadn't told anyone of his decision to go on the expedition yet, but this seemed as good a time as any. Not to mention, the sooner he did, the less likely he was to talk himself out of going. Leonora would need him. That much became clearer every time he interacted with Mr. Flemming. He couldn't allow anything to keep him from being there for her.

Mr. Brighton turned to Marcus. "Wonderful! It will be nice to have as many of our group as possible go on the expedition. I thought your job prevented you from going on longer trips, though."

Marcus shifted from trying to tune out Mr. Flemming's

boastful stories drifting over from the other table to explaining his new freedom without revealing his family's shameful reality. "My brother has recently taken a more active role in handling family matters, which has freed up my time a bit." He paused, his heart thumping as he contemplated his next words. If he was going to start making decisions for himself, he would have to reveal his true passion to his friends at some point. "I can even bring my survey equipment to help once we get to the site."

Curiosity radiated from Leonora. Marcus could feel it in her gaze. She didn't press him for answers now, but no doubt, she would. "That sounds wonderful. I didn't know your interest in surveying had become a hobby, but it will be so beneficial to the expedition. I'll add your name to our list. Will you be able to come camping with us?"

After setting down another cooking pot fragment, Marcus shifted to face Leonora. "I was hoping to. Will there be enough space and supplies for me to go along?"

He was aware of how low his voice had dropped, of how intimate the conversation turned when Mr. Brighton and Mrs. Adler both focused their attention to some activity at the other table, which Marcus couldn't care less about at that moment.

Leonora ran her tongue over her lips before responding. "Of course. I'm so pleased you'll be able to go, after all. I'll be sure to increase the number of supplies on our list to account for another person. I take it Eli's engagement brought about his interest in running your father's estate? It's nice to see him maturing."

Marcus had told her years ago that his mother and brother had no interest in managing what his father had left behind upon his death, which was true. He'd simply left out the part about Mother being swindled out of that inheritance before Marcus took over. As far as anyone knew—Leonora included—the family fortune was intact. Everyone around him believed he worked at the bank out of an interest in financial dealings and a desire to fill his free time with hard work.

There was no way to tell her Eli wanted Marcus to step back because his brother was only interested in helping their family if it meant he could control a fortune. So he offered a tight smile. "It certainly is."

If only that were true. If only Marcus could take pride in the way his brother was choosing to step into his role as the oldest sibling. For ten years, Marcus had been the one keeping them from ruin when Eli should have shouldered that responsibility from the start. But he and Mother had both claimed that Marcus was less likely to garner scorn from society for choosing a career. Eli would be shunned if he took on a career when he was supposed to be inheriting a fortune.

So Marcus had done what his family needed. And he'd endured their derision the entire time while doing so. Well, no more. He was making decisions for himself now. He was going to figure out a way to pursue what he wanted to do, not what he had to do for others.

In the week since Eli's engagement, Marcus had assessed the money he'd been putting back from his pay for himself and decided he would stay at the bank up until the expedition, then quit. Once they returned, he would find work surveying. Maybe he would even be able to survey for archeological teams uncovering sites around Wisconsin, rather than for crews laying out roads, railroad tracks, and property lines around town.

And once he had everything established and stable, he was going to pursue Leonora. He would be free to travel when he wanted if he was working on his own terms and he could prove to her that she could have her adventures and fall in love too. *He* could take her on adventures. *He* could be the man who gave her what she longed for. Everything he'd dreamed of but never thought could happen was almost within his grasp.

~

*E*motions flickered behind Marcus's glasses—worry, excitement, pride, uncertainty, and more. What was prompting the play of emotions?

For years, she'd struggled to understand Marcus's relationship with his family. He seemed to care about them while at the same time feeling beholden to them. She'd even thought he might be angry at them quite often, but still, he spent time doing things for them. She'd never understood Mrs. Turner's refusal to take care of her sons or Eli's apparent disinterest in his family's business. But maybe all that was changing.

Marcus seemed to be changing before her eyes—that she was certain of. Leonora had never known him to be so confident, so ready to stand up to his family or someone like Mr. Flemming. It was a type of strength she admired, the ability to hold fast to what was right in the face of blatant opposition. And seeing that quality in Marcus made a flurry of emotions well up in her chest. Desire, attraction, deeper feelings that might border on a love that was more than friendly.

Those were feelings she absolutely could not have. Not for Marcus.

But there was that moment in the confectionary when she knew he'd been about to kiss her. And a myriad of other points recently when he'd looked at her with such intensity. It wouldn't be difficult to let herself believe his feelings were deepening alongside hers.

Mr. Marion and Mr. Howard had opened the final crate of Peruvian artifacts, and the group was finishing their work. An array of beautiful pottery items including pots, jars, flat dishes, and bowls now covered the two tables. A few artifacts were intact, but many were broken in some way. A pile of pieces waited to be sorted and matched.

As she surveyed the entire collection, it became clear there were two distinct styles represented. Some were red clay items decorated with geometric patterns in multiple colors, then there were lighter clay pieces with red paint depicting mostly animals and people. Marcus was right. Not all of the artifacts were Incan.

That meant Mr. Flemming was wrong.

It irked Leonora to admit that the man was not only getting under her skin more all the time, but he was also wrong quite often. His boastful words frequently covered absolute ineptitude. So why was she putting her club members in his hands for this expedition?

It took some thought as the group thanked Mr. Marion and said their goodbyes before heading home, but she finally realized why she was hesitant to call off their participation in the expedition—because God had placed Mr. Flemming in her path. He had brought the explorer at the perfect time, when questions about Papa's death had been raised in her mind. He had provided this opportunity to get her moving onto the path He had planned for her.

Plus, wasn't everyone wrong at some point? Leonora made plenty of mistakes herself. She didn't choose to handle them with arrogance like Mr. Flemming did, but it wasn't as if anyone could expect him to be perfect.

Despite her faith, the questions still stuck with Leonora throughout the next week. One day she would be certain she should call off the trip. But the next, she would have herself convinced again that it was their only foreseeable opportunity to get such an experience. Maybe Mr. Flemming wasn't the most proficient guide, but he had navigated multiple trips to South America. The crew he worked with must be capable enough to save him from himself.

By Thursday, the morning of the next club meeting, Leonora had decided to go ahead with their plans. The experience they would gain and the chance to do something good in the world and show the light of Jesus to others was worth dealing with Mr. Flemming for a few more months. Wasn't it?

Leonora was heading down the dim hallway toward the back door to take a stroll around the garden when her mother came out of the parlor. Mother's face crinkled into a smile when she saw Leonora. "My dear, I was hoping to see you this morning. You've been gone quite a bit these last few weeks."

Leonora leaned back against the stairway banister, releasing a deep breath. The reminder of how much she was trying to get done was enough to make her even lungs weary. "Yes, along with fundraising and preparations for the expedition, I've been spending a good amount of time at the church teaching classes. There are so many immigrants who need help learning English, but they're always more of a blessing to me than I imagine I could be to them."

Mother's eyes softened, and approval emanated from her. "I'm so proud of your work there, my dear. But remember that their success in this country doesn't rest on your shoulders alone. It won't do any good if you spend every moment helping them and tire yourself out until you take ill. Especially not with your expedition coming up."

They hadn't spoken much about the expedition, just the two of them. Usually, one or the other of Leonora's siblings was present when the matter came up. She tilted her head, searching her mother's face for evidence of her feelings about the trip. "I'll take care of myself—don't worry. We've been rather short-handed on volunteers with illnesses going around, but it seems I'm healthy as a horse."

They shared a smile.

Then Leonora took the opportunity afforded her. "Mother, what do you think about this expedition? Really think, I mean, not what you've said in front of Cassia and Felix."

Mother's smile faltered, her lips tightening and eyebrows drawing together for a moment before she relaxed her expression. "I'm happy to see you finally doing what you've always wanted to do. I'm worried, of course. Especially considering the location. Anyone would be after what happened to your father. But my dear, my confidence in your strength and good character, knowing that the Lord has His hand on your life, and the fact that you're traveling with trusted friends provides enough peace to overcome the worry."

By trusted friends, Mother meant all the club members. But Leonora could only think of what it might be like to travel with Marcus. They would be spending every waking moment together, working side by side, exploring, and experiencing a world beyond anything they'd known to this point in their lives. Would she be able to keep her feelings to herself throughout all that? Or would she let something slip that would strain their relationship?

Pulling her mind back to the moment, Leonora nodded. "Thank you, Mother. I'm grateful for your confidence."

Leonora pushed away from the banister while Mother took the first few steps up. Then she paused and gestured at the narrow table that sat near the front door. "I nearly forgot. A letter arrived for you. It's there with the other mail."

As Mother ascended the stairs, Leonora casually took the envelope from the silver tray and slipped it into her pocket, the familiar tidy handwriting listing her name and address making her heart race. Since receiving the first letter, Leonora had compared the handwriting to that of all her family, the club members—anyone she could think of. As far as she could tell, this was truly a stranger sending the missives.

Outside, the mid-March weather had turned warmer than usual, and she was determined to enjoy as much of it as possible before the likely return of sporadic cold. Spring in Wisconsin was hardly predictable, so taking advantage of nice days when they flitted in between snowstorms was always a good way to clear her thoughts.

Leonora made her way to the stone bench at the very back of the garden and took a few moments to look for any bits of green peeking out from the ground, hoping some of the early flowers and plants might be ready to start springing up. Finding nothing yet, she glanced back toward the house, then slid the envelope out. She tore into it and withdrew the page inside but paused for a breath before unfolding it.

> *Dear Miss Thornton,*
>
> *So you've heeded my words at last.*
>
> *There will be perils on your journey, but the truth will be worth any difficulties in uncovering it. Your father, respected as he was amongst his fellow explorers, deserves to have a legacy untainted by lies. He would be proud of the steps you're taking toward securing that legacy.*
>
> *As someone who has many connections in the world you are about to enter, take my word that the expedition you have planned is in the best of hands. I'm sure some doubt your ability to make it a success, but you cannot allow their skepticism to hold you back. They are wrong. Anyone who knew your father could look at you and see that the same strength, bravery, and curiosity that drove him also resides in you. Hold fast to those qualities and the doubters will be proven wrong.*
>
> *With great respect,*
>
> *An Observer*

Just as with the other letters, reading that mysterious signature made Leonora feel suddenly exposed. The prospect of someone out there watching her every move was disturbing, despite the encouraging words in the letter.

Still, Leonora couldn't help grasping at the clear approval of her choices. Would Papa have been as proud as the anonymous writer seemed to think? She could imagine he would have. She was doing what God was calling her to, despite her fear. She was leading her friends and making this monumental trip happen for all of them. Mother was proud of her, so Papa surely would have been, as well.

And that knowledge was strengthening enough to help her overlook Mr. Flemming's faults and trust that since this was the right path, God would make the way.

CHAPTER 11

$\mathcal{I}$nside Barrow Brothers' department store, Marcus followed Leonora around display after display of outdoor supplies, the shelves loaded with everything from tents to driving goggles to fishing waders to refrigerated lunch baskets. The morning was warm, creating a stifling canopy of warm air inside the store. The situation was not improved by the armful of items Marcus was holding, things Leonora couldn't decide whether they needed for the camping trip or not.

The group would leave Milwaukee that evening, so Marcus had decided to take the entire day off from work, something he rarely did. It had taken some effort not to worry about the effect it would have on his family's finances, but Marcus was getting better at reminding himself that was no longer his problem. He could do what he liked with his time, and Eli could worry about the money for once.

So he'd volunteered to help Leonora purchase the supplies they would need for the trip. Most of the club members had some equipment they were able to contribute, but Leonora had volunteered to gather the food and anything they were missing. Marcus raised his head to look over the top of the pile of fleece blankets she had stacked on top of the other items he was attempting to balance. "How many things are still on your list? I'm not sure my arms or the club's budget can handle much more."

When his hip bumped against the corner of a low display table that had been blocked from his view by the blankets, a grunt slid out with the words.

Leonora glanced back at him and raised her eyebrows, lifting the much smaller load she carried as if to show it off. "Are you telling me a little shopping is enough to make you whine like that? This trip is going to be a terrible disappointment for you, in that case."

Marcus could see well enough to catch the teasing glint in her eyes and the smile that played around the corners of her lips. She was gorgeous when she was playful.

That thought—and the fact that he nearly said the words aloud—erased any answering smile from Marcus's face and dropped a chill over him. He couldn't reveal thoughts like that to her. Not yet, anyway. He had a plan all prepared. First, he was going to quit his job at the bank before they went on the expedition. When they returned, he would begin taking on surveying jobs. And once he had settled into his new career enough to feel confident that he could support a family, he would declare his feelings to Leonora. Going out of order would only bring unnecessary complications to the process.

So for the moment, his feelings had to remain only in his mind. He shifted the load to keep it from toppling and stopped near one of the counters. "Can we at least decide on some of this so I can free up my arms for more things you pick out?"

"If you insist." Laughing, Leonora rushed to help him lay the blankets and other things they carried on the counter. They went through the items together, and in the end, Marcus took the blankets, three folding stools, and several aluminum pots and pans and handed them to an employee, who piled them with the other things they intended to purchase. Then they returned to the store floor to check off the rest of her list.

An hour later, they loaded their purchases into the Oldsmobile Leonora had borrowed from Felix for the morning and returned to the Thorntons' house. The club would gather there to pack up and head to the campsite. Mr. Brighton had recently purchased a car camping kit for his Ford Model T which would create a large tent for the ladies to use, while the men would sleep in a regular tent. The Bauer sisters would drive their father's car, providing enough space for all the passengers and supplies.

The club members began arriving by midafternoon. Mr. Brighton was first, with his black-and-gold touring car all shined up. Not that it would stay that way for long out in the woods. A friend of Mr. Howard's had permitted them to camp on his property, but it was likely to be very rough going.

While Marcus and Mr. Brighton stared at the stack of supplies, trying to decide how they were going to split it all between the cars, the Bauers pulled up with Mr. Howard riding along. They jumped out and joined the rest, increasing the level of excited chatter substantially. Once both vehicles were present, Marcus and the other two men were able to sort everything into two piles based on the available space in each one.

"Oh look, there's Mr. Flemming." Miss Alice's calm, even words caused everyone to glance down the street. Sure enough, Mr. Flemming was walking toward them from the direction of the nearby streetcar stop with a leather bag in one hand.

Miss Charlotte leaned across Leonora to get a better look. "He's so dapper. I can hardly believe a man exists who cares enough to dress that well for a trip into the woods. I'm not sure if it's commendable or foolish."

Marcus would definitely have described it as foolish if anyone asked his opinion. But the ladies went on chatting while Marcus, Mr. Brighton, and Mr. Howard stacked supplies next to the cars. Instead of stopping to help the other men pack as he should, Mr. Flemming passed right by them and joined the women on the sidewalk. "Ladies, how are you on this fine afternoon?"

He took Leonora's hand and leaned over to kiss it, which would have bothered Marcus if anyone had done it, but considering the tension that was already between them about Mr. Flemming, the man's gesture rankled Marcus to the core. It took every ounce of his self-control to remember that he didn't have a say in who Leonora allowed to touch her. Not yet.

From the corner of his eye, Marcus saw Leonora yank her hand away to wrap her arm around Miss Charlotte's shoulders while taking a step back toward Miss Alice, almost as if using the other women as a shield. "I'm very grateful for this fine weather. Outdoor activities can be tricky at this time of year in Wisconsin. The paper predicted unseasonably warm temperatures for the next several days, although it will still get quite cold at night."

Mr. Flemming nodded, then slipped both hands into his pockets. Silence fell over their little group. Now maybe Mr. Flemming might finally move to join Marcus and the other two men. Instead, he turned to watch them, rocking back and forward on his heels as if completely unconcerned.

After a few minutes of silence, Leonora declared firmly, "I'm going to help move things to the cars. 'Many hands make light work,' you know."

Miss Alice and Miss Charlotte followed her, and they began handing items to Marcus and Mr. Brighton, who filled every available nook and cranny in the cars with food and camping supplies. And all the while, Mr. Flemming stood looking on, as if he was the overseer of a work crew. At one point, Leonora handed Marcus a box of food, and he met her gaze, shifting his eyes toward Mr. Flemming and then rolling them. They both grinned, words being completely unnecessary for either of them to understand what the other was thinking.

That was the way it had always been between them. Comfortable. Easy. Understanding. That was the basis Marcus would build on when he was ready to declare himself to Leonora. A niggling thought tickled the back of his mind, a question of whether that comfort might make it difficult to move from friends into romantic territory. But Marcus pushed it aside. He had a plan. If he followed it, everything would fall into place. There was no reason to worry about things that wouldn't happen.

~

The drive to the property where Mr. Howard had secured permission to camp was tedious. Leonora had chosen to ride with the Bauers, thinking that it was her responsibility to keep an eye on the women who were part of her club. Mr. Flemming had a smooth way about him that seemed to draw the eyes of some ladies, and Leonora intended to protect Charlotte's and Alice's reputations as carefully as their parents might.

But while her choice of vehicle had at first seemed like a wise one, it turned out to be one of the most irritating hours of Leonora's life.

"It's generally accepted that this is an excellent time to invest." Mr. Flemming smacked the palm of his hand against the side of the open touring car while addressing all the ladies in general. "Steel. That's what I put my money on. The way the automobile industry is taking off, it's sure to raise the value of steel beyond our wildest expectations."

Mr. Flemming's droning voice was enough to nearly cause Leonora to nod off where she sat. The only thing keeping her awake was the way the car's wheels seemed to find every single rough spot in the road, thus jerking them around. Alice's and Charlotte's blank stares and occasional polite smiles confirmed they felt the same. The only person on the trip who might have had a passing interest in Mr. Flemming's long-winded monologue was Marcus, with his banking career and all.

Although, it occurred to Leonora that Marcus didn't usually enjoy talking about banking. He sometimes discussed financial matters with Felix and Paul, but only when they asked for advice. He seemed to rather dislike the subject, otherwise. What on earth made him continue working at the bank, then?

Eventually, Mr. Brighton turned off onto a dirt path that cut through an area choked with thick woods and underbrush. Charlotte slowed her car to a stop behind Mr. Brighton's when the path came to an end in a clearing. There weren't many leaves out yet, but the trees and briar patches were crowded close enough to make the location feel completely secluded and as separate from busy Milwaukee as possible. Leonora loved it.

As soon as Charlotte turned off the car, Leonora hopped out and immediately began walking toward a trail that led into the trees. She called over her shoulder, "The property owner mentioned a creek not far into the woods where we can draw fresh water. I'm going to make sure it's as he described before we unload everything."

The moment the trees swallowed her up, blocking the others from her sight and hearing, Leonora released a sigh of relief. The silence was so much better than Mr. Flemming's chatter that she was tempted to stay there for the entire weekend.

But the peace was short-lived, as footsteps behind her

revealed the presence of one of her companions who must not have gotten the message that she needed to be alone. Thankfully, she turned to find Marcus catching up to her, a knowing smile on his lips. "I take it your ride here wasn't as relaxed—or quiet—as mine?"

Leonora let herself smile in return. Marcus fell into step beside her, and she bumped his arm with her elbow. "I hope it wasn't obvious to everyone else, but I needed a bit of time without constant commentary on things that are interesting to absolutely no one."

"And what happens on the expedition when our leader's bragging gets to be too much? We'll be stuck together for a much longer time, then."

Was he attempting to convince Leonora to abandon the expedition? While Marcus had decided to join them, Leonora had gotten the feeling he still didn't believe it was a good idea. And he had strong suspicions about Mr. Flemming's trustworthiness. Honestly, she'd never expected Marcus to agree to go at all, given how he'd already tried to persuade her that his feelings were right.

But what real reason did Marcus have to suspect Mr. Flemming of being anything other than a bit abrasive, full of himself, and not the most helpful? He had the connections to find a good crew. Not to mention, the man was experienced and a member of the Explorers Club, the same as Papa. They must have a process for confirming the legitimacy and character of their members, as Leonora did for her club. Such a prestigious organization wouldn't have admitted someone who was a fraud.

But Marcus was right about one thing—spending all day for weeks on end with Mr. Flemming was going to be a trial. "We'll figure it out. I'm sure once we're busy traveling and then occupied with the work of uncovering a historical site, he won't have so much time to talk about himself."

Marcus lifted one shoulder and looked away. It was something of a relief that he wasn't going to push the same argument they'd had before, but his closed-off indifference was a bit frustrating. She was starting to miss the easy way they'd always interacted before Vernon Flemming came to town.

A few steps later, however, a rushing sound she hadn't expected in the hushed forest distracted Leonora. She rounded a large tree and stopped, gasping. Marcus bumped against her back, and his hands wrapped around her arms to stabilize both of them. But she was too captivated by the view to worry about falling. "Oh, Marcus. Look how beautiful this is."

The property owner had vastly understated the water source they would find. Instead of a small, rocky creek as she'd been expecting, Leonora and Marcus stood at the base of an actual waterfall. Large rocks were strewn about the clearing, and spray from the falling water dampened everything. Sunlight streamed through the bare branches overhead, reflecting off the airborne water droplets, and Leonora could envision how lovely this grove would be in the dappled shade of summer.

Behind her, Marcus hadn't moved, still gripping her upper arms with his body only a breath away from her back. If she hadn't still been wearing her long duster jacket from the drive, she might have felt the warmth from his chest as it rose and fell.

A different heat rushed up her neck and spread across her face. This was silly. She was acting like a lovesick schoolgirl instead of a woman capable of helping to lead a team into the jungle. She—reluctantly—took several steps toward the waterfall, regretting the loss of Marcus's touch on her arms the moment his hands fell away.

Crouching on one of the huge rocks around the pool at the base of the waterfall, Leonora cupped her hand and let it fill with water. A small tremor shook her fingers, but she wasn't in danger of the panic taking over as long as she knew without a doubt that she wouldn't have to enter the water. This was quite different from the moment she was dreading—when she would have to step foot on a steamship that would take them out onto the endless ocean.

Reminding herself that was a worry for another day, Leonora raised her hand to her lips and sipped. Then she stood, waving her hand around to dry it while turning back to Marcus. "The water is good. Very cold for washing, but it tastes clean and should do fine for our needs—" The words stuck in her throat when she saw the look on his face. His eyes had locked onto her lips, his mouth open as if he was struggling to breathe.

His expression held...longing.

For her?

Maybe she hadn't imagined that he wanted to kiss her at the confectionery weeks ago as she'd convinced herself since. Maybe she'd been wrong to assume that he had never returned the romantic interest she'd felt as a younger girl. Was it possible that Marcus—dedicated, loyal, responsible Marcus—might have the same desires she'd told herself were hers alone?

Marcus glanced away, his lips pressing into a tight line. For a time, they stood in silence while the water crashed down. Would he explain the expression she'd caught? If she waited long enough, would he declare feelings for her that went beyond the friendship they'd always shared?

Instead of fulfilling the longing that suddenly pressed down against her chest, Marcus offered Leonora his hand with a grim expression. "Now that we know there's good water, we should get back to the others. Darkness will come sooner than we expect this deep in the woods, and we'll want to have every-thing set up."

Leonora let him hold her hand long enough to step down from the slippery rocks surrounding the waterfall. But she withdrew her fingers as soon as possible. Once again, she'd misread the situation. Why did her heart keep running away with such wild assumptions? And how was she going to manage to keep herself level-headed and focused on the expedition when at any moment she might slip and reveal that Marcus wasn't just her dearest friend any longer?

CHAPTER 12

On the second day of their camping excursion, Marcus hefted a fourth split log, resting the whole stack on his shoulder. That was the most he could carry at once from the pile Mr. Howard's friend had laid in near the waterfall back to the clearing where they'd set up their tents. It appeared the property owner liked to camp near the waterfall, but with the automobile tent they'd brought along, the Exploration Society had to remain closer to the end of the road.

Not that Marcus minded the frequent opportunities to disappear into the quiet woods. Mr. Flemming never stopped boasting. He went on about his questionable camping expertise and what he claimed to be successful archeological digs. Through all of it, he never included others in discussion, rather choosing to sing his own praises or lecture. It was tiresome.

The one bright spot in the trip was that Leonora also seemed tired of Flemming's constant barrage of arrogance. Marcus had caught her exasperated sighs on several occasions, and more than once, she'd met his gaze and shook her head in commiseration. Marcus rested a bit easier knowing things were going as he'd hoped. She would see the truth behind Mr. Flemming's false swagger and withdraw their club from his doomed expedition. And Marcus certainly wouldn't point out that he'd tried to warn her.

When Marcus stepped through the last trees and back into the clearing where their camp was set up, Mr. Flemming's complaints cut through all the gentle sounds of the woods. The others were attempting to prepare lunch, but it was plain to see that the explorer kept getting in the way. Irritated all over again, Marcus marched up, pushed right past Mr. Flemming, and added the wood to a pile sitting a bit away from the fire. Then he turned to Mr. Howard, who was in charge of the meal. "What can I do to help?"

A sniff came from behind him, followed by Mr. Flemming's grating voice. "In my camps, we hire local women to do all our cooking. That's what will happen on the expedition, so I see no reason why you men are attempting to cook here."

Marcus refused to give the man the satisfaction of stopping what he was doing to turn around. Instead, he took the long ladle Mr. Howard offered and stirred the stew bubbling in a pot that hung on a metal hook over the fire. "Self-sufficiency is never a bad thing. In this club, we prefer to make sure every member can survive in case something goes wrong on a trip. If I get lost in the woods, I'd hate to starve because there wasn't a woman there to cook for me."

Leonora's snicker sent a warm wave of satisfaction through Marcus. He allowed himself a glance over his shoulder, getting a nice look at Mr. Flemming's outraged face before turning back around to ladle the stew into bowls Leonora held out.

The group all settled on logs placed around the fire to eat. This meal was more peaceful than the previous day's dinner, or breakfast that morning, during which Mr. Flemming had turned any attempt at conversation back to himself. Now, he sat quietly—sullen, if Marcus read his mood right—which allowed the others to talk with ease.

Miss Charlotte chewed and swallowed a mouthful of the hearty stew while swiveling her head to examine the whole clearing, then sighed. "Is there anything as marvelous as the peacefulness of the woods?"

Across the fire from her, Mr. Brighton shrugged. "Sure, it's peaceful now. Wait until the snipes come out when dusk falls."

Miss Alice paled, but her sister scoffed. "No animals were poking around last night, so why would any appear tonight?"

Mr. Brighton tipped his head, careless and relaxed, but Marcus's angle allowed him to see the other man sneak a covert wink at Leonora. "They're shy at first, not sure about humans. But they get comfortable after a time—and curious about our food."

Would Mr. Flemming ruin the fun, thanks to his foul mood? But the explorer only shook his head and stood, dropping his bowl next to the log seat he'd vacated before marching off across the clearing. The Bauer sisters paid him no attention, riveted by Mr. Brighton's tale. Despite Miss Charlotte's skepticism, they both seemed fascinated by his description of the snipe's needle-sharp beak and massive size. As the only ones in the current group who had never gone on an overnight camping trip, the twins were due for the practical joke that served as a rite of passage for many campers.

Next to Marcus, Leonora leaned back a bit on her log, clasping her hands in her lap. Her eyes twinkled in a way Marcus loved. If either of the Bauers looked at her now, though, the joke would be up. So, under the guise of taking her empty bowl, Marcus leaned close to whisper near her ear, "Watch your face or you'll give it away."

He gathered other bowls and took the stack to the tub they'd set up for washing. Unexpectedly, Leonora followed, taking up a cloth and scrubbing each dish under the water. She handed the first clean bowl to Marcus to dry, finally speaking in a low voice "Charlotte might suspect something, but Alice will be the easiest target of a snipe hunt to ever exist."

Marcus prodded her side with his elbow. "If I remember right, you fell for it without much effort too. With all the traveling your father did, I was so shocked that he had never attempted the joke on you."

Leonora chuckled, wringing more contentment out of Marcus than he'd ever imagined possible while deep in the woods. He'd always been involved in the Exploration Society for Leonora's sake. Now that he had more freedom to decide what he wanted to do with himself, the adventures were already growing on him.

With her eyes still glowing and her perfect lips turned up in a playful smile, Leonora nudged him back. "You were so serious back in those days that I never dreamed you'd play a practical joke on anyone, much less that I would fall for it."

The memory of the snipe hunt he'd sent her on the first time the club had gone camping sobered him a bit. She'd been baffled when he disappeared as they trekked a particularly rough trail. Marcus had watched her through the trees, waiting for the right moment to rustle the branches and make her think a snipe was about to jump out and attack her. But instead of pushing bravely forward as he expected, Leonora had stopped in the middle of the trail and turned in a full circle, her eyes brimming with uncertainty. He'd felt too terrible to scare her, instead shoving a few rocks in the bag he held and rejoining her with the claim that he'd caught a snipe. Her relieved laughter when she opened the sack and realized the joke had lodged in his memory ever since.

Now she was looking up at him with the same sort of amusement, the kind that spoke of her complete trust in him. How on earth would he ever live up to the view she had of him? Even with some of his family issues now set aside, could he be the man she needed in her life?

They finished cleaning up the meal while listening to the jovial conversation behind them. The group—minus Mr. Flemming—gathered to take an afternoon hike. Without Mr. Flemming to immediately demand the lead as he often did, Marcus gave directions, wanting to take them past the waterfall to see what lay beyond. He had found a sturdy stick earlier, which he used to hold aside intrusive undergrowth or tree branches for the ladies to pass along the path.

They spent some time admiring the waterfall before returning to their journey. The afternoon passed in a relaxed fashion. Marcus tried to stick to trails carved out by the deer that roamed the woods, occasionally needing to hold back or crush down some brush to allow them passage.

"Look at that, will you?" Mr. Howard dropped into a crouch at the edge of the trail. He'd proved to be adept at noticing small things in the woods that the others missed. All five of them moved in close to see what he'd found.

Miss Alice paled again, staring as Mr. Howard extracted a long, grayish-brown feather from the emerging undergrowth. "Is it a snipe feather? Please tell me it isn't."

Taking pity on her, Marcus smiled. "It's not. I would say that belonged to a wild turkey at some point."

Leonora beamed as she examined it. "I agree. Excellent find, Mr. Howard! Look at the size of that feather. I wish I was as astute at seeing those details. You'll be the one to find our first artifact in the jungle, I'm certain of it."

The Bauer sisters nodded in unison, and Mr. Howard stood taller under the approval of the group. Marcus's throat grew thick at the way Leonora's encouragement always brightened the mood. She was an excellent leader for their club, and he longed to see her take charge of the expedition. It would be so much easier for all of them if he could convince her to leave Mr. Flemming out altogether and organize the trip herself.

But then Leonora's shoulder grazed Marcus's, and thoughts of pursuing his own goal fled. She was in her element. She radiated joy and contentment. He would try not to sully that by bringing up the explorer's name. Instead, he let himself enjoy her delight and dream about ways he could bring that same look to her face every single day.

~

*L*eonora had believed she knew everything about Marcus Turner.

She'd been there when his voice started cracking and deepening. She'd seen the change in his features the first time he shaved. She could still remember the brief period of time when she'd been the slightest bit taller than him. They had experienced all the pains of growing up together.

They'd been on plenty of hikes and camping trips together in the past. But something about the way Marcus took charge with a natural ease this time was different. He seemed stronger, more confident.

And decidedly more masculine.

Watching him lead their group and take on the task of ensuring everyone was comfortable and able to keep up was a new level of charm she'd never seen in him before. The way he jumped in to help with even the most menial work that came with camping captivated her. And it didn't hurt that he'd somehow grown a great deal more muscular than she'd realized, which was shown off to the fullest by all the physical tasks he took on around the campsite and the fact that none of the men bothered to wear jackets.

It was difficult not to stare so she didn't miss a moment of it.

What was it about this particular trip that had her seeing a side of him she'd never noticed before? While Marcus certainly hadn't told her everything relating to his family, something had changed that gave him some release from their expectations. Had that also freed him up to be more assertive, to take charge?

Or was it Mr. Flemming's presence and behavior? Did Marcus feel he needed to make up for the explorer's unpleasant demeanor? Was he trying to save the trip for her?

It didn't matter what the root cause might be. Leonora's heart swelled with pride as he tromped off the path to approach an animal burrow they'd stumbled across. He and Mr. Howard examined it with caution before Marcus turned and waved the rest of them over to talk about what they thought might have built it.

The remainder of the hike was much the same. Marcus led without being pushy or bossy. He watched out for each member of the party. He even moved faster than Leonora would have guessed possible to catch Alice when she began to slip on some loose rocks in one section of the path.

They returned to the campsite before the evening meal, flushed and jovial, the entire group laughing as Mr. Brighton led them in tripping over a tongue twister. But the amusement halted in its tracks when they noticed Mr. Flemming scowling at them from a spot next to the fire. "Whose turn is it to cook? I've tended the fire all afternoon while you traipsed about."

Leonora forced back a surge of defensiveness and made her voice as kind and even as she could manage to keep it. "It's Marcus's turn. You should have come along. It was a beautiful afternoon for a hike, and this property is perfect for exploring."

Mr. Flemming muttered under his breath while poking at the fire with a stick, so Leonora shrugged and turned to Marcus. "How can we help you with supper?"

Marcus sent a warm look her way, his eyes darker than usual, yet softer at the same time. "You don't have to do a thing. I can handle it."

It was all Leonora could do to find a log to drop onto rather than melting straight on the ground. The way Marcus's voice had deepened...what did that mean? Her body seemed to understand even as her mind didn't, an uncontrollable longing to wrap her arms around his waist racing through her. She swallowed hard and prayed none of the others had noticed the exchange.

While the three women and Mr. Howard sat and talked—and Mr. Flemming sulked—Marcus and Mr. Brighton worked together to prepare the meal, beginning with stirring the beans that had been simmering while they were away. Once the food was dished up and handed out, Leonora offered a prayer of thanks.

After swallowing his first bite, Mr. Brighton grinned at the Bauers. "Ladies, are you ready for your first night hike? The sun still sets rather early this time of year, so we'll have plenty of time to enjoy the woods in the dark."

The twins exchanged a nervous glance. Charlotte gathered herself first and squared her shoulders. "I can't imagine that's wise. Wouldn't you agree, Leonora? To go out there in the dark when there are...wild animals around. Bears and such."

Attempting to restrain a smile at how completely Mr. Brighton had convinced the two that snipes would be out to get them, Leonora patted Charlotte's arm. "Don't worry about wild animals. We can scare them away with trail songs. Do you know any rousing tunes we could belt out to keep them back?"

The sisters began discussing the best songs for that purpose, and Leonora glanced across the fire at Marcus. He was beaming, his eyes brighter than she might have ever seen them. But it wasn't the sisters he was watching with such delight. He was staring straight at her, his eyes intent and oh, so warm.

A shiver passed over Leonora, driven not by the temperature but by Marcus. If she was this taken with him during a simple camping trip, how was she going to avoid falling irrevocably in love with him on the expedition?

The moment the word *love* passed through her thoughts, Leonora was hit hard with a truth she'd likely been denying for a long time. It was already too late. She loved Marcus. And not as her dear childhood companion, or as her best friend now. She loved him as the strong, capable, kind, handsome man that he was.

She was devastatingly in love with Marcus.

Leonora looked away from him before he saw the truth in her eyes. She focused on the ground in front of her feet while thoughts whirled through her mind. What on earth was she supposed to do with this knowledge? She couldn't tell him. That would be far too awkward for their friendship to survive. But she knew without a doubt that this shift in her heart had also changed their friendship forever.

Because she wanted so much more than his friendship now.

And what if he didn't? What if he found out, didn't feel the same way, and then resented her for changing their relationship?

No, she would have to hide it. Somehow.

The meal dragged on for longer than Leonora would have liked. The others seemed content to lounge by the fire, putting off finishing their food. But she was restless, anxious to stand, move, clean up, do *something*. When her friends finally began gathering plates, she jumped up and rushed to the women's tent, needing a few moments alone before they ventured out into the woods again.

Leonora stood in the middle of the tent and took a few deep breaths. Maybe she could avoid Marcus for the rest of the trip. Yes, there were only six other people present to keep between herself and him. But surely, she could manage the feat. She didn't have many other options. She refused to ruin their relationship with her wayward feelings.

As soon as she stepped out of the tent, however, all her intentions flew into the dusk. The camp site was still and silent, save for the occasional pop of coals from the dying fire. And then there was Marcus, standing right by the tent and waiting for her. "The others went ahead, but they're going to wait for us at the waterfall. I knew you wouldn't want to miss the hike."

He examined her with raised eyebrows, his arms folded across his chest making his shoulders look impossibly broad. Leonora had a sudden urge to reveal all her thoughts and feelings, to drop them at his feet and see what he would do in response. She immediately quelled that notion, shoving it as far back into the recesses of her mind as possible. She would not test Marcus's newfound confidence by straining their relationship on this trip. She wouldn't.

If she could help it.

"Did everyone go? Including Mr. Flemming?"

Marcus nodded, his lips lifting in a half smile that sent her stomach into somersaults. Awareness that they were completely alone at the campsite dropped onto Leonora like a heavy coat. She reached back inside to take hold of her thick cardigan, pretending it was the reason for her escape to the tent. "Then we better catch up before anyone wonders about us."

She ignored Marcus's quizzical expression as she passed him on her way out of the tent, instead focusing on marching toward the woods. Just before stepping onto the trail, Marcus rested his hand on her shoulder. Leonora's jumpy heart caused her to stop dead in her tracks. She couldn't look up at him, though. He would see all her emotions in her eyes.

So she stared at his chest when he stepped very close and lowered his voice. "I thought you'd want to be part of the prank, so I told the others we'd walk at the back and let them get ahead, then go into the woods and pretend to be the snipe."

Leonora hardly heard the words over the thundering in her

ears. How had she been this close to him so many times before without feeling such overwhelming awareness? Unable to speak without risking saying something she would regret, Leonora nodded and began walking again, trying to clear her mind enough to enjoy the fun of playing a prank on the Bauer sisters.

They arrived at the waterfall and found the others as Marcus had described, lined up and ready to continue their walk in the dark. They were going to use one of the deer paths they'd explored in the afternoon so they would be sure not to stumble across anything too dangerous in the dark. Charlotte was standing tall and stiff while Alice twisted her skirt in her fingers, glancing sharply at every sound in the trees. If she hadn't known it was all in good fun, Leonora might have taken pity on poor Alice, especially. But without a doubt, both sisters would enjoy the laugh once all was revealed, as well as having the tale to tell later.

Marcus stepped in line behind Mr. Flemming, and Leonora followed him. She offered a tight smile in response to Mr. Brighton's jovial wink when he slipped in front of them. Mr. Howard began leading the way along the inconspicuous deer trail, their feet rustling through the cover of damp leaves that remained from the fall. The woods looked different at night, something that always intrigued Leonora. The trees seemed to loom higher, and the bare branches took on an almost sinister quality.

Although she knew Marcus intended to signal her to break away from the others, she was so taken with the night that it was a shock when she was suddenly whisked backward and around the trunk of a large maple tree. His warm hands spanned her waist, and the contact distracted her enough to keep from gasping as the others continued. Within seconds, it was just the two of them in the shadowy woods with silence falling around them and Marcus holding her close.

On any other day, the surprise of his method might have been funny enough to bring a giggle bubbling out of her. But at that moment, Leonora knew she wasn't going to be able to keep her feelings to herself. There was nothing she could do to stop this night from changing their friendship forever.

CHAPTER 13

*M*arcus had only intended to pull Leonora back a bit from the group so they could let their friends get ahead before sneaking back up on them through the woods. But the moment she looked up at him with shining, desire-filled eyes while her ribcage expanded under his hands with every short breath she took, he knew he'd made a grave mistake.

It wasn't because he feared what the others thought if someone were to stumble across the two of them in an embrace. His intentions were as honest as could be.

Not because kissing her would lead her on. He intended to follow through on any promises a kiss in the woods might make to her.

And it certainly wasn't because he feared letting the moment get out of control. He would never take advantage of Leonora.

It was that he'd been hoping to make her—their—first kiss a special moment, something she could remember for the rest of their lives. He hadn't meant for it to happen on a silly snipe hunt in the dark woods where he could barely make out her expression.

But he felt her response to his nearness down to his toes. She'd been looking at him in a new way all day, with such warmth and approval and even pride. Leonora had always been a supportive friend, but the way she watched him now felt like so much more than that.

So instead of releasing her when he'd spun them off the path, he slid his hands around to her back and leaned her against the tree that also provided privacy. He gave her a moment to get accustomed to the intimacy, then dipped his head closer to hers. "Leonora, I'd like to kiss you. If you want me to, that is."

She hesitated, her tongue darting out to wet her lips. Marcus pressed his own lips tight together to keep from stealing the kiss before she had a chance to respond. He wouldn't ever push her for more than she was willing to give.

But heaven help him, he prayed she would allow it. Now that the moment had come, he wasn't sure he would survive without discovering how her lips felt under his.

Leonora met his gaze, searching his face as much as one could in the growing dark. The only sounds around them were the distant tramping of their friends and the little noises of the frogs and insects that came out in the night. In a hushed tone, she finally answered, "Are you sure, Marcus? What if we can't ever be friends again because of it?"

That wasn't where he'd expected her thoughts to be going. "Why would a kiss destroy all the years we've cared about each other?"

She glanced down, seemingly trying to gather the right words. "If this doesn't work as something other than friends, we couldn't return to that same relationship again."

Marcus touched her chin with one finger, raising her head

so she would look at him. "Leonora, I always wanted something other than friends for us. Can you see me as a man you'd consider marrying when the time is right? Because I have no doubt our friendship could transform into a wonderful courtship."

Waiting for the answer to that question was far more nerve-wracking than Marcus had expected. His heart thumped hard, and he had to fight to swallow. But finally, Leonora's pretty lips curved up into a smile. She placed one soft hand on his chest, right over his pounding heart. "Of course, Marcus. Without hesitation."

She tilted her head back and raised her other hand to slide around the back of his neck, granting him the permission he'd been desperate for. Marcus let his lips hover over hers until her fingers flexed against his skin as if she wanted to pull him closer. Then he moved the last inch and let himself drown in the reality of kissing Leonora.

He'd imagined this over the years, although he tried not to. But no vision in his mind could compare to the real feeling of her soft lips, the sound of her breathing speeding up, the way her fingers slid into his hair. He tightened his arms around her, pulling her closer until they were pressed together from head to toe.

Leonora responded to his kiss the way she responded to everything in life. She threw herself into it, moving her lips, searching out the best angle, even parting them for him without hesitation. Marcus could get lost in the sheer wonder of Leonora letting him kiss her.

But there would be time for more later. He squeezed her tighter for a brief second, then broke the kiss with a great deal of reluctance, letting his forehead drop against hers so there wasn't immediate space between them. He could see enough to make out the way she smiled, her eyes brimming with trust, delight, and a handful of other emotions he was a little afraid to examine.

"I'm sorry, Leonora. I shouldn't have...I mean, I know you want to establish your career as an explorer before you make time for romance. I've always known that and tried to respect it. But I got caught up in the moment and—"

She stopped the flow of words with a light caress of his cheek. "Marcus, that was divine. And I haven't been worried about that for years. I know I can have both. I want both."

Her words almost sent his lips crashing back down onto hers, but instead, he ran his hands up and down her arms and smiled at her. "Then I hope there will be many more kisses like that in our future."

Moving her head back to search his face again, she nodded. "Our future. I like the sound of that."

Nothing in Marcus's life had ever made his heart soar like those simple words from Leonora. A ridiculous grin broke across his face that he couldn't stop it if he wanted to. He slid his hand around hers, threading their fingers together, then pulled her toward the denser woods. "We should catch up so we can play our part in the snipe hunt before the ladies notice we're not with them."

She allowed Marcus to continue holding her hand while he guided them through the trees in the darkness. It wasn't long before they caught a glimpse of the group, which had stopped in the path. Marcus crouched in the brush as silently as possible, close enough to see Miss Alice's hand flutter around the collar of her serviceable shirtwaist. He could almost feel the compassion emanating from Leonora as Miss Charlotte shook her head at her sister. "Alice, you needn't be so anxious. We're capable of handling anything that comes out of the woods."

"Not a bear. And not a snipe, according to Mr. Brighton's tales."

Miss Alice's voice was high and strained, sending a pang of remorse through Marcus.

Standing a bit behind the others, Mr. Flemming heaved a long-suffering sigh.

Mr. Howard glanced back and forth between the two women. "Ladies, I assure you that I won't allow anything to happen to a single member of our party. And no matter what exaggerated campfire stories Mr. Brighton has told, a snipe has never actually hurt a person. They're quite shy. We'll make more noise, and that will be enough to keep them far away."

When Miss Charlotte burst out into a loud rendition of "By the Light of the Silvery Moon," Miss Alice startled with a gasp. It was all Marcus could do not to laugh, and he used every ounce of his willpower to keep from glancing at Leonora. If she was so much as smiling, he would lose the ability to continue the ruse.

But the levity was short-lived. Miss Charlotte glanced around and paused her boisterous singing. "Where did Leonora and Mr. Turner go?"

All color drained from Miss Alice's face, and she shrieked, "A snipe got them!"

They might have waited a bit too long to begin the final phase of the prank. As if she could read his thoughts, Leonora croaked out a sound that was something like a frog choking on a bird. Marcus had to cover his mouth to keep from laughing at the absurdity of it. Even though it was dark, he was close enough to make out her challenging glare, silently asking if he could do any better. He reached above her head and rustled a nearby sapling, causing it to shudder while Miss Charlotte and Miss Alice yelped. On the path, the men burst out laughing.

The joke was played out, but Marcus had grown too distracted by the ease of moving past friendship with Leonora to mind. He should have kissed her years ago. How could he have ever doubted that she could care for him as more than a friend when they'd always been so close, so comfortable with each other? Their friendship would only make for a stronger romantic relationship. Nothing would stop his plans for their future now.

~

*L*eonora floated through the rest of the camping trip.

Marcus had kissed her, and it had not ruined their friendship, but instead felt like the most natural thing in the world, the obvious progression of years of closeness. How had she ever imagined Marcus would rebuff her, having seen his feelings written on his face several times before? She hadn't realized it was the look of a man who was thinking about kissing her, or she would have encouraged the contact far sooner.

The snipe hunt had ended in much laughter, once Alice and Charlotte realized they'd been good-naturedly duped and they could then enjoy being part of the joke. Leonora had savored all the little moments with Marcus—heated glances across the fire, a brief goodnight hug when the others were busy, the sensation of their hands grazing each other when they passed while packing up the camp.

Now, pressed against his side in the front seat as Mr. Brighton drove them back to Milwaukee, impatience rose. She'd been anticipating the expedition since the first mention of it, of course. But now that she and Marcus would get to go as...more than friends, well, the time for departure couldn't come fast enough.

One point of contention remained in her mind, however. The more time she spent in Mr. Flemming's company, the more the man's behavior wore on Leonora's nerves. He seemed incapable of allowing anyone else to do things without his input, even though his opinion was wrong more often than not. How did he not see how ridiculous he was?

But the bigger question was, how were they going to endure months of his behavior on the expedition? Especially on a trip where he was in charge, he would likely be insufferable.

Why was she agreeing to subject herself and her friends to his presence for so long? If Mr. Flemming was wrong so much of the time, how could he plan a safe, successful expedition? If they were following his questionable lead, would he take them straight into danger in the jungle? If he didn't listen to them in these situations now, was there any possibility he would listen to native guides when they were traveling?

The doubts plagued her the rest of the way home, keeping her from enjoying Marcus's company as much as she would have liked. Once the cars pulled up in front of Leonora's house, the Exploration Society members unloaded the equipment Leonora was going to store for their next excursion. As they prepared to part ways, Mr. Howard hovered near Alice, speaking to her in a low voice Leonora couldn't hear. Sweet, pretty Alice looked quite flattered by whatever he said. How interesting.

After saying goodbye to everyone, Charlotte and Alice left with Mr. Howard and Mr. Flemming, who they would drop off at their respective residences. Mr. Brighton drove off with a jaunty wave, and Leonora and Marcus were left alone on the sidewalk.

Together, they took the pile of equipment into the house, and Marcus helped her hoist it all into the attic space Leonora had cleared the week before. Finally, they retreated to the parlor, where Leonora's mother was waiting for them. As soon as they appeared in the doorway, she clicked her tongue at them. "You both look quite tired. Was the trip that draining?"

"It was an adventure, which is what we intended, I suppose." As she spoke, Leonora dropped onto the sofa next to her, while Marcus took the chair on Leonora's other side. They shared a glance, and a burst of longing to be alone with him caught her off guard. She rather wished she was sharing the sofa with him instead of with Mother.

But of course, while they might be able to sneak a moment alone here or there while on a trip, in her family's house, there was almost always someone around. They were unlikely to ever have that parlor to themselves.

When Leonora turned back to her mother, however, the older woman was watching her and Marcus with narrowed eyes, a slight smile lifting the corner of her lips. "I see. Perhaps you could tell me more about what adventures exactly the two of you got into while you were away."

Oh dear. She should have sent Marcus home and brought in all the equipment herself. There was no world in which her mother wouldn't notice the change in their longstanding relationship. And they hadn't even discussed what it all meant yet. Mother's questions would make Marcus uncomfortable, at the least. Would it be enough to run him off?

But instead of denying anything had happened or becoming tense and awkward, Marcus reached across the arm of his chair to take Leonora's hand in his and smiled right at Mother. "Mrs. Thornton, you should know that Leonora..." He paused to glance her way, then continued with more confidence as if bolstered by the sight of her. "Leonora has always been important to me as a dear friend. But those feelings have begun to change of late, and I think I can speak for both of us when I say we'd like our relationship to change, as well."

With her stomach churning, Leonora scrutinized her mother's response. She hadn't thought far enough ahead to wonder how Mother might react to such news, but the giddiness of relief rose in her chest when the other woman clasped her hands together in front of her chest and laughed.

"Finally! Oh, I've waited so long for you two to sort this out. That's the best news I could have hoped for from your excursion."

Marcus squeezed Leonora's fingers, and she glanced over again to smile at him. This was a wonderful moment, but Leonora did find herself wishing for some time alone to think through everything that was happening, all that was changing so quickly.

Of course, she was thrilled that Marcus seemed to feel the same way she did. But would their strong friendship be completely replaced by this new development? Would things become difficult between them rather than easy as their relationship had always been?

Already, the new feelings had led her to react with extreme emotion rather than logic back at the campsite before they kissed. How were they to navigate this new landscape?

Thankfully, Marcus seemed to be reading her thoughts as he watched her face. "It's been an exhausting trip. I'll go now and allow us both to get some rest. Leonora, I'll see you when we meet with Mr. Flemming to finish arranging details for the expedition, correct?"

Leonora nodded and Marcus released her hand. He bid her mother goodnight and showed himself to the door. For a long time, the two of them sat in silence. It was a relief to let her mind clear a little.

But Mother wasn't going to allow her to remain in her thoughts forever. "Would you like to tell me more about this change with Marcus?"

Leonora let her head drop onto the back of the sofa, slouching to find the right spot to rest it. "I saw him in such a new light over these last few days. He's free from the influence of his family, and that's given him a confidence and strength that I've always known was there but never had the privilege to witness. It brought to light feelings I've likely had for some time but wouldn't let myself admit. He kissed me, Mother. And it was all I could have ever hoped for."

Her mother's soft smile brimmed with compassion as if she understood the thoughts Leonora couldn't express. "But you're still concerned?"

Leonora jumped up and paced between the chair Marcus had vacated and the bookcase by the door. "What if we lose our friendship to this change? I don't know what I'd do if our relationship became strained, if we lost the ability to discuss anything, to depend on each other completely. I need Marcus in my life as he's always been. What if that all gets replaced with awkwardness and difficulty speaking our minds and fear of hurting the other person?"

Mother rose and stood in Leonora's path, stopping her pacing. "My dear, you're still the same people, and as you mentioned, these feelings you're now admitting have likely been there for quite some time. For both of you. Yes, things might change. But it's certain to be in a way that deepens and strengthens your relationship. Marcus is not the kind of man to play games with a woman's feelings, and you aren't the kind of woman to refrain from speaking your mind. You two will figure it out together."

The relief was instant when those words, ringing with God's truth, pierced the fog of worry in Leonora's mind. She let her shoulders relax and drew her first deep breath since returning to Milwaukee. Of course, they didn't need to have everything figured out right that moment. Hopefully, they had the rest of their lives to build the kind of relationship that was perfect for both of them. "You're right as always. Thank you for sharing your wisdom, Mother."

Mother returned to her chair and picked up a piece of embroidery she'd been working on. But a bothersome thought occurred to Leonora that kept her from sitting down again, instead adding to the restless tension in her chest.

She felt on occasion as if Marcus was holding something back from her, but in truth, she was the one with a secret. And since he was helping her plan the expedition, that untold information now impacted him. Eventually, she would have to tell him about the anonymous letters and her real reason for pushing forward with the trip. She could only pray that he would understand and see it as she did, not only as the fulfillment of her dreams and a good opportunity for the club but also as the best method to confirm what had happened to Papa.

CHAPTER 14

"Mr. Flemming, are you certain we can't find a safe, clean hotel for those first few nights in Peru? The money we've raised allows for more than camping, and we'll be living out of tents in the jungle for weeks after that."

Marcus found Leonora's attempts to hide her exasperation admirable, but her jaw clenched, and the toes of one foot tapped on the thick carpet of the Thorntons' parlor. The Exploration Society members were leaving for Peru in only ten days, and they needed to settle the final plans. But Mr. Flemming and Leonora were more at odds over the details than ever. Not that Marcus could blame her. The man was impossible to reason with. In fact, Marcus was rather glad to see her standing up for the choices she felt weren't the best.

"Miss Thornton, your lack of experience is showing. It's unlikely that there will be a hotel in any of the Peruvian villages we'll be traveling through, or that if one exists, it would provide better conditions than a tent." The explorer shook his head while lounging in his chair, looking every bit as if this was a relaxed, easy conversation. To an outsider, it might appear they were a group of friends catching up.

But anyone who set foot in that room would feel the kind of tension that immediately made shoulders tense and jaws tighten. And they still had a great deal of items to check off the list.

In the name of making some kind of progress and giving Leonora a chance to recover from Mr. Flemming's unkind remark, Marcus jotted a note next to that line on the notepad in his lap and looked over the next item. "Is there anything we need to arrange regarding our methods of travel? Steamboat tickets? Train timetables? Local translators or guides once we arrive?"

Mr. Flemming picked an invisible speck from the leg of his trousers. "We'll use my usual guides, of course. I've already telegraphed to inform them of our arrival date, along with some former crew members who will meet us in California. I have an acquaintance who has agreed to take us on his steamship for quite a discounted price. He's familiar with the route, as he hauls cargo back and forth regularly."

Leonora blanched, and Marcus steeled himself for more conflict. Her spine straightened as she leaned forward, her rigid posture the complete opposite of Mr. Flemming's. "I insist that we find a passenger boat. I will not subject my friends to a rough trading ship for this journey, especially young ladies like Charlotte and Alice. Find a reputable passenger ship, Mr. Flemming, or we're done."

Pride expanded in Marcus's chest, bringing a slight smile to his lips. She was a sight to behold when she stood up for those she cared about. If she had been the leader of this expedition, he had no doubt it would be a much smoother experience. Instead, they had to suffer through Mr. Flemming's arrogance and argue his terrible choices.

But it was nice to see Leonora putting her foot down. Ever

since Mr. Flemming came to town, she'd deferred to him far more than he deserved. Had the change in the relationship between her and Marcus given her the resolve to fight again? The thought warmed every inch of him.

Mr. Flemming watched Leonora with narrowed eyes for a long moment, then finally waved his hand in the air. "Fine. I'll arrange for a different ship."

A smile played around Leonora's lips, and Marcus's rose in response. She gave a brusque nod, then glanced over at Marcus's list. "So, from the research I've done, once we depart on the morning of April fourth, we'll travel by train to Chicago, then to San Francisco, which should take about two days. There we'll board an ocean liner. How long will that portion of the journey take, Mr. Flemming?"

The other man sat forward, appearing somewhat invested in the conversation for the first time that evening. "Actually, my preferred method is to travel from New Orleans to Panama, crossing by way of the rail from Colón to Panama City. Then we would board another ship to finish the journey to Lima."

Leonora's brow creased. "Mr. Flemming, I've done enough reading to know that using the transcontinental railroad to California is by far the most efficient way to get to the Pacific and points southward of there. Crossing at Panama would add at least a few days—most likely, even a week—to our travel time."

Mr. Flemming shrugged. "I'm attempting to make wise use of the funds your club worked so hard to raise. If you prefer to overspend on the journey, I'll defer to you."

The man's eyes sharpened, giving him a shrewd look that reminded Marcus of those tense, frustrating visits his mother had received from the swindler who later absconded with their fortune. Morgan Baptiste would sometimes let that same expression slip in moments when he thought no one was looking. But Marcus had always been watching. His mother might have missed it, but he hadn't. Whatever Mr. Flemming's plan was for this expedition, it was important to him to make arrangements that cost the least, regardless of quality, comfort, or speed. And that was suspicious.

Thankfully, unlike his mother, Leonora seemed to be on guard against Mr. Flemming's underlying motives. "Thank you. We'll take the overland route, then. We'll still have enough money for the entire expedition if we take care with our expenses in other areas."

For once true to his word, Mr. Flemming did indeed allow Leonora to lay out the rest of her plan for the journey without argument as Marcus made notes. Someone would have to check in the coming days that Mr. Flemming followed through on the items they discussed. The meeting was finished in no time once Leonora took over, and soon enough, she returned from walking Mr. Flemming out and dropped onto the sofa next to Marcus—so close he could smell her soap. He would have been content to sit there with her forever.

After a few minutes of blessed silence, Leonora released a deep sigh. "Marcus, am I making a mistake in allowing Mr. Flemming to direct our trip?"

Options for a response flitted through Marcus's mind. On one hand, he'd been hoping for a clear opening to talk her out of going with Flemming. He hadn't wanted to nag her, which could cause her to resist all over again and allow the man more leeway because she didn't want to be wrong.

On the other hand, things were different between them since the camping trip. No matter how much Marcus had intended for their friendship to remain intact, something had shifted the moment they'd returned to Milwaukee after kissing each other. Leonora was seeking his opinion more often than she ever had before. And a desire to watch her shine had grown in Marcus to the point that he couldn't imagine using her trust in him to sway her. He wanted to let her lead their group and prove to herself and others that she was capable of doing it well.

At this moment, he had to decide whether to use her question to press his own opinion or trust her to decide the right path by herself.

In the end, there was no choice at all. "You're doing very well dealing with a difficult man, Leonora. You're watching out for our group, and that's enough. The trip will be a success because of you."

She regarded him with those intuitive eyes, her lips twisted to the side as she thought through his words. "But you don't trust him—I know that. Marcus, none of us like him as a person, but what caused you to immediately distrust him? You knew before any of us that he would be so challenging to work with. How?"

It had been naïve for Marcus to think she wouldn't ask how he could read a man like Flemming so quickly. Most people didn't notice the little things Marcus did. But he couldn't explain to her how he knew the man was untrustworthy without also explaining the past experience that had taught him to spot the clear signs. "Uh, well, a banker must determine if people are honest, you know. If they're telling the truth about why they need a loan, or that they've come by large sums of money in legitimate ways. It's a learned skill."

Sweat broke out along Marcus's collar as Leonora's eyes narrowed. She didn't believe his flimsy excuse. He wouldn't have believed it, either, to be honest. While it was true in theory, it wasn't the whole truth. And didn't the woman he wanted to marry deserve to know the whole truth?

But that wasn't his story to tell. His mother would never forgive him if he revealed their family's shame. Even to Leonora. He would have a hard enough road to travel trying to balance his family's reactions to Leonora joining the family. She brought no financial or social gain to the table, like Eli's intended. She was strong and opinionated and didn't care at all about social standing, none of which his mother would appreciate.

Given all that, how could he add revealing his mother's past mistakes without first getting her approval?

He would share everything, though, at the right time. He would speak with Mother after the expedition so he could then tell Leonora the entire story before asking her to commit her life to him. For now, he would have to keep the truth hidden, but he wouldn't go into marriage with this amazing woman with a secret hanging between them.

He could only pray she wouldn't object to waiting a little longer for the truth.

~

*M*arcus was lying to her.

The pinch in Leonora's heart told her all she needed to know. He'd made up an excuse for his distrust of Mr. Flemming. But why? Why would he feel the need to hide his reasons?

She longed to trust him as she always had, but that was going to be quite difficult if he continued to hide some secret from her, one that felt as if it could be big and important.

How could he claim to want a future life with her while keeping secrets?

A twinge of remorse mixed with the pain in her heart when she thought of the stack of letters hidden in the drawer in her room. What would she want to hear when the time came that she was ready to share them with him?

"Marcus, you can tell me anything. I won't hold it against you, and I wouldn't dream of revealing something to others that you would like to remain quiet. Please tell me what's going on."

Marcus swallowed hard, his throat working with the effort

of doing so. Unease settled over Leonora. But he composed himself fast enough to make her doubt if she'd seen it at all. "I know that, Leonora. I promise you, I do. For now, I need you to trust that I'm doing my best with what I've been given. I've been living with a situation not of my making, and I'm trying to manage it as well as possible, but it isn't something I can discuss at the moment. Can you trust that I'm doing the right thing?"

She was doing what she felt was right, too, and she longed for him to understand when he finally learned the full story behind this expedition. Could she give him the same gift of understanding?

Deep in his eyes, under the hesitancy and worry, she caught a glimpse of desperation. A fierce desire to help welled up in her chest, overcoming the pinch of hurt. This was Marcus. Dear, steadfast, trustworthy Marcus. She would try to believe that whatever his reasons for hiding something from her, they were noble. She would choose to hold fast to that hope while praying he would feel free to reveal the truth sooner rather than later.

"Of course, Marcus. I trust you."

The relief that flooded his expression increased the tightness in her chest. She should prove her trust by telling him now about the letters. He was leaving behind everything he'd known for his entire life to spend three months traveling with her. Didn't he deserve to know the real reason she'd chosen to go now, and why she was depending on Mr. Flemming when she and Marcus both knew he wasn't trustworthy?

What if he didn't understand, though? What if he convinced the others that the expedition was a bad idea and she lost her chance? Or worse, what if the truth caused a rift between them that ruined this beautiful new turn in their relationship?

Before she could sort out any of those questions, Marcus

reached over to take her hand in his, and all thoughts of the letters flew from her mind. His thumb caressed the back of her hand, leaving trails of awareness on her skin. If this change in their relationship wasn't so new, she might have snuggled herself close to his side, maybe even lifted his arm to wrap around her shoulders. Being closer to him was all she could think of.

"Leonora, we haven't had much opportunity to discuss what's happening between us. I hope you know my intentions are honorable. And long-term. But I don't want to rush anything simply because we've known each other most of our lives. I'm hoping after we return from the expedition, you'll consider what kind of role you want me to have in your future."

Marcus's voice dropped deeper as he spoke, and the direct nature of his statements made the conversation feel quite intimate, enough that a flush crept up her neck. But she met his gaze, trying to record the moment in her memory. "I already know I want you in my life forever, Marcus. I think deep down, I've always known."

Sliding one hand over her shoulder to rest at the back of her neck, Marcus leaned in and pressed his lips to hers. Every inch of Leonora's body relaxed, loosening at the wonder of his kiss. For a moment, he was still, as if allowing her to get her bearings. Then he moved his mouth over hers, and Leonora completely lost herself in him.

In no time, she'd slid back against the sofa, and Marcus leaned over her, deepening the kiss. Their surroundings faded, and all she knew was his touch. His hand cradling the back of her head. The heat of his body at her side, almost pressed over the top of her but held back by his restraint. And his glorious lips creating sensations she'd never imagined possible.

Eventually, he pulled back, and she almost grumbled from the loss of his touch. Sitting up, she straightened her shirtwaist and smoothed her hair. But when she glanced over at Marcus, she found him attempting to hold back a grin. "You might as well retire for the evening. You look thoroughly kissed, and no amount of patting your hair will hide that."

Leonora shoved at his arm. "You shouldn't tease a lady when her mussed condition is your fault."

His soft chuckle slid over her like a blanket, warm and comforting. "I'm going to go before I'm tempted to give you another good night kiss. Sleep well, Leonora. I'm expected for dinner on Sunday, aren't I?"

She could only nod, a little intrigued by the idea of Marcus needing to leave before he lost himself in kissing her. He paused in the parlor doorway to wink at her with a knowing grin, proving he was somehow aware of the direction of her thoughts.

But he couldn't have known that as soon as the front door closed, her thoughts once against returned to the letters. She should have told him. How could they begin this exciting new adventure—both in their relationship and with the expedition—while a secret stood between them?

The anguished look on Marcus's face only a bit ago flashed through Leonora's mind, reminding her that there was more than one secret in their way. What could he be hiding? She'd thought she knew everything about Marcus. How on earth could he have hidden something that seemed quite monumental from her without her ever having an inkling of it before now? And for that matter, how long *had* he been hiding it? Months? Years?

The swirling questions began to overwhelm Leonora, and she jumped up from the sofa. There was no way she would be able to sleep with so much on her mind, so she took her cream wool cardigan from the hall closet and went out the back door into the garden.

It was still early enough in the spring that none of the plants had gotten very tall, but even in the darkness, she could see things were growing, beginning to show signs of the beauty that would soon be upon them. April, May, and June would bring explosions of life and color, and she would miss all of it. What did those months look like in the jungle? That was something her father had never tended to notice, so she had no idea. He had always been focused on discoveries—the buildings, artifacts, and people he'd encountered and learned from.

There was so much she didn't know, both about what was to come on the expedition and about her future with Marcus. And there was one thing she'd been neglecting to do recently, with all the activity of preparing for the trip and the changes in her life. Dropping onto the bench tucked into a bed of herbs, Leonora ignored the cold seeping from the wood through her skirts and bowed her head. She asked the Lord for wisdom to navigate all the shifting elements, for direction in how to unravel the secrets between herself and Marcus, and for strength to stand up to Mr. Flemming when it was needed.

But most importantly, she prayed for a long time that the Exploration Society would not only make discoveries on their expedition but that they would reflect God's goodness and love to everyone they met. Her father had always intended for his travels to leave a trail of changed hearts, people who saw his faithfulness to God and were inspired to believe too.

Leonora wanted that just as much as she wanted the expedition to be a success. So she set aside all the worries, all the questions, and refocused her mind on the only One who could help her navigate everything that stood before her.

CHAPTER 15

The night before the expedition began, Marcus stood in his room, surrounded by piles of items he was debating whether or not to pack. Basic survey equipment was a given, along with a wooden lap desk that would make it easier to take notes and record findings in remote locations. It was the amount of clothing he was unsure about. Would he need more than one jacket? Their days in the jungle wouldn't require the same proper clothing that working at the bank did.

His mother hovered in the open doorway wringing her hands, which wasn't helping him make decisions. "But Marcus, whyever do you have to leave us?"

Her whining tone had begun grating on his last nerve an hour ago, but he tried to be patient. Mother had never been good with significant changes. They tended to make her sensitive and prone to tears. The last thing he needed was her sobbing on his shoulder while he tried to get his bag packed. "I'm not leaving forever, Mother. I'll be back before you know it. And anyway, you have Eli's wedding events to help plan. The time will fly by with all that to occupy your attention."

"But what if you die in that jungle? What will I do without you?"

Tears were beginning to well up in her eyes, so Marcus dropped the shirt he'd been folding onto his bed and went to her side. He waited until she looked up into his eyes and used the gentlest tone he could. "I can't promise nothing will happen on the trip. But I'm as likely to die crossing the street here in Milwaukee, or from catching an illness, or any number of other everyday situations. Focus on Eli's wedding so you don't worry too much about things you can't control."

She sniffled but then raised her handkerchief to her nose, squared her shoulders, and nodded. "I will. But you must promise not to take unnecessary risks. Especially not things that Thornton girl tries to talk you into. She's far too wild and impetuous for anyone's good."

Marcus could only shake his head in response. He hadn't told her yet about his intentions with Leonora. That would be a discussion for another time, after he'd returned and Eli was married, giving Marcus even more freedom to leave if their reaction was as negative as he expected. So he returned to his packing, relieved when he heard Mother's footsteps shuffle away down the hall.

Throughout the night, Marcus couldn't still his body or his racing thoughts, leaving him bleary when he rose, well before his mother or Eli would even consider waking up. He dressed and gathered his bag, then left the silent house without a glance back. The cold air helped wake him up as he walked to the streetcar stop and rode to the train station.

The Everett Street Depot was already teeming with people, even before the sun had broken the horizon. Striding under a stone archway set below the soaring clock tower, Marcus was immediately overwhelmed by the noise and chaos. To his relief, Leonora, Mr. Flemming, and the Bauer sisters were waiting at the ticket counter, exactly where Leonora said they should all gather. The mere sight of her in a practical tan skirt and light jacket calmed him, but it was the warmth of the smile she greeted him with that truly allowed him to relax.

As soon as he reached her side, Leonora leaned close, speaking for his ears only. "Good morning, Marcus. I'm so relieved you're here. I worried that something would come up at the last second with your family."

Distaste for the secret he had to keep rose in his throat. Not knowing all the details about his family's situation had caused Leonora to worry, and the weight of that knowledge settled onto his shoulders. "No, thankfully. While Mother was quite distraught last night, I was able to calm her enough that she didn't hinder my departure."

Excited waving from Miss Charlotte signaled the arrival of Mr. Howard and Mr. Brighton, completing their group. Tickets were disbursed and bags checked over, everyone ensuring they had what they needed. Mr. Flemming started marching toward the waiting train until Leonora stopped him. "Wait a moment, everyone, if you please."

They all paused, their attention on her, although Mr. Flemming complied with a roll of his eyes that only Marcus seemed to notice.

Leonora glanced at each of them while speaking loud enough to be heard over the other travelers. "We ought to begin this trip with a prayer for safety, health, and success. If any of you would rather not participate, I understand, but it can't hurt, and I believe it will help more than a little."

Marcus hadn't expected that. While Leonora was active in church and had a strong faith, she'd rarely brought it into the Exploration Society. It felt a bit strange to bow his head there in the middle of the busy platform, but the others did it, so he did too.

"Lord, we ask for Your protection as we travel. Please help the trip to go well and for us all to remain healthy and safe as we travel. Give us success in this venture, both in our objectives and in showing Your light to those we travel and work with. In Jesus' name, amen."

At some point during the brief prayer, Marcus's eyes shot up to Leonora, drawn by the sweet earnestness in her voice. He struggled to look away after she finished. While the others gathered their things and followed Mr. Flemming toward the train, Marcus's entire focus was locked on the beautiful, glowing woman walking next to him. How was he going to pay attention to anything except her while they traveled if she kept looking so content and happy?

When she glanced up and found him staring at her, a pretty pink colored her cheeks. "Why are you looking at me like that?"

Marcus leaned close to brush his lips across her heated cheek while at the same time reaching over to take her heavy bag from her hands. "Because I'm very, very glad I was able to join you on this trip. I can't imagine the great disappointment of never seeing you this much in your element."

A shy smile stretched across her face, adding even more to the radiance she was projecting. Straightening her shoulders, she marched across the platform and made sure all their companions made it onto the train, looking as if his words had given her the confidence to take charge. If a simple compliment could give her that much strength, Marcus determined to give them out freely throughout the entire expedition. And the rest of their lives.

The seven of them climbed the steps onto the train and found a group of seats together. It wasn't long before the engine pulled away from the station and they were rushing through Milwaukee. Sitting between Marcus and the dusty window, Leonora watched the town in delight. "We have many days of train travel ahead of us. Do you think I'll tire of it? Because at this moment, I'm not sure anything could make me happier than the sound of that train whistle as it carries me into a new adventure."

Marcus tried to mutter something coherent, but her words struck his heart. Combined with the joy on her face all morning, it was obvious that she was as thrilled with the reality of leaving her hometown as she'd imagined. If she fell even more in love with travel and adventure, would Marcus be enough to keep her satisfied once they returned? Hopefully, they would be able to take trips together, maybe even more exploratory expeditions. But he would also have to work somehow to support them. They couldn't travel all the time.

And what if they had children at some point? Would Leonora resent staying in Milwaukee while they raised a family? Marcus knew as well as anyone that children needed and deserved parents who were present and cared for them. Would Leonora desire to have children with him if it meant not traveling?

Leonora's calming presence was no longer doing the trick, and Marcus lost himself in questions he wasn't sure he could ever answer.

∼

The thrill of leaving Wisconsin for the first time in her life sustained Leonora through the morning. But as she stood in the bustling Chicago Wells Street Station arguing with Mr. Flemming over the next leg of their journey, the excitement gave way to frustration.

"Miss Thornton, I am the experienced traveler here. Please allow me to make the arrangements, as we agreed."

Leonora clenched her hands into fists behind her back in an effort to contain the anger rising in her chest. "We agreed to make arrangements that are suitable for all of us, not ones based on your preference. Why on earth would we take a longer route through Los Angeles when we have the option of taking the Overland Limited straight to San Francisco?"

As it tended to more and more often, Mr. Flemming's tone took on a patronizing quality. "Because it will save us money. Your club was quite helpful in raising the funds we need for this expedition, but these trips are very costly, especially with so many unqualified people going. We still need an experienced crew, but now we'll have to hire them *and* pay for your club members' supplies and accommodations. Any opportunity to save some of our funds should be considered."

Mr. Flemming's scornful description of her and her friends as unqualified seared her heart. Leonora glanced at Marcus, who still seemed as distracted as he'd been since they first boarded the train in Milwaukee. "Marcus, what do you think? A longer train ride to save money or a shorter route to save time?"

Shaking his head as if bringing himself out of deep thoughts, Marcus held out his hand for the train timetable she'd been examining. After studying it for a moment, he looked back at her with a shrug. "In this case, saving money might not be so bad. This says the Los Angeles route should only take a few hours longer, and it will save us a decent amount on tickets."

Mr. Flemming cocked a smug eyebrow at her and took the timetable from Marcus with a flourish. "Thank you for seeing reason, Mr. Turner. I'll go purchase our tickets."

Leonora aimed a glare at Marcus. "I thought you would support me. We have so much travel ahead, I hate to spend any more time on a train than we have to."

Marcus finally focused his full attention on her, his expression gentling while he adjusted his glasses. "I didn't mean to contradict you, but I saw a chance to give Mr. Flemming something he wanted without sacrificing our safety or comfort too much. That will give us leverage to fight him when he tries to cut costs in more extreme ways, as I expect he will."

When he put it that way, Leonora's ire began to fade. She allowed a small smile, just for him. "I see your point. Thank you for looking at the situation from angles I didn't see."

Holding out his arm for her to take, Marcus winked. "I'm right, in other words."

She found herself giggling, a surprise after the tension that had been hovering between her and Mr. Flemming the entire day. The sound caught the attention of their companions, causing Charlotte and Alice to stop mid-conversation to stare at Leonora and Marcus.

Her heart dropped. She'd thought it wouldn't be difficult to hide their changing relationship until the expedition was over and they could discuss what their future might look like. How could she have believed it would be easy to keep between the two of them when they would spend so much time in close quarters with their friends?

Once Mr. Flemming returned with their tickets, the group waited on the platform for the next train to arrive. Mr. Brighton grumbled, "If we'd taken the cars, we'd be driving right now instead of waiting on a train."

To Leonora's surprise, the usually quiet Alice immediately retorted, "If we'd taken the cars, we'd have had to pull over and repair something by now. Not to mention stopping to eat, sleep, and refuel. Plus, what would we do with them in San Fransisco while we continue on to South America?"

Rather than appearing offended by her reproachful tone, Mr. Brighton grinned, his eyes never leaving her face. "You do make some excellent points, Miss Bauer. I'll contain my impatience with our method of travel from here on out."

A light flush washed across Alice's cheeks, and Leonora couldn't help smiling to match the pair. Perhaps she and Marcus weren't the only ones with a changing relationship.

A piercing whistle in the distance signaled the arriving train, so the group gathered their things and waited, ready to board. The ground vibrated as the engine grew closer, the sounds of grinding metal and clanking wheels filling the air and making conversation difficult. The train clamored to a stop in front of the platform, and the expedition group boarded along with the other passengers.

There was an immediate difference in the quality of this train compared with the one they'd taken from Milwaukee. This line was newer but hadn't placed the same amount of care on designing their second-class cars for comfort. Padding was sparse on the bench seats, and the fabric was thin and rough. It was dark inside, thanks to very small windows and only a few gas lights spaced so far apart they hardly helped brighten the space at all. Everything felt cramped and dingy.

But as the president of the Exploration Society, Leonora was determined to set a good example on this expedition. The second-class tickets were an even greater savings to go along with the route Mr. Flemming chose. Papa wouldn't have complained about unpleasantness while traveling. He had been an expert at making the best of things. She could and would follow in his footsteps.

So she marched down the narrow aisle and found the sections where they would sit during the day, then have the seats made up into berths at night for sleeping. Nothing about it was as luxurious as the Pullman cars for the first-class customers, but Leonora would find something to enjoy in it.

For this leg of the journey, she made a deliberate effort to sit with Charlotte and Alice, rather than Marcus. Their companions might realize sooner rather than later that there was more than friendship between them now, but she didn't want to neglect the others in favor of spending all her time with Marcus. Even as tempting as the thought of hours and hours by his side was.

When Leonora finally had herself settled next to Alice, with Charlotte on the seat across from them, she realized the sisters were deep in a rather intense conversation. Alice, in particular, looked a bit stricken. "Is everything all right?" Leonora asked. "I know this train isn't as nice as the last one, but I suppose explorers don't get to travel in luxury most of the time."

The twins exchanged a glance that seemed to contain a great deal of communication without a word being spoken between them. Charlotte leaned forward so Leonora could hear her hushed words. "Alice is worried about a man who was lurking around us at the station. We lost sight of him during the boarding, but now he's seated right back there."

Leonora had the presence of mind not to turn and seek out a glimpse of the man in question, although she wished she could. "And what makes you so concerned, Alice? Many people were standing close to us while we waited for the train."

Alice licked her lips and swallowed hard. "He was in Milwaukee too. And he kept staring at you. I don't think he noticed that I saw him because he was so focused on you."

A chill raced up Leonora's spine. Had she been so focused on Marcus that she missed a situation she should have seen right away? "And he's here, in this car with us?"

Charlotte nodded. "About three rows behind the men. He's not looking at you now, but he was until I glanced that way. If you get a chance to look, there's very little to distinguish him from any other man traveling today, but he has a pin on his lapel that looks quite interesting, although I can't make out much of it from this distance."

Leonora swallowed back her own rising worry and tried to muster a reassuring smile for the other women. "Thank you for mentioning it. I'll be sure to keep an eye out."

Alice's hand fluttered around her collar. "I think we should tell the men. I don't want to be in this train car for days with that fellow watching us."

Charlotte reached across the section to tap Alice's hand,

stopping the fluttering. "What are they going to do about it? He hasn't done anything wrong or even improper."

Leonora settled back against the seat, even though every fiber of her being screamed at her to figure out what was going on. She had to help these two realize that they were strong enough to handle whatever came their way. "We'll be fine, Alice. If he's still around when we reach the connecting train in Los Angeles, then we'll ask the men to intervene. There are quite a few stops before that where he might disembark. Until then, let's try to ignore him and enjoy this part of our journey. I imagine it will be one of the less demanding portions."

The sisters seemed pacified. Alice began working on an embroidery piece she'd had in her lap. Charlotte turned her attention to updating the diary she hoped to keep during the journey. Pulling a book from her brown leather valise, Leonora opened it and attempted to focus on the words for at least a minute or two. But her thoughts were centered instead on the potential situation at hand and how she might handle it in a way that didn't make her seem weak or incapable of leading the group. Mr. Flemming might be the experienced traveler, but Leonora was responsible for her friends—he'd made that clear. More than ever, she wished Papa could have been there to advise her.

CHAPTER 16

*B*y the end of the first day on the train, Marcus regretted going along with Mr. Flemming on the choice of which line to take.

The hard seats were difficult to sit on for any amount of time, much less two-and-a-half days. The berths that pulled down to form beds were no better, hardly more than a thin mat on hard metal. And the constant noise and movement of the train all night left Marcus and the rest of the club members on the cranky side for their second morning of travel.

Dropping into a seat next to Leonora, Marcus rolled his shoulders, hoping to ease some of the tight soreness in them. Somehow, she appeared as cheerful as ever. She also looked beautiful, with her hair in a looser pompadour than usual and the jacket from her suit removed, allowing the pale cream shirt-waist she wore underneath to set off her complexion. His heart lurched at the realization that he was witnessing a side of her he never had before, the moments right after she woke.

"Good morning, Marcus. I trust you slept well."

He blinked at her a few times, clearing the fogginess from his mind while trying to understand how she could ask such a question. Perhaps the women had been given better beds than the men. Maybe she actually *had* slept well. "Not particularly, but I'll be glad to get this day underway so we can be that much closer to the end of the train ride."

Raising an eyebrow, Leonora smirked at him. "We might have fared better on the other train, don't you suppose?"

Coming from anyone else, that might have caused him to grumble. But he couldn't be put out with Leonora, especially when she looked so fetching. He bumped her arm with his elbow and tried to smile. "I'll give you that one. But now we have even more reasons to hold our ground the next time Mr. Flemming tries to make the cheap, uncomfortable choice."

She tilted her head to rest it on his shoulder, sending a thrill through Marcus and leaving him wishing he could wrap his arm around her and pull her closer. "Thank you for seeing things in ways I wouldn't have. It does feel good to know we can at least use this discomfort to our advantage if we need to."

They stayed that way for a long time, while their companions trickled in from the buffet car where the second-class passengers ate. Marcus's heart warmed at the fact that Leonora didn't bother to lift her head even when their friends exchanged curious glances. She didn't seem to mind if people knew their relationship had changed, and that increased Marcus's confidence in ways he would never have expected.

The morning wore on without much to fill the time. Mr. Flemming stopped by for a moment to explain that he had a headache and would be spending the day trying to rest in the quieter gentleman's club car. So the rest of the group attempted to occupy themselves with games the Bauer sisters suggested. It turned out to be rather fun, with many laughs coming from their seats at the end of the train car. But the twins kept casting furtive looks at something behind Marcus.

A surreptitious glance didn't reveal anything unusual. There were a decent number of passengers in the car, enough to make it feel full but not overcrowded. They all seemed to be minding their own business, chatting with companions, reading, or napping. Although how anyone could sleep on the uncomfortable seats, Marcus would never understand.

But Miss Alice grew more agitated as time went on. After they went to the buffet car for lunch, it grew worse. She could hardly be pulled from staring toward the back of the car to participate in the conversation or any of the games her sister tried to start. Marcus scanned the car several more times but couldn't detect anything that would warrant such distraction.

About an hour before supper time, he couldn't stand it anymore. Leaning forward, Marcus waited until the woman noticed his gaze and met it. "Miss Alice, something has been bothering you all day, but I can't discern what it might be. What's going on?"

Across the aisle from Marcus, Mr. Brighton perked up. "Is something wrong, Alice? How can I help?"

The other man's distressed tone caught Marcus's attention. He might not have guessed love would rise between those two, in particular, but it wasn't surprising that others in their group were seeing each other in a romantic light, as he and Leonora were now. He didn't dare let a smile lift his lips at the realization, though. Miss Alice looked distraught, and it wouldn't help if she thought he was laughing at whatever her plight might be.

Biting her lower lip, Miss Alice glanced toward Leonora, who reached forward to pat the younger woman's hand. "I can explain it, Alice." Leonora turned to Marcus, Mr. Brighton, and Mr. Howard, who had also leaned in to listen with great interest. "Alice and Charlotte noticed a man watching us a bit too closely yesterday. He was also in Milwaukee before we left, and he's in the same car we're in most of the time."

"He stares at Leonora more than anyone, which is how Alice has been able to watch him and notice all the times he's in our vicinity. The whole thing is quite odd," Miss Charlotte interjected, her chin jutting out as if she intended to confront the man herself for upsetting her sister.

Mr. Brighton halfway rose from his seat, his gaze sweeping the train car. But Miss Alice stopped him. "Please don't confront him, any of you. He hasn't done anything wrong. It's...well, as Charlotte said, it's odd the way he watches Leonora so much. She doesn't know him. So why is he always staring at her?"

Now it was Marcus's turn to force himself to remain seated. Why *would* a strange man be watching Leonora and following them? He wasn't sure what he expected, but the pensive expression that settled on Leonora's face seemed odd. "Are you worried about him, too, Leonora? I'll go speak to him if you'd like."

She shook her head, an insincere smile lifting her lips without reaching her eyes. "Oh, no. Please don't do anything like that. I'm sure it's a passenger with far too much time to waste. We'll never see him again once we reach Los Angeles."

But Marcus wasn't so sure she meant the words. Leonora continued to wear that thoughtful, uncertain look until they rose from their seats to move to the buffet car, and he caught flashes of it throughout the evening. In the thin gaslight glow, the furrows on her forehead appeared dramatic and ominous. Did she have an idea why someone would be watching her that she wasn't sharing? After all, there were other things she wasn't sharing...

~

By the time the club members retired to their sleeping berths that evening, Leonora was ready to be alone with her thoughts. After lunch, she'd found another letter tucked into her valise, the same as the ones she'd received at home. Of course, with her companions sitting right there with her, she hadn't had a chance to read it. What the afternoon had given her was too much time to worry about who the letter was from and how it had gotten into her bag without her noticing.

When Marcus asked Alice about why she was so nervous, a thought had lodged in Leonora's mind that she wasn't able to shake. Was the man watching her the connection? Had he found a way to slip the letter in with her things? Was he the one who wrote them or just the one making the delivery? What would happen if she approached him?

Nestled into the private space of the upper berth, Leonora read the letter with growing frustration. Unlike the others, this letter seemed intent on convincing her the expedition was a bad idea. The writer questioned her courage, her ability to adapt to the challenges of the trip, even her suitability based on the delicate nature of females. It was strange, considering the other letters had all but dared her to come. If not for the same handwriting and signature, she would have questioned if this one even came from the original author.

But her exasperation wasn't so much related to the content as it was to what *wasn't* in the letter. It revealed nothing about the man or how the delivery was made. She pored over the words until late into the night, turning them over in her mind even after extinguishing the gas lamp in the berth. But to no avail. This letter didn't give her more specifics than any of the others.

By the time the train finally pulled into the station in Los Angeles the next evening, Leonora had to admit she'd missed her chance to find out the answer to any of her questions. The suspicious man hadn't reappeared that day, either hiding in another car or having disembarked at some point when she'd been distracted. She tried to look for him as the passengers emerged from the train, but steam billowed around the platform, and too many people darted this way and that to pick him out.

"Leonora? Are you ready to get on the connecting train to San Francisco?" Marcus was watching her, probably having noticed how distracted she was. She needed to pull herself together, or she might make a mistake that could harm her friends.

Forcing a smile, she gave a brisk nod. "Of course. Let's get this train travel finished. I'll be glad to board the steamship where at least we can walk around more."

Marcus's hand came to rest on her lower back as they followed the others through the busy station, sending shivers up and down her spine. He lowered his voice so only she could hear. "I didn't think I'd ever hear you say those words, not after what you told me about your feelings for water."

It was too crowded for Leonora to tell him how she'd been having nightmares about drowning, the dark waves pulling her inexorably toward certain death. She couldn't explain that statements like that were a front she put on to cover the fear so their companions wouldn't have reason to doubt her.

Instead, she shrugged. "I'm facing the fear and hoping that having you at my side will keep me from the usual reaction."

The train ride from Los Angeles to San Francisco was short —a blessing, to be sure. They spent the night in a hotel Mr. Flemming had obviously chosen. To say the beds were uncomfortable was an understatement, and the shared bathrooms were not ideal. But she was more determined than ever to make this expedition a success, and the leader's attitude played a vital role in that. She refused to let her expectations regarding their accommodations be a point of failure.

After all, as an explorer, shouldn't she be unconcerned with the quality of the bed or availability of running water? She ought to be tougher than that. Papa would never have complained—or likely, even noticed—if a hotel was shabby and the pillows possibly infested with something. She needed to refocus her mind on their purpose—discovery.

That determination only held until morning, close to deserting her when she stood on the dock in San Fransisco Bay staring up at a small but sleek steamship with the name *Minden* painted in large white letters. It might look clean and well-maintained enough, but it was not quite the large, sturdy, even luxurious vessel she'd expected Mr. Flemming to purchase passage on when they'd made plans back in Milwaukee.

In all honesty, though, that fact paled in comparison to the fear threatening to paralyze her before she could even step foot on board.

The others didn't seem bothered as they passed Leonora on the dock, heading off to get a closer look at the ocean. Marcus stopped at her side, though. "Will you be able to manage this?"

A wild urge to laugh rose in Leonora's throat, but she forced it down. She would only look hysterical if she let it loose, and that wouldn't help the situation any.

So instead, she spun around so none of the others could see the state she was in even thinking about going near that vast expanse. "Marcus, it goes so far. I can't see anything except water. How am I going to get myself on that ship?"

His arm came around her, which would usually be comforting. But at that moment, she very nearly threw off the restricting touch so she could attempt to draw a full breath. But that was ridiculous, so she let him hold her with her back pressed against his chest, sending up prayers for strength that seemed to bounce right off the clouds.

Marcus's soft voice in her ear, however, brought a reassuring calm that settled her frayed nerves. "Think about it like this. You're not actually in the water. You're in a vessel. It's taking you on the adventure you've dreamed about your entire life. You wouldn't let a little fear get in the way of that, would you? The Leonora Thornton I know wouldn't."

To her surprise, something solid brushed her hand. She

glanced down to find Marcus handing her a box emblazoned *Ghirardelli* in shining gilded letters. "What's this?"

The glow in Marcus's eyes belied his nonchalant shrug. "I thought a treat might distract you a little. I was told by the clerk at the hotel that this shop makes the best chocolates in the state. But I suppose you'll have to try one to find out if you agree."

He'd bought her chocolates. Like a real courting couple. Leonora's heart melted, and all the tension drained out of her. With this darling man at her side and God guiding her steps, couldn't she face a little fear, as he'd said? "Thank you, Marcus. Let's test them, then."

She tore back the paper covering the box and slid the lid off. Then she broke a precious piece in two and offered half to Marcus. He took it and lifted it to his lips with his warm gaze locked on her, making the moment feel far more intimate than the busy dock would usually allow.

The mix of sweet and bitter on her tongue delighted Leonora. "The clerk might have been right. This is the best chocolate I've ever tasted."

Marcus adjusted his glasses before tipping his head toward the steamship. "Do you think you can do this now?"

It was the strangest thing, but maybe she could. Not that the chocolate held any magical strengthening qualities, of course. But knowing she didn't have to face this portion of the journey alone and that Marcus had worried about this for her...that was somehow bolstering to her courage. "I do. As long as you're next to me."

With a slow half smile tilting his lips, Marcus took her hand and led her down the dock, closer to the water but also toward their friends. A group of strangers gathered a few feet away from the club members, speaking with Mr. Flemming.

When Marcus and Leonora approached, Mr. Flemming introduced the group on his right as part of his hired crew, who would travel the rest of the way with them. The six men included a naturalist, an archeologist, and four others who would help the club members dig, carry, or cart whatever was needed. Or so Mr. Flemming explained, anyway. They all looked rough and acted uncouth, not at all like the educated professionals Leonora would have expected.

Then Mr. Flemming presented the man on his left. "This is Captain Reginald Artois. I've known him several years, and he's quite capable of getting to our destination without issue."

Leonora wouldn't take Mr. Flemming's word for anything right then, but she chose to inspect the captain instead of taking issue with the explorer. The short, rotund man seemed pleasant, from a broad smile to thinning white hair that stood on end to the colorful combination of a purple vest with a red-lined coat and dingy green trousers. He looked every bit the eccentric sea captain she imagined from her father's travel stories.

She shook his hand, refusing to act like a woman who needed to be cared for and rather like an equal to Mr. Flemming.

Once the introductions were complete, Captain Artois puffed out his chest and gestured toward his vessel. "Welcome to the *Minden*. I'll lead the way aboard if you're all ready to go."

Ready was the last thing Leonora would claim to be when faced with walking onto a ship, even one moored at the dock in rather shallow water. But she'd come this far. She couldn't abandon the expedition now.

Clenching her fingers around the handle of her valise, Leonora remained still and let the captain lead the others up the gangplank. Marcus waited at the base of the ramp, giving her time to decide if she would be able to succeed. For too long, she stood frozen with her heart pounding so hard, the others could probably see it from the ship's railing.

With every ounce of will in her being, Leonora fixed her

eyes on Marcus's face and took a step forward. He nodded, his eyes warming. That hint of approval was enough to push her another step forward. Then another.

As she passed him and took the first step onto the gangplank, Leonora whispered, "I'm doing it. I can do this."

Marcus fell into step behind her, close enough she could feel his supportive presence. "I never doubted it. One step at a time and you'll get to the top."

With that praise echoing in her mind, Leonora forced back any stray thought about the water that lurked beneath them and pressed on. Finally, she reached the top of the gangplank, as Marcus said she would, and a waiting sailor reached out to help her step down onto the ship's deck.

Instant relief made her almost sag back against Marcus's chest. She'd made it onto the ship. Forcing herself to get this far had been the most difficult part. Now that she was aboard, she had no choice but to manage the water crossing. Even if they didn't find Incan treasure or an important historical site, she could at least claim that she'd stood up in the face of immense fear and conquered it. All thanks to Marcus's support.

CHAPTER 17

*A*long with the other Exploration Society members, Marcus entered the ship's dining room that evening to find there were few other passengers on board. The *Minden* was a small enough ship that the crew ate alongside the thirty or so passengers. Marcus wasn't concerned about class or mixing with the ship's crew, but he was quite annoyed with the raucous laughter and crude jokes flying from the corner where Mr. Flemming and his new crewmen sat. Marcus was immediately wary of anyone Mr. Flemming claimed to trust. Was this another way the explorer was trying to hold onto money, by hiring a fake crew of lackeys? Or were these the type of men he always associated with?

By the time the food was served, Marcus was ready to stand up and let the crew know their behavior was uncouth with ladies present, as few ladies as there were.

But Marcus soon had a bigger concern to distract him. As the meal went on, it became clear that something was wrong with Leonora. She picked at her food and barely interacted with their friends. Was her mood related to being on the ship? The ocean was calm enough that evening that one might almost forget about it, but every now and then, a wave would rock the vessel enough to be noticeable. Was the movement affecting her? Bringing back her fear?

Finally, he couldn't bear to watch her mince the fish on her plate without eating any longer. He leaned against her side, tilting his head down to whisper, "Is something wrong? You're not eating."

Leonora looked at up him, startled as if she'd forgotten there were others around. She slid her hand over Marcus's where it was clenched into a fist on top of the worn wooden table. "I need to acclimate myself to conditions I'm not used to, I think. After all, the life of an explorer is rarely comfortable."

Marcus turned his hand over to grasp her fingers as fear and uncertainty resurfaced in her eyes. Leonora looked so out of place in this rough environment, surrounded by men who used words she was unaccustomed to hearing. He wanted nothing more than to whisk her away to a more elegant ship that would have fine linens and staff to attend to her every need. That might have been enough to distract her from the method of travel she'd dreaded for so long. "Do you want to leave the dining room and find a quieter spot?"

Tilting her head, Leonora blinked a few times. "If you think that would help, I suppose I don't feel like eating, anyway."

Prepared to do whatever it took to help Leonora through this, Marcus stood and tugged on her hand to encourage her to follow him. They made their way out of the dining room, and he pulled her around a corner outside. It was quieter there, far enough away from the railing that she couldn't see the water, but where the lights of San Francisco were visible, growing smaller in the distance.

Leaning against the cold steel wall covered in white paint, Marcus pulled Leonora around to face him instead of the endless ocean and gave in to the urge to run his fingers over her soft cheek. "The farther we travel, the more I learn about the kind of strength it takes to live like this. All of us have fears we're going to have to face on this trip. Yours might have been the first one, that's all."

Her eyes softened at his touch, and his heart drummed against his ribs when she turned her cheek to rest against his hand. "I'm not sure about that. You don't seem to be afraid of anything, while having you at my side is all that's getting me through."

"I have far more to be afraid of than you realize." For the hundredth time since Vernon Flemming appeared in Milwaukee, Marcus wished he could tell Leonora everything. If she thought he didn't live most moments of his life terrified, then she didn't know him at all. How could they start a life together when he was hiding such a large part of himself?

But even as they left behind everything they'd known down to their very country, Marcus still felt bound by his promise to never reveal his mother's shame. When they returned—if they returned safely—he would tell his mother that Leonora would be his wife, and as such, she would know the full truth about what happened after his father's death. Until then, he had to continue trying to protect her while asking her to trust him.

Unaware of his inner turmoil, Leonora leaned back, removing herself from his touch to glance toward the railing with a hard swallow. "I thought getting on the ship would be enough to drive the fear out completely. But I'm still shaky and on the verge of freezing at any moment. How will I get through all the weeks that we'll be on board like this?"

He hesitated in the face of her utter trust in him. Even though she knew he was keeping things from her, she still turned to him in her fear. "Consider that the fear might not disappear all at once. All this time on the ship could be the perfect remedy. I'll help you work on it a little at a time. After all, I came for you, to be here if you need me. To be by your side for the adventure you've dreamed of for so long. It's all for you."

He'd never spoken truer words, and he found himself praying that she would see that.

To his relief, a slight smile lifted the corners of her lips again, and her shoulders relaxed. "That means so much to me, Marcus. I know this expedition isn't something you would have undertaken on your own, but I'm so glad you're here."

Swallowing back a wave of emotion, he reached for her hand, lifting it to his lips and kissing the soft skin. "As am I."

They spent a large portion of the evening on the deck, although far from the railing. As they talked, their friends joined them, and Leonora grew less tense. Perhaps she even forgot the water for a bit. Pride welled in his heart as he watched her grow despite her fear. If she could do it, maybe he could conquer the shadows that plagued him too.

The next morning, however, Marcus was once again reminded of what they were up against. Mr. Flemming asked all the Exploration Society members and the crewmen to meet him in the empty dining room after breakfast. It was the last thing Marcus wanted to do. He'd hoped to spend as little time with Flemming and his friends as possible while on the ship. They would be stuck in very close quarters for the next few months, so it would be prudent to take advantage of being away from them while he could.

But Marcus was there for Leonora. So he attempted to be polite and turned his attention to listening while Mr. Flemming made his announcement. "After speaking with the captain about our journey, we have decided to stop next week at the Mexican port of Mazatlán. From there, we will continue on with the planned schedule—two more weeks on the ship to reach Port Callao, near Lima, then donkeys and carts into the interior of the country."

Leonora's brow furrowed. "Why are we stopping so soon in the journey? Is something wrong? You never mentioned the possibility of a stop in Mexico before."

Mr. Flemming's nostrils flared as he drew a breath. "Nothing is wrong, Miss Thornton. If you would like fresh food for the journey inland, we'll have to stop and get it on the way."

With cheeks flushing, Leonora gave a sharp nod.

Marcus's fingers clenched at the way Flemming had embarrassed her, speaking to her as if she was a child. But he wouldn't make a scene. For her sake, he refused to make it worse.

Mr. Brighton tapped the paper he was taking notes on with the end of his pencil. "So three weeks to get to Peru, including the stop in Mexico, then how long do you suppose we'll be traveling inland before reaching our destination?"

Mr. Flemming pursed his lips, crossing his arms with a glare. "I've never given a specific timeline for that because it's impossible. Everything depends on the weather and the path our guide chooses."

Miss Charlotte smiled toward Mr. Flemming, seeming to be unaware of the rising tension in the room. "And what will we—"

Mr. Flemming threw up his hands. "So many questions!" The exclamation caused the rest of them to freeze in place. "We went over all the pertinent information before leaving Milwaukee. Miss Thornton has as many details as I do. Ask her everything you want to know."

Leonora slipped her arm around the crestfallen Miss Charlotte's shoulders while Mr. Flemming ended the meeting and marched from the room with his new crew members following, stopping anyone from asking for more clarifications.

Across the table from Marcus, Leonora looked rather shocked by the explorer's behavior, but she pulled herself together to address their group. "Well, that was a rousing start to the day."

When no one laughed at her attempt at lightheartedness, Leonora pushed up from her seat and offered a tight smile. "We've known for some time that our leader is not the most personable man. But keep our goal in mind. In less than a month, we'll be traversing the Peruvian jungle. We could even have made some discoveries by then."

That perked up their friends, and they left the dining room chattering with a little more excitement about what might lie ahead. But, despite his intentions to support her, Marcus couldn't help being more concerned than ever about Mr. Flemming and his bad leadership. Refusal to answer legitimate questions was a sure sign of someone hiding his true intentions, in Marcus's experience.

Sitting alone in the dining room while the others went on, Marcus removed his glasses to rub the pounding spot above his right eye. Pressure built in his chest until he wasn't sure he could draw a full breath if he had to. He was as helpless to stop Mr. Flemming from hurting Leonora as he had been to help his mother ten years ago.

With no other options in sight, Marcus could only cry out in silent prayer, hoping God would rescue them. God might not have kept Marcus from suffering all these years, but maybe Leonora's faith would be enough to gain His favor for all of them.

$\sim$

A week later, Leonora stood on deck, proud as could be that she was hardly shaking at all with the water so nearby.

Grumbling from the crew as they went about their work on deck, however, ruined the moment. It also made Leonora wonder why they didn't get their supplies in Peru when the stop in Mexico was such an obvious imposition. But the prospect of getting off the rocking ship and onto solid ground was such a relief that she refused to question the decision. She would enjoy the break and not worry about the delay.

As they disembarked at the busy port, Leonora relaxed a bit. Enjoying the stop wasn't going to be difficult at all. The coastal city of Mazatlán was beautiful. The area around the docks was clear of most vegetation, but towering palm trees scattered throughout the city beginning only a few streets away. The sound of the ocean waves lapping at the nearby sea wall mingled with the ships' pneumatic horns and steam whistles. The shouts of sailors going about their work added to the thrilling energy that accompanied it all.

The Exploration Society members had packed smaller bags with necessities for two nights on shore, which they now carried as they followed one of the ship's crewmen through the bustling streets. Spanish conversations mingled with another language Leonora couldn't identify as they passed groups of locals. Picking up her pace to catch up to the guide, she tapped his shoulder to get his attention. "Are there many Europeans in Mazatlán?"

The man sent her a wide smile. "Just Germans, which you must have noticed. A whole group of them moved here years ago."

Fascinating. While she was experiencing leaving her home and culture behind for a few months, she couldn't help imagining what it would be like to do so permanently. "What do you suppose brought them to this town, of all the places in the world?"

Next to her, Mr. Flemming shrugged. "Whatever the reason, they've established a brewery that would rival what you have in Milwaukee. I intend to visit that establishment later."

Disgust roiled through Leonora at Mr. Flemming's crass tone, along with the knowing chuckles of the new expedition crew members who were walking with him. If he intended to drink himself into a stupor with his friends, she would have to take charge of her group. They would not be sitting around the hotel waiting for him for the entire two days. And they would certainly not be visiting the brewery.

As if he read her thoughts, Mr. Flemming glanced sideways at Leonora again. "The lot of you might prefer a sightseeing excursion, I suppose."

On Leonora's other side, Mr. Howard nodded with vigor. "Yes, that's very much of interest. Are there any spots you suggest we see before leaving?"

Mr. Flemming jerked his thumb behind them, toward the south end of the city. "I'm sure that hill out there would interest you."

As if he didn't hear the other man's sarcastic tone, one of the new crewmen added, "There's also the beach by the sea wall."

Mr. Howard began asking the sailor leading the way how much time he'd spent in Mazatlán, but Leonora turned her attention to the architecture that stood out to her as they moved through the city. Many elements were clearly inspired by other cultures that must have been present in the area throughout its history. Colorful paint on the buildings gave the whole town a cheerful atmosphere, especially when combined with bright smiles from the locals they passed. Yes, she was going to enjoy this unexpected delay, after all.

They reached the hotel without any trouble. For once, Mr. Flemming's penchant for finding economical options wasn't a detriment. Located on a quiet side street, the compact building was well cared for and charming, with arches lining the front and a beautiful balcony wrapped around the entire second story.

Inside, the lobby was simply decorated. Cream-colored walls held a few paintings, and several potted plants were tucked into corners. There was a large fireplace on one side, flanked by four padded chairs, and the clerk's counter took up most of the opposite wall. The stairway up to the guest rooms was centered straight across from the entrance.

Leonora gave her friends instructions to meet there again in the morning so they could begin exploring the city. Before following Alice and Charlotte to their shared room, Leonora was stopped by Mr. Flemming's hard grip on her upper arm. "Miss Thornton, a moment."

Out of the corner of her eye, Leonora saw Marcus watching them with an intense frown. She smiled in his direction to alleviate the worry that was obvious in his expression and gestured for him to go with the others, then turned her back so she could look at Mr. Flemming. "Yes?"

Facing her, Mr. Flemming's eyes were oddly bright, unsettling Leonora's stomach. "I'm making quite a few arrangements for this group as we go, which would be much easier if I held onto *all* the expedition funds from here on out. Including everything raised in Milwaukee."

She hadn't expected him to ask for the money the club had gathered, which she kept close by at all times. Hesitation caused her to clutch the handle of her valise tighter. "It's worked fine before now. Why change what we've been doing?"

A dark shadow crossed Mr. Flemming's face, and his voice turned cold. "Because I'm the leader of this expedition. It undermines my authority to ask a woman for money to pay for food and lodging or to pay my crew. That is why it needs to change."

In the face of his brusqueness, Leonora wished she hadn't made Marcus feel confident enough to leave her alone with this man. Her mind raced. The last thing she wanted was to give him the money hidden deep in her valise. But she didn't have a good reason not to. She was the one who had been convincing Marcus for months that this man was trustworthy. It would be hypocritical of her to balk at giving him what he needed to be the leader they expected him to be.

Forcing aside her reluctance, Leonora unclasped her bag and reached inside, finding the folded leather packet by feel.

She separated what she hoped was enough money to cover the expenses the Exploration Society members might incur the next day while they went off on their own. Then she drew a deep breath and held out the packet that held the rest of what they'd raised in Milwaukee.

The moment she placed it in his hand, Mr. Flemming's demeanor lightened. "I knew you'd see reason. Enjoy whatever excursions you decide to take tomorrow. I'll be here in town with my crew."

Without giving her a chance to reply, Mr. Flemming whisked himself out the front door and disappeared down the street. Leonora tried to gather her sinking heart before retiring, but it was a long night spent worrying if she'd done the right thing.

Morning dawned bright and warm. Though Leonora woke feeling unrested, she refused to dwell on what she'd done the evening before. Instead, she led the group to a charming local restaurant a block away that the hotel owner had recommended. It sat across the street from a lovely plaza that Leonora intended for them to explore after they ate.

Breakfast was delicious. A lovely woman with a wide smile brought out plates mounded with fluffy eggs with green chili peppers mixed in and warm tortillas on the side. Bowls contained some fruits they were familiar with, but also some the group had never seen, like a sweet, bright-yellow fruit the waitress called mango.

They struggled to communicate with the restaurant staff until the waitress brought over a young man who looked to be around thirteen years old. He was slim, with inquisitive dark-brown eyes and neatly combed brown hair. "Good morning and welcome," he said in heavily accented but discernable English. "I am Manuel."

Swallowing a large mouthful of eggs, Mr. Howard leaned

forward, his eyes glowing. "Excellent, now we can learn more about this delightful location."

During the course of the meal, the group asked Manuel all the questions they could think of. In turn, he told them about a theatre nearby and the cathedral they could see from the restaurant's large front window, along with many tidbits of the town's history. As they were finishing up, Mr. Howard pulled out his notepad once again. "What places in town should we try to see before leaving, Manuel?"

Manuel tilted his head to one side, squinting as he considered the question. "The *observatorio* is interesting. It is near Crestón Island, the large hill. You might like the *faro*...ah...lighthouse at the top also."

Mr. Howard grinned. "Yes, those do sound interesting. We want to learn about your history and culture, not just see the popular sights."

Charlotte and Alice exchanged glances, communicating without words as they often did. Then Charlotte addressed their new friend. "We heard there's a nice beach by the sea wall, though. Do you recommend a visit there, as well?"

The boy tipped his chin forward. "If you want to see the sea wall or sit in the sand, yes, that beach is fine. But if you like history, you might like the old carvings on a beach to the north."

Like the rest of the group, Leonora perked up at the sound of that. "Carvings? How far north is it? Can we walk there?"

Manuel shook his head. "No, too far. But a man I know has come to own an automobile, and he can take you. It will still take several hours."

After some discussion, the group decided to make the northern beach an overnight excursion, to allow plenty of time for exploring after the long drive. Marcus asked Manuel to find the man with the car while the rest of them returned to the hotel to get everything they would need.

They then explored the plaza by the restaurant while waiting on Manuel, enjoying the scent of the blossoms that were beginning to open on a row of orange trees and the lovely stonework. As the others walked around together, Marcus pulled Leonora into an intricately designed wrought-iron gazebo. He held both her hands, gazing into her eyes with such a soft expression that her mouth went dry. "I love watching you interact with the locals. You're kind, respectful, and curious. Everything a good explorer should be."

Warm delight spread through Leonora at his approval. "You always know how to speak to my heart, Marcus Turner."

Grinning, Marcus dropped his head closer to hers. "I've had years to observe you and learn what you like, my darling."

Leonora raised her lips to meet his. While unexpected, the kiss was most welcome. She'd missed his touch while they'd been busy getting their bearings. Marcus's arm slid around her waist and pulled her closer, lining up their bodies in a way that made her marvel at all the sensations assailing her at once.

Feeling bolstered by his sweet words and captivating touch, Leonora slid her hands up his shoulders to sink into the hair along his neck. Before she was ready, he pulled back, raising one eyebrow. "We should join the others."

She shot him a teasing glance. "Or we could stay here. I've learned something about myself. I'd rather improve my kissing skills than walk around a plaza, no matter how beautiful or historic it is."

Chuckling, Marcus started to move back in for another kiss until the blaring of a car horn broke in. Pulling apart with a rueful glance, they went to join their friends and begin the day's adventure. Despite the interruption, the moment with Marcus had been just what Leonora needed. Her confidence was restored, and she was once again certain she hadn't made a mistake by trusting Mr. Flemming.

CHAPTER 18

*T*he road out of Mazatlán—if one could call it a road —was little more than a rutted dirt cart path. The lack of infrastructure shouldn't have surprised Marcus. He'd already seen that cars weren't widely used in the city yet.

Still, in no time at all, the jostling of the car brought Marcus close to losing the large breakfast he now regretted eating. It didn't help that the group was packed into too few seats. It was necessary in order to get all six of them in the car with the driver, Juan, and Manuel, who had agreed to come along to translate for them. But it was uncomfortable, nonetheless.

Only an hour into the half-day drive, Juan pulled to a stop dead in the center of the path. Relief cleared away a little of the nausea. It was time for a break. Marcus started to reach over to help Leonora stand when men materialized out of the trees lining the road. Everyone in the car went still.

Behind Marcus, Manuel whispered, "Guerilla fighters. They roam the jungles."

The men stalked closer, every one of them armed. Heavily. Time slowed while Marcus struggled to draw full breaths.

Juan spoke to the men, although what he said Marcus

would never know. Manuel had fallen silent, as if he didn't want to draw attention to himself. One man, who appeared to be the leader, waved his rifle, gesturing with it while he spoke. From the back seat, a muffled whimper escaped Miss Alice.

They'd been warned to expect unrest in Mexico, but Marcus hadn't imagined they would be anywhere near it. If these men opened fire, what could he do? His thoughts rattled around in his skull, hollow, ineffective, no matter how much he wanted to protect his friends and, especially, how desperate he was to protect Leonora.

The conversation continued between Juan and the leader while several of the other men advanced toward the car, looking over the Americans in a way that lifted the hairs on the back of Marcus's neck.

Suddenly, the leader spat one last comment at Juan and waved off his men. They disappeared, slinking back into the trees and leaving the clearing looking as if nothing had ever happened.

Without hesitation, Juan slammed his foot on the accelerator, causing the car to lurch into motion. They flew down the road for several miles, jolting wildly, before he finally slowed to the previous reasonable pace.

Mr. Brighton leaned forward and spoke to Manuel. "Why did they stop us and then let us go?"

Manuel and Juan spoke for several minutes in Spanish before Manuel began his explanation. "There is much conflict here right now. Many groups who want to lead Mexico. Those men are waiting for government officials, hoping to ambush them. It's good they didn't want anything to do with us."

Next to Marcus, Leonora released a long breath. "Thank goodness God protected us."

Marcus pushed his glasses up on his head to rub his eyes. As much as he wanted to trust that God would protect them, his inability to do anything in that situation would likely haunt him forever. Why had he believed he was capable of this kind of travel? He was no asset to Leonora out here. He was a mild banker who was powerless in the face of real danger.

Silence prevailed for the rest of the drive as they all considered how close they'd come to tragedy. After several more hours, Juan turned off the road and pulled to a stop. Ahead of them, at the edge of the ocean, a wide swath of large dark-gray rocks ringed a narrow strip of pristine sand. The rocks appeared to grow bigger as they trailed away from the spot where Juan had parked. And, most exciting of all, some of the closest ones did indeed have what looked like ancient carvings etched on their surfaces.

As they all disentangled themselves, climbed from the car, and stretched cramped limbs, most of the others seemed to have recovered from their ordeal. Marcus grabbed the wooden case he'd brought which opened up into a lap desk, and Leonora pulled her bag of supplies from the floorboard of the car and slung it over her shoulder. She grinned at Marcus. "I can't wait to see your surveying work in action. Getting to watch you do what you love most is a pleasure I haven't experienced."

Marcus swallowed hard. That expectant glint in her eyes was a lot to live up to. But her glowing expression almost made the terrifying trip worthwhile. Almost.

Manuel spoke in rapid Spanish with Juan for a few minutes before turning to the group. "He says this place is where the people...ah, travelers...used to stop. We call it *las labradas*."

Leonora scrunched up her face, trying to decipher Manuel's words. "Travelers. Nomads? People who traveled all the time?"

The boy nodded vigorously.

Leonora continued, "And does the name refer to the carvings?"

Another pleased nod from Manuel.

Reaching in her bag, Leonora handed out tracing paper and charcoals to the others. Then she looked around the group, her eyes lingering on Marcus before sweeping across everyone else. "Let's explore and meet back here in a few hours to compare what we've found."

With so many rocks, there were endless nooks and crannies for them to examine. Marcus followed Leonora while the others broke off in pairs as well. Even with three groups of them, they were hardly going to get through much of the long stretch of rocky beach. There were glyphs everywhere.

Leonora started with the driest area. She dropped down to sit on a rock next to one of the carvings. She placed a sheet of tracing paper over the glyph and lightly rubbed her charcoal across it, bringing the swirled design to life on the paper. After ensuring that the entire glyph had transferred onto the paper, she moved on to the next carving.

While Leonora recorded what was on the rocks, Marcus pulled out his own tools. He hadn't been able to bring any large surveying equipment on the expedition, but he did have a set of chains for measuring distances and his theodolite, which would measure the angles he needed to complete mathematical equations that would help him map each rock's location on the beach with precise accuracy.

Before beginning, Marcus had Manuel help him establish a baseline using the chain, then he was able to begin marking the location of Leonora's rocks on paper stored in his lap desk. They worked that way through noon, with Leonora concentrating on the designs and physical features of the carvings and Marcus mapping them. Across the beach, the others followed similar pursuits. They stopped briefly to eat the lunch they'd bought from the restaurant that morning, which consisted of what Manuel called *tortas*—seasoned chicken stuffed into bread like sandwiches—along with more fruit. Then they returned to their areas, anxious to keep going. While they wouldn't be able to cover all the glyphs in one day, it was good practice. And enjoyable enough to wash away the remaining tendrils of fear from the morning.

As always, Marcus was amazed at how pleasant it was to work alongside Leonora. Every so often, she would glance up from her task and smile when he caught her gaze. At one point, she stood, arching her back to loosen it from all the bending she had to do to see the rocks well. Walking over to where Marcus was mapping her previous rock, she peeked at his notes. "It's amazing to me how accurate these simple tools are, Marcus." Her voice roughened a bit, as if with emotion. "I'm sure it helps that this is something you've practiced. I think you must be quite good at it."

Stopping to give her his attention, Marcus let everything he was feeling show in his eyes. There was no way something as plain as words could do it justice. "Thank you for believing in me and championing what I love to do. I've...well, I haven't had that from anyone since my father died."

Dropping her head against his shoulder, Leonora let her touch speak, a conversation Marcus was coming to understand and appreciate more than he would have thought possible. After a few moments, she headed to the next rock while he returned to his work. But the contentment of knowing someone supported him remained.

When the incoming tide brought white-foamed waves crashing up to the rocks they were working on, the group gathered up their tools and met back by Juan's car. The sun hung low in the sky, bathing everything in pink and gold. Manuel had been busy while they explored, setting up an organized campsite with the supplies they'd brought, the three tents erected in a semi-circle with the box of food and water in between them. They all sat down around the fire he'd started to eat the simple meal of tamales they'd brought along with their lunch.

While they ate, Mr. Howard and Miss Charlotte asked their

new local friends all about their lives. They learned that Juan and his wife spent most days selling fruit in the large central market in Mazatlán. He talked about his three grown children and the five grandchildren they'd given him so far.

Juan told tales of his hometown as the sunset burned brilliant hues across the sky, the clouds holding the color for a long time, as if hesitant to surrender to darkness. The older man spoke of the many conflicts in his seventy years due to different Mexican leaders fighting for control of the country. He told of the famed opera singer, Angela Peralta, who had arrived to perform in the theatre in Mazatlán but succumbed to illness before she could. He went on for quite some time about the beauty of her voice when she managed one last song from the balcony of her hotel room.

It was quite late when Miss Alice stifled a yawn, then nudged her sister with an elbow. "We should get some sleep, don't you think?"

The ladies rose, so the men did too. A chorus of goodnights echoed around the campfire. Marcus, however, walked with Leonora to the tent the ladies had claimed. Once the Bauer sisters disappeared inside, he wrapped his arms around Leonora, smiling down at her. "Despite the rocky start, this has been a good day. See what a good expedition leader you are?"

She giggled a little, a reaction Marcus found incredibly endearing. Dropping his head, he placed a kiss on her forehead before releasing her. Leonora lingered at his side, though, looking up at him with wide eyes. "Do you still think I should have left Mr. Flemming out completely and arranged everything myself?"

Marcus nodded. Having faced the possibility of death that day, what reason was there to hide his true feelings? "Without a doubt."

A frown marred her face. "But I don't have his connections and experience."

Trying to communicate his complete faith in her, Marcus tipped her chin up, holding her gaze. "But you have kindness, intelligence, curiosity, and persistence. Those things will bring you connections. And his amount of experience is debatable."

Without responding, Leonora gave him one last hug, then followed the twins into the tent, her forehead still furrowed. While waiting for sleep to claim him that night, Marcus tried to pray that she would see what he saw—how capable she was and the way she inspired others with her genuine care for them. But instead, he could only envision the hard, angry face of the guerrilla leader. His body alternated between too hot and too cold, leaving his skin uncomfortably clammy as he tossed and turned under a blanket. Would they be stopped again on the return trip? And if they were, would they survive the encounter, or would their powerlessness lead to tragedy?

～

*W*aves crashing against the rocks on the beach woke Leonora the next morning.

She could tell even before opening her eyes that the weather that day was not going to cooperate with their plan to explore the glyphs for a few hours before driving back in the afternoon. Moisture hung heavy on the air, and wind whipped around their tent, causing the canvas sides to heave. A tendril of worry curled through her.

Charlotte and Alice were still asleep somehow, so Leonora dressed as quietly as possible and slipped out of the tent. She would make whatever arrangements she could before the entire crew woke. That way, she would look competent and inspire their confidence. In her memory, Papa had always had everything under control, never scrambling for a solution. She would be the same. She had to be.

Outside, under dark, roiling clouds, Marcus, Manuel, and

Juan had already gathered by the car. Leonora marched over through a spray of cold raindrops and addressed them with as much poise as she could muster. "Juan, can we make the drive back this morning instead of waiting? I'm concerned about this weather."

Juan and Manuel spoke for a moment before Manuel turned to her to relay Juan's words. "He says with so much rain, there will be too much mud. The car will get stuck."

Marcus paled. "The guerrillas are out there between here and Mazatlán. I don't think we should take that risk."

Leonora's stomach clenched. The tents wouldn't be secure enough to shelter them in the storm, and driving back now wasn't feasible. But was there anywhere safer in such a remote area? "Juan, do you know of anywhere nearby where we could take shelter?"

Manuel consulted with him again before answering, "There is a small village not far. We could ask for shelter there."

With Manuel's help, Leonora inquired about the village and its location. As it was their only option in this remote area, Leonora went to wake Charlotte and Alice while Marcus roused the other men. They worked together to get the camp-site taken apart and packed up, but they were all still drenched by the time they piled into the car, with the top now unfolded to provide what protection they could get. Marcus, thoughtful as ever, spread blankets over as much of their bodies as possible, though it didn't help against the blustering storm with the open sides of the car.

It was a very slow, cautious drive from the beach to the edge of what was indeed a very small village. Nestled against a large hill, Barras de Piaxtla followed the sharp curve of the shore. The architecture was a fascinating combination of thatched fishing huts interspersed with a few larger homes painted in pristine white. But what drew Leonora's interest was a small stone building with a cross mounted atop a plain wooden spire.

"There's a church. Perhaps that would be a good option, rather than imposing on any of these people's homes."

Juan directed the car that way and parked close to the church. They all rushed to climb from the car and used the blankets to provide what shelter they could on the way to the door. Leonora tugged on the carved wooden handle, thankful when it opened without resistance.

Once the door closed behind them, although they could still hear the wind roaring outside, everything else grew quiet. They spoke in hushed voices and took light, almost tiptoeing steps into the empty sanctuary. But Leonora couldn't hold back a gasp when they emerged from under a low ceiling at the entry and the entire room came into view.

A picture rail running around the three walls held frames every few feet that contained paintings of various Biblical scenes, most of which Leonora could identify. Handmade wooden benches lined both sides of the rectangular room, leaving one aisle up the middle. Spaced across the high ceiling were beautiful round beams that gave extra support to the structure.

The room itself was lovely in its simplicity, but the altar area stole her breath. Behind a railing, built up on a raised platform, sat a narrow table covered in a pretty linen cloth and set with floral arrangements and candelabras. Behind that, though, rising from the floor to the ceiling, a skillfully carved wooden altarpiece covered the entire wall. Sculpted columns flanked each side of it, with different intricate borders marking off a grid of smaller sections. Paintings of what she assumed to be Catholic saints filled in these panels, the quality of those works rivaling anything she'd seen in museums.

Charlotte, Alice, and Mr. Brighton took seats in the back pew, while Leonora, Marcus, and Mr. Howard roamed the room, taking in the reverent beauty of every piece that adorned it. Before they'd finished, a door to the side of the altar opened, and a priest stepped out, startling when he saw them. He spoke in rapid Spanish, which Manuel hurried to translate for Leonora. "He asks, do you need prayer?"

Leonora couldn't help smiling. "Don't we always?"

When Manuel relayed her words, the priest also smiled, and Leonora relaxed a bit, glad he wasn't upset by the intrusion of eight strangers. Manuel explained their situation to the priest, who then gestured for them to sit with him. Using Manuel's translations, Leonora spoke to the man. "Your church is beautiful and so peaceful."

The creases on the older man's face deepened when he smiled again. "Many thanks. It serves the village well."

How different this space was from the often large and elaborate churches in Milwaukee. While there were also many modest places of worship like this, the larger buildings drew more people—and more influential ones, at that. What made them choose lavishness over simple peace? "I'd like to worship in a place like this. I wish more American churches were this way."

"Isn't God's spirit everywhere, from big to small, wealthy to poor? I am sure you can find Him where you are placed."

Blinking a few times, Leonora let those wise words fill her mind. Wherever she was placed? She'd been feeling so unsure of herself and the choices she was making. When Mr. Flemming first arrived in Milwaukee, she had been certain the expedition was God's will for her. Now, she worried that she might have missed His direction somehow. Was God with her even if she chose wrong? Even if she'd trusted the wrong person?

At that moment, in the modest little sanctuary, Leonora pondered the tension that she'd been forcing back ever since she agreed to raise money for Mr. Flemming in exchange for their club being included in this trip. God must have had a reason for bringing them here, for putting Mr. Flemming in their path. Maybe she hadn't been as wrong to trust him as Marcus made it seem.

But if that was true, why was she still so unsure? Shouldn't following God's will bring peace?

Outside, the storm still raged. The priest told them to stay as long as they needed, then shuffled back through the door, which presumably led to his office. Hoping to get away from the questions she couldn't answer, Leonora joined the others at the back of the sanctuary. Mr. Brighton was in the middle of telling a lively story. Alice, in particular, was hanging on his every word. Leonora smiled as a lovestruck expression crossed the younger woman's face. It was so very sweet.

As the conversation moved on, Leonora slid closer to Alice and leaned in. "I don't want to pry, but if you want to talk with someone about, say, any feelings developing between you and one of our gallant gentlemen, I'm happy to listen."

A flush crept across Alice's cheeks, but she smiled. "Is it that obvious? I suppose I shouldn't be surprised. I know what I'm feeling, and sometimes it seems ready to burst out of me."

Leonora understood that deep inside. The same sensation filled her chest every time she thought about a future with Marcus. It had replaced the excitement she used to feel over planning her global adventures. That realization should have shaken her, but in some way, it felt inevitable. Marcus had been in her life for so long, and she'd cared for him always. "I know just what you mean."

Now it was Alice's turn to pry. "Because of your relationship with Mr. Turner? He's quite the catch, being from such a prominent family."

"You know very well I'm drawn to him because he's a good man, not because of his family. Anyway, he doesn't like to depend on their money or status."

Alice nodded. "That's a fine quality in a man, to be sure.

And a good thing, since there have been rumors that they don't have the fortune they're alleged to."

Narrowing her eyes, Leonora tried to sort out what on earth Alice could be talking about. "What would make anyone think that?"

"Oh, you know how the old gossips are. They say Mrs. Turner used to be quite fashionable, but my mother and her friends have mentioned many times over the last few years that she's been seen in gowns that are obviously remade from ones that she wore seasons ago. I'm not astute with fashion, but Mother never forgets a gown."

"And reusing old gowns means the family is lying about their financial situation?"

Alice's forehead wrinkled as her eyebrows drew together. "Oh no, that's not the only reason. I would never have heeded the gossip over that one thing. It's also because items from the Turner estate have shown up in the homes of *nouveau riche* recently, and they released nearly all their staff two years ago without hiring any more. Haven't you ever wondered why Mr. Turner is so devoted to a family that seems to be a trial for him? Most people have concluded he's supporting them with that job."

Leonora's head swiveled until she could see Marcus. He chuckled at whatever witty comment Mr. Howard had made, looking handsome and completely at ease. Was Alice's claim the truth? Had he been working so hard because his family needed the money? Did he remain with his indifferent mother and brother out of obligation to them?

But why would he hide that from her? He had to know she didn't care in the least about his family's financial or social standing. Was there more to the story? He'd asked her to trust him until he could tell her what hid beneath the surface of his sometimes-secretive behavior. Was this it? Was the loss of his family's money the only thing he'd been keeping from her?

And when would he trust her enough to reveal if it was?

As they whiled away the morning in the church, a weight began to press on Leonora's heart. Wasn't she keeping a secret the same as Marcus seemed to be? Hadn't she kept the letters and the real reason she continued to let Mr. Flemming lead their expedition from him?

By the time the storm let up, she'd come to a decision. It was time to tell Marcus everything. Past time, really, but she prayed he would forgive her for that. She could no longer allow any walls to stand between them. Before they left Mazatlán the next day on the steamer, she would explain the letters and her hopes for revealing any hidden details about her father's death.

CHAPTER 19

*D*uring the course of the morning and while they enjoyed lunch with the priest and his wife in their small home, Marcus's chest had tightened until he thought his lungs might cease to function altogether. The possibility of encountering the guerrillas again was high. What if they decided to interrogate the group, or take them as hostages, or something much worse? The sooner they left and got through the drive back to Mazatlán, the easier Marcus would be able to breathe.

The rain had finally stopped completely when they exited the priest's abode in the early afternoon. After thanking the priest again and waving goodbye for longer than Marcus thought necessary, the group piled into Juan's car, squeezing tight together again, and prepared for the long drive back to Mazatlán.

Marcus clasped his hands together most of the way back to keep them from shaking. But it helped that he wasn't the only one affected. When they reached the spot where the guerrillas had appeared the day before, Juan's eyes darted back and forth to scan the tree line on either side of the road, and the group fell silent, as if they were holding their breaths. Thankfully, they passed through without incident. Two hours later, the outskirts of Mazatlán were a welcome sight, proving that the sense of foreboding Marcus had woken with that morning was irrational, after all.

Deep dusk blanketed the city when the car finally stopped in front of the hotel. The passengers unloaded from the close confines of the car and took a few minutes to stretch out after being in such awkward positions for hours. Meanwhile, Leonora tried to pay Juan for driving them, though the kind man shoved the money back into her hand and folded her fingers over it, waving off her arguments with a smile and a cheerful "adios!" as he drove away.

Leonora had paid Manuel before they left to act as their translator on the two-day excursion, so now they all said their goodbyes to him as well, thanking him profusely for his help. Then it was only their original group of six Exploration Society members standing in front of the hotel.

Unable to imagine being able to rest after the day they'd had, Marcus gestured toward the plaza they'd explored the morning before. "I hear music and voices. Should we go see what this town holds on a Friday evening?"

Joyful agreement from every one of his friends proved none of them had been any more ready to go inside than Marcus had been. In high spirits, the group made their way by following the sounds of revelry. When they turned a corner and the plaza came into view, decorations covered every surface—lush flowers and fabric banners that ruffled in the light breeze. After all the rain that had gone through Mazatlán as well as the village they'd been in, everything had a clean, fresh feel.

It soon became evident that they had walked into a wedding celebration. In the center of the activity was a beaming young woman in a gown made of many tiers of colorful fabric all covered in beautiful floral embroidery. She clutched the arm of a man in a suit with a short jacket and beaded embroidery running from his shoulders down to his shoes. At his neck, a wide tie formed a floppy bow. The large crowd gathered in the plaza seemed to be dressed in their best clothing, creating a bright, colorful display as they mingled and danced. But the groom only had eyes for his bride. Understandable. Marcus had enough experience with staring in awe at Leonora to know what the groom must be feeling.

At first, the group of Americans held back, not wanting to interfere in an event to which they hadn't been invited. Marcus made sure to place himself next to Leonora, as close as he could without taking her in his arms. He was fascinated by the emotions crossing her face as she took in every detail of the joyous celebration.

Before long, a stately older man approached them. He and Marcus tried a few times to speak to each other, but this man didn't know English, and Marcus had only picked up a few words in Spanish over the last two days, none of which were helpful. Finally, the man gestured them toward the party with a wide smile that was impossible to interpret as anything but a request for them to join in.

In no time, Mr. Brighton had asked Miss Alice to dance. An eager young man presented his hand to Miss Charlotte, which she accepted with a blushing giggle, and they also took to the dance floor. Mr. Howard claimed an empty seat at a long table and pulled out his ever-present notebook to record his observations.

That left Marcus alone with Leonora. He nudged her side with his elbow. "Would you like to dance with me, Miss Thornton?"

Raising her face toward his, she nodded, more solemn than he expected. "I would love to."

Marcus took her soft hand in his and led the way onto the dance floor, which was essentially the entire plaza. Bright, happy music filled the air thanks to a mariachi band tucked into a corner of the outdoor space. All around them, people laughed and talked while dancing. It was different from the more sedate society balls he was used to but in the best way possible.

Leonora, however, seemed to have grown melancholy since they returned to town. She still let him tug her close, even though the current song was too lively for that kind of dancing. But Marcus didn't care. He wanted to hold her. And if there was anything he enjoyed about this expedition more than he'd imagined beforehand, it was the freedom from other people's expectations. No one cared if he was following strict social guidelines for courting Leonora. No one noticed if he held her closer or longer than was necessary. Knowing he could do what he wanted to was a heady feeling.

But an unintended result of sliding his arm around her back was that Marcus could feel tension in Leonora's shoulders. She had stopped exclaiming with glee over the decorations, the outfits, and the music and had dropped her head to his shoulder. "Leonora, is something wrong?"

She raised her head and stared up at him for a moment, biting her lower lip. Worry threaded through Marcus, displacing some of his enjoyment of the evening. "There's something I need to tell you."

That didn't sound like a good thing. "You should know you can tell me anything, anytime."

Still she hesitated, letting her gaze wander around the festive celebration for a long time while Marcus moved them through the other dancing couples in a slow sway. Finally, she drew a deep breath and spoke with quiet, deliberate words. "I haven't been honest with you about the reason I insisted on participating in this specific expedition, despite your feelings about Mr. Flemming."

Marcus's stomach dropped. "What do you mean? It's been

clear the entire time that you want to go where your father went. We could have managed it without Flemming, but we all understand your desire to continue your father's work."

But she shook her head. "That's a bit of it, of course. But there's more. You see, I've been getting these letters. They're delivered anonymously and only signed 'an observer.' This person knew and respected my father, and the letters raised all these questions about the validity of the story of his death that the Explorers Club reported to us. Once I started to wonder, Marcus, I had to come for myself and find out if anything had been covered up. I need to know the truth."

A bitter taste filled Marcus's mouth. He stopped moving them and dropped his hands from her back. Leonora's eyebrows pulled together, and her lips parted, but her words had thrown him off balance, negating his natural concern over her response. "You dragged us all this way—with several months of travel, difficulty, and danger still to go—because some fool who's too afraid to reveal their identity suggested that the esteemed Explorers Club covered up details about your father's death?"

"Now, don't sound so dismissive, Marcus. You didn't read those letters. They're very compelling. I have good reasons for us to be here."

A heavy weight crashed down on Marcus. He began to back away, desperate for some space to think. "No, I didn't read the letters, did I? Because you chose to hide them, to bring us out here on false pretenses."

Leonora's pained flinch caused him to pause a moment. Was it right for him to be so hurtful when he was hiding his own secret, one she knew he had and had trusted him to share when he could?

But this was different. She hadn't promised anyone to protect this information like he had. She'd chosen not to include him, or any of their friends. A memory of the guns the rebels had held the day before flashed through his mind. She was putting all of them at risk and hadn't bothered to give them the information they needed to make an informed decision about the potential costs of this trip.

They remained at a standstill in the middle of the dancers, staring at each other until Miss Charlotte rushed over, wide-eyed and still accompanied by the same young man, but now with Manuel trailing along too. "Leonora, the ship left this morning. Mr. Flemming has stranded us here!"

~

At first, Leonora couldn't fathom the meaning of the breathless words pouring from Charlotte's mouth. The ship was leaving tomorrow morning. Why on earth would anyone claim it was gone?

But her brain caught up all too soon as the horrible reality became clear. Still, how could it be possible? "Charlotte, dear, slow down. Why don't you catch your breath for a moment and then tell us everything?" Leonora pushed Charlotte into the chair she'd vacated.

Charlotte glanced back and forth between Leonora and Marcus. "I know it sounds beyond belief. But Antonio is certain he saw the *Minden* leaving the dock a little before noon. Manuel spoke to the hotel owner, who is also here, and he confirmed that Mr. Flemming checked out early this morning. We've been abandoned here."

Charlotte fanned herself with one hand, but it didn't seem to help her intense agitation. The state she was in made the situation all the more real for Leonora. Alice was the sister most likely to panic at such a discovery. Charlotte generally maintained a more pragmatic outlook. So the fact that this twin was so distraught...well, Leonora had to take her words to heart.

Turning to Manuel, she gathered any information he knew about the whereabouts of the ship and crew while the Expedition Society members had been out of town. It sounded as bad from his account as it did from Charlotte's. At Leonora's request, Manuel ran off through the revelers and returned a few minutes later with the hotel owner trailing behind him.

With Manuel translating for them, Leonora spoke to the man who had been so gracious during the one night they'd been at the hotel. "Please tell me what happened with Mr. Flemming, our leader."

She couldn't spit out the word *leader* fast enough. It hardly fit the man anymore. No leader would desert his crew in a strange place. No leader would swindle people who only wanted to learn from his experience. Bitterness began welling up in her heart, and Leonora struggled to find any desire to contain it. Mr. Flemming deserved her contempt if this situation was what it appeared to be.

Sweat glistened on the hotel owner's creased face as he spoke to Manuel, who then repeated his words in English for the rest of the group. "The explorer came to me this morning, after sunrise. He wanted to pay for his room. I asked him about the rest of you, and he said you had decided not to go on, that you were too frightened and were finding a way to go back to America. He said you would return to pay for all of the rooms later today." The man swallowed hard, his throat constricting.

On impulse, Leonora rested her hand on his forearm. The man finally met her eyes and calmed, placing his weathered hand over hers. As much as she didn't want to, Leonora pushed forward, needing to know everything. "And did you see the ship leave?"

The man shook his head while Manuel translated. "No, but when it grew late and you did not return to pay, I went out to see if I could find you. I went past the dock in case you were there and noticed the ship was gone. I apologize for being angry when I thought you disappeared without paying."

And then one more condemning detail crashed down on Leonora—the choice she'd made in naivety that now caused her heart to plummet. In her mind, she could see the moment when they'd first arrived in Mazatlán and Mr. Flemming convinced her to give him the majority of the expedition funds. He'd never returned the thick envelope of bills to her.

They had been abandoned in a foreign country with no money and no way of negotiating their own trip home.

Vernon Flemming had truly betrayed them.

Leonora couldn't draw air into her lungs. She groped behind her for something to hold onto, finding an empty chair and dropping into it with a thump. Around her, Manuel, the hotel owner, and Marcus all hovered close, asking if she was all right. But their voices sounded muffled and distant as if they were separated by glass. She couldn't respond, managing only to wave off their concerns before covering her face with both hands.

Despite her arguments over the past few months that they could trust Mr. Flemming, despite Marcus's assertion that she was smart and capable enough to lead this expedition even without the explorer, she'd made the worst possible mistake. No, several of the worst possible mistakes.

She'd trusted the wrong man. She'd defended a scoundrel. She'd given him their money, for goodness' sake. And worst of all, she'd ignored Marcus's concerns, even while claiming she trusted him.

Not only had her choices placed her in a terrible situation, but as Marcus had just accused her, she'd dragged her friends along. The words he'd flung at her had hurt a few minutes ago. Now, however, she could see the impact of what she'd done. He was right to be angry with her. And it was all because she'd gotten wrapped up in some silly anonymous letters.

The author of those letters had been right too. She wasn't experienced enough to lead an expedition on her own. She wasn't intelligent or worldly enough. She had led her club members into this and now had no idea how to get them out.

Marcus's hands on her knees alerted Leonora that he'd crouched in front of her, which should have felt intimate but barely pierced the veil of her growing panic. He said her name in a low, calm voice. It was quiet in the midst of the revelry, but enough to make her open her eyes.

Then she wished she hadn't. The entire group of Exploration Society members stood around her, staring with various levels of worry on their faces. The people they had met during their time in Mazatlán also stood close by—Manuel, the hotel owner, and even Juan had appeared. Everyone she knew in this place was witnessing her utter failure.

Her instincts spurred her to stand, though she regretted the loss of Marcus's touch as soon as his hands dropped from her legs. But there were more important things to think about now than romance. She had problems to solve. They had very little money and no plan for how to return to the United States. Their only way of communicating was through Manuel. How was she going to get them out of this mess she'd created?

Possible solutions raced through her mind, but Leonora attempted to focus on the first problem at hand. They needed a place to stay that night, and they owed the kind hotel owner for the last two nights, even though they hadn't used their rooms for one of those. But everything in her balked at publicly admitting they didn't have enough money to pay for those rooms, much less passage home. Could she save what was left of her dignity while getting them out of this mess?

As he tended to do, Marcus came to her rescue, although he didn't know this time how much she needed saving. He spoke low in her ear, his nearness sending shivers up her spine despite her distracted state. "Maybe we should get some sleep before attempting to unravel everything."

They couldn't pay for another night at the hotel. But what choice was there? He was right. They needed sleep. They were already in debt to the hotel owner. They didn't have many options except to continue on and manage the consequences in the morning. "Manuel, please tell our host we'll settle our account in the morning if that's acceptable to him. Everything will become clearer after some rest, I'm sure."

When Manuel finished translating, the hotel owner nodded, patted her shoulder, then returned to the celebration that was somehow still going on around them. Leonora thanked Manuel for his help and he, too, disappeared into the wedding guests. In contradiction to the joyous atmosphere, a hard twinge squeezed Leonora's heart at the reality that a deadline was now ticking ever closer. She had to figure out a solution to their lack of funds by morning if she was going to prove she was capable of being the expedition leader she wanted so badly to be.

The six of them trudged back to the hotel in silence. Thankfully, the others seemed to share her current introspective mood. She wasn't sure she could stand questions about what they were going to do when she didn't have a single answer. And the others didn't even know the extent of the trouble they were in. Their lack of money was a fact she planned to shoulder alone. She would figure out something, even if it took all night. She would *not* let anyone see how much she'd failed them.

CHAPTER 20

*M*arcus hated that he'd been right. He hadn't wanted to be. He really had hoped Mr. Flemming would turn out to be an honest man and a better explorer and expedition leader than he'd seemed to be. But now, thanks to Marcus's inability to convince Leonora, they were stuck in a very unstable situation.

Following the others back to the hotel, he was thankful they at least had a place to stay. The owner seemed like a kind man who was concerned about their predicament. Even if it took some time to arrange their journey home, they could take comfort in having safe lodging available. The funds they'd raised for this expedition had been significant enough to allow them to stay for at least a week or two and still have enough to cover even an exorbitant price for passage back to California.

Marcus's bigger concern now was how this would affect his relationship with Leonora. She was more upset than he'd seen her since her father died. How had Mr. Flemming's betrayal been such a blow to her? She'd already admitted that he wasn't as upstanding and qualified as she'd initially thought, so this turn of events shouldn't be shocking enough to demoralize her so completely.

Was she more upset because of the way Marcus had responded when she told him about those letters? Was that the underlying cause of the way all light had been snuffed out from her eyes?

If it was, no one could blame her. He was the worst kind of cad for standing in front of her with his own secrets while throwing out angry words because of hers.

Back at the hotel, they all stopped inside the hotel lobby, as if none of them quite knew how to end a day filled with such unexpected twists and turns. Miss Alice was clutching Mr. Brighton's hand, which was almost sweet enough to make Marcus smile a little. Perhaps something good would come out of this mess, after all, if a couple was brought closer and learned to lean on each other through it.

Glancing toward Leonora, he couldn't help wishing she would reach for him that way. But instead, she remained a few feet away from him and addressed the group in a flat voice. "We should attempt to get some rest. Tomorrow, I'll see what can be done about finding a ship returning to California. One good thing is that we know the port here is popular for ships coming from and going to California. By this time tomorrow, I think we'll have a plan. Good night, everyone."

Without making eye contact with any of them, Leonora strode across the common area and hastened up the stairs, disappearing around the corner before the rest of them quite knew what to do. The others glanced around, Mr. Howard shifting from one foot to the other while Miss Alice chewed hard on her lower lip.

Miss Charlotte shook off the discomfort left in Leonora's wake first and broke the silence. "Well, she's acting odd, even considering this situation."

Miss Alice's eyes widened and she nodded in agreement. "While she's usually quite good at taking charge, right now she seems cold and unemotional, and that's not like her."

Mr. Howard tapped his ever-present pencil against one palm. "Perhaps the strain of feeling responsible for this is too much for her. It must be a heavy burden to know the trip she planned and was helping to execute has become such a tragic predicament."

Marcus pushed up his glasses and rubbed his chin, letting their observations fit into place with his own. Was that the true cause behind her sudden coldness? His heart lifted with the possibility that he might not have destroyed their budding relationship, after all. "You might be right. Maybe instead of waiting for her to arrange everything for us, we should take some responsibility and help fix this."

The others nodded while looking around at each other. As he had when his mother had confided in him about the swindler at the young age of seventeen and begged for his help, he felt compelled to step up and leave his comfortable circumstances to do something for a person he loved.

So Marcus drew a breath and shared his plan. "I'll go talk to her and let her know we want to help, that she doesn't need to handle everything on her own. If she'll give me our expedition funds, then tomorrow Mr. Howard and I will ask Manuel to help us figure out how to find a ship for the return trip. If you ladies and Mr. Brighton can keep Leonora from worrying too much, we'll be heading home again in no time."

While he wasn't sure those words were the truth, having a plan seemed to lift everyone's spirits. The other four settled into a group of chairs near the unlit fireplace in the lobby while Marcus headed toward the stairs. Standing outside the room Leonora shared with the Bauer sisters, he paused.

It seemed too intimate to knock on that door, knowing he

and Leonora were currently the only ones from their group upstairs. What if she was already preparing for bed? Maybe he should wait until morning. She might be sitting in there stewing over how much of what had happened was his fault or reliving the angry words he'd said about the letters. He should have had Miss Charlotte ask her for the money instead.

But then he envisioned Leonora's face when she'd turned to come up. In the cold, hard expression, he'd caught a glimpse of her quivering chin. She would not sleep well, if at all, with the responsibility for their situation hanging over her. She was most likely in there worrying and fretting. And he couldn't stand the thought of leaving her like that all night.

So he knocked softly. There was silence for a moment, then shuffling inside. Then the door cracked open, and Leonora's red eyes and tear-stained cheeks came into view.

"Oh, Leonora, darling. Please come out and talk to me." Marcus held out his arms, instinct driving him to do anything he could to repair this for her.

His legs went weak for a moment when she rushed into his embrace. He held her while she sniffled, and her tears dampened his shirt. He relished the feeling, even as he felt bad for enjoying it when she was upset enough to cry.

He couldn't be sure how long they stood there, but eventually, she swiped at her eyes with the back of one hand and stepped out of his embrace. "I'm sorry, Marcus. I'm so sorry for not listening to you."

So she hadn't been blaming him, but herself. He should have known she would take all the responsibility. "Don't apologize. You did what you felt was best. You aren't to blame for a man taking advantage of people."

"But you told me more than once. And I acted as though I knew better than you did. How you knew, I'm not sure, but the truth remains that you did."

Marcus shook his head before she even finished speaking. "And I've been telling myself that if only I had explained how I knew Mr. Flemming wasn't honest, things would have been different. We can both blame ourselves for the rest of our lives. Or we can look forward and figure out what to do next. I came up here to see if you would allow me to take the money we raised so the rest of us can handle the arrangements for you. It's hard for us to see you feeling so responsible for something that's not your fault, and we want to take some of that burden for you."

Leonora's gaze shifted away while she chewed on her lower lip. "That's a very sweet gesture, and I do appreciate it. But no. I'll go to the dock in the morning."

Softening his voice in hopes of showing her how much he and their friends wanted to help, Marcus took Leonora's hand. "I insist that you let us do this for you. Not because we think you can't, but because we don't want all of this to fall on your shoulders. We're a team."

To his shock, Leonora tugged her hand away, wrapping her arms around her waist. "I said I would handle it, Marcus. I can and will fix this. You needn't insist on anything."

Something was terribly wrong, and it seemed to be more than just her reacting to Mr. Flemming's betrayal. She was never so short with anyone. Marcus tried a different approach. "All right, then. I'll go with you. First thing in the morning, we'll visit the dock and see—"

"For the last time, Marcus, I said I would do it. The rest of you should focus on packing up and having your things ready to go in the morning."

"It's unlikely that a ship will be available tomorrow. Why would we leave here before we have passage arranged?"

"Because we already have to figure out how we're going to pay for these two nights, much less more of them! We don't have any money, Marcus." Leonora threw both hands in the air, her voice rising to an almost hysterical level as she spat the words at him.

A horrible, familiar sinking feeling washed over Marcus. He could remember every detail of a moment all too similar to this when another woman he cared about told him there was no money. That night in Father's study when his mother had finally revealed why she'd been crying in her room for days would be burned into his memory forever. She'd been duped by a man who said he would invest their money so they would be financially secure for the rest of her life, only to abscond with everything Marcus's father had left for them.

But this was Leonora. She was nothing like his mother. She was smart and strong and had been aware that Flemming wasn't the most reliable person. What had happened? "He stole the money? We can go to the authorities, then. We have a reason to involve law enforcement and see that he's arrested and charged with a crime."

Instead of perking up at the little bit of golden lining in a terrible situation, Leonora only looked more miserable. "No, he didn't steal it. I...I gave it to him. When we first arrived here."

The full reality of their situation now crashed down on Marcus. They were penniless and stuck in a dangerous country where they could barely communicate. Just like ten years ago, he was facing a situation he hadn't created, and that he had no idea how to fix. He wanted to. More than anything, he wanted to make this right for Leonora and the rest of them.

He reached for Leonora. No comforting words came to mind, but maybe his touch would be enough to start repairing the situation.

This time, instead of accepting his futile attempt to ease her pain, Leonora stepped back into the doorway of her room, gripping the edge of the door with one hand as if it was her lifeline.

An all-too-familiar hopelessness crashed over Marcus. Almost numb with it, he watched her shut the door. It took several moments of standing alone in the hallway before he managed to wander down the stairs, aware enough to know he needed to tell the others they would have to change their plan in the morning.

He found them all waiting in the lobby, right where he'd left them, as if the world hadn't fallen apart. They all looked at him expectantly, but what could he say? "I...I think we'll need to rethink the plan in the morning. Leonora—" His voice cracked on her name, bringing heat rushing up his neck. "We'll just have to handle this in the morning. Try to get some sleep." He turned to escape, hoping for some privacy before the other men returned to the room they shared.

Privacy was not to be found, though. Both men followed Marcus, Mr. Brighton closing the door behind them once they reached the room. It wasn't large, anyway, and with four beds packed in, space was at a premium. Marcus ground his teeth together. He didn't want to add lashing out at his friends on top of everything else he regretted, but why couldn't they give him a few minutes alone?

The other two men didn't look as if they noticed his growing frustration, though. They dropped onto their beds, Mr. Brighton leaning forward with his elbows propped on his thighs and Mr. Howard crossing one ankle over the opposite knee.

Mr. Brighton began. "I assume it didn't go well?"

Marcus shook his head. "No, I certainly wouldn't say it went well." He flinched at the scorn in his words. That hadn't been necessary.

Mr. Howard's gaze sharpened. "We're here as your friends, who need to know what's happening if we're going to help. You needn't snap at us."

He was right. What Marcus had been doing for the last ten years—bottling up his worries and shouldering everything alone—had ceased to work. Maybe it never had. Was it time to let others into his private life so they could help him through a time like this?

Marcus swallowed against the dryness in his mouth and drew a deep breath. "Mr. Flemming not only left us here, but he had also been holding all our money. Or most of it, anyway. So we're well and truly stuck here unless we can figure something out."

Marcus stared at a spot in the corner where the plaster wall was flaking, unable to meet the other men's eyes. But he looked back across at them when Mr. Brighton hummed. "I don't find that too difficult to believe."

The complete understanding in his tone, with no hint of censure or blame, eased the tightness in Marcus's chest. "No," he agreed, "it isn't exactly unexpected."

For a few minutes, they sat without speaking. Marcus's anger had receded, replaced by wildly tumbling thoughts and partial solutions that didn't solve their problem.

Mr. Howard eventually resumed the conversation. "And how is Miss Thornton handling this betrayal?"

Marcus jumped from the bed to pace the few feet of open floor, running one hand through his hair and adjusting his glasses. "Not well at all. And I very likely made things much worse. She told me something else earlier, and I reacted without considering how it would make her feel. That must have made learning about Mr. Flemming's betrayal all the worse for her. I'm afraid she'll never forgive me for how badly I've acted tonight."

Mr. Brighton nodded sagely. "You could choose to believe that. Or you could trust that she'll come to understand."

"It can't be that easy, though. Just believe, and it will happen? That's never worked for me, not in troubling situations in my life or in my faith."

Mr. Howard tilted his head to one side, regarding Marcus with serious eyes. "It *is* hard to have faith that God cares enough about each of us to redeem things that don't work out how we expect. But it doesn't change the truth that He does."

Mr. Brighton straightened. "Certainly. Why, all of us have times when God doesn't seem to be listening to our prayers, but that's the very meaning of faith. We have to choose to believe that He's still good, even when it doesn't look like it."

The truth they spoke settled around Marcus like a heavy blanket, comforting and significant. But could he let himself believe it? "But what if *nothing* in my life looks like God cares?"

Mr. Brighton's eyebrows shot up. "I don't think you're looking hard enough. You're healthy, as are your mother and brother. You have friends in us. And you have Leonora. Isn't she enough to make you believe God has *something* good planned for your life? I know being blessed with the gift of Alice's love would sustain my faith for the rest of my days."

Marcus dropped back to sit on his bed again, and the other men let him consider all they'd said. In light of their words, he could see the lies he'd been telling himself for years. Just because something bad happened, it didn't mean God didn't love him as much as others or didn't listen to his prayers as He did theirs. Marcus had been living his entire life based on deceptive thoughts.

And it was time to make a change before he lost the biggest blessing God could have granted him.

❧

It had been terrible when Charlotte had come to Leonora and revealed that Mr. Flemming had left them. Worse when Leonora realized her stupidity had stranded them with no money and a debt owed to the hotel owner. But watching Marcus's trusting expression shatter in the hallway was a devastation she never could have prepared for.

She couldn't accept his comfort, though. She'd done too

much damage as the expedition leader. And now she faced the knowledge that she might have done irreparable harm to her relationship with Marcus as well. He'd always had such faith in her, but after this, he would never see her as a strong, capable woman again. He would always look at her and remember one of the worst moments of their lives.

Curled in a ball on the bed, Leonora clutched an already wrinkled letter, still sealed in its envelope. She'd found it at the foot of her bed upon entering the room earlier, but she hadn't gathered enough courage to open it before Marcus knocked. The handwriting wasn't the neat, flowing script she'd come to expect in the letters. Instead, it was heavy and hurriedly scrawled. And her stomach sank with suspicions about the source.

Now, with nothing left to lose, she slid her finger under the flap to loosen it. Her gaze jumped around the words at first, but she read enough to confirm her worst fears, even without a signature. Vernon Flemming had tricked her from the very start.

He'd planned every step. He was a real explorer, apparently, but he'd decided it was far too much work for too little money. This scheme had started months ago, when he'd been at a restaurant in New York City and overhead several men from the Explorers Club membership committee discussing a letter she'd sent that asked them to consider opening their ranks to women as well as men. Their mention of her father had piqued Mr. Flemming's interest, and after some research into Papa's accident, he'd decided to take advantage of her pain by setting into motion a plan to get her to raise money for him.

He had arranged lectures in Milwaukee and once there, had hired a woman to write out the letters while he dictated them so no one would connect the handwriting. Leonora was more tenacious than he'd assumed, though. The letter explained that he thought she would raise funds to send him on the expedition but that she would never gather the courage to go. Then he would disappear with the money. Instead, she'd begun the journey with her friends in tow, so he had to devise a way to get rid of them while he kept the money. Thus, the unscheduled stop in Mazatlán.

The way he explained his motives with such brazen thoroughness—as if certain she couldn't harm him even with the truth written out—rankled almost as much as knowing that every moment of it had been preventable. If only she'd trusted Marcus more, she would have made different choices. Instead, she'd let her pride get in the way and entangled them in a mess she couldn't get them out of.

She'd been so certain this was God's will, the path He'd opened up for her to achieve the dream she'd cherished for so long. Why had He given her such an interest in exploration if this disaster was going to be the result? And it wasn't as if she wanted to pursue exploration for her own benefit. She didn't want fame or fortune. She wanted to shed light on history and spread God's love to those who may not have heard it. Why would He create her with that desire and bring her so far to then leave her stranded when He could have prevented all of it?

All night long, Leonora went over and over the details of everything that had happened since she received the first letter. All her mistakes piled heavy on her heart, and the anger building there kept her from turning to God with them, as she normally would have. By the time weak light broke the horizon the next morning, her heart had shattered. All she wanted was to stay in that bed until someone else fixed the situation.

But there was no one else. She'd destroyed Marcus's faith in her and let down her friends, and she was the only one who could fix that.

So she dragged herself up, noticing halfheartedly that Charlotte and Alice had already left the room. She pulled on a skirt and waist without bothering to check if they matched or were even on straight, then made her way downstairs with heavy steps. It was very early and very quiet in the hotel, but that was for the best. The first item on her list was to explain the full situation to the hotel owner and request time to figure out how they would pay for their stay. She would much rather face that conversation without an audience.

However, when she rounded the corner in the staircase, she stopped short at the sight that awaited her. Marcus was already at the counter speaking with their host, with Manuel at his side. As she approached, she couldn't help overhearing Marcus explaining the situation. "Since that swindler left with our money, we're in a difficult situation. But we appreciate your kindness and understanding."

With those words, Marcus reached out and handed the owner a stack of bills. Leonora blinked for a moment as her mind fought to understand. Had he somehow gotten their money back? Where had that come from?

She must have made some sort of sound because all three of them turned her way. Manuel nodded a greeting. The hotel owner smiled, his expression filled with enough understanding to make tears burn in Leonora's eyes.

But it was Marcus she couldn't look away from. She'd been certain he would never again look at her with the adoration she'd been growing used to. But there it was, as strong as ever. His strained lips softened into a half smile, and his gaze roamed her face. He reached out for her hands with both of his while he walked toward her. "Leonora, I'm sorry for how we left things last night. I feel terrible that you must have worried all night. I shouldn't have left you in such a state."

After everything she'd done, the way she'd doubted him, Marcus's first concern was for her feelings? He was too good for her. A sniffle snuck out of her before she could stop it, the tears now brimming over. Marcus raised a hand to rest on her cheek, and that was too much. Leonora pressed her face against his chest and let the tears fall, let all her roiling emotions out, despite their audience.

Once the tears began to dry up, one question refused to remain in Leonora's thoughts. She raised her head, trying not to be overcome again by the love that shone in his eyes. "Marcus, where did that money come from?"

His smile widened. "It amazes me that you still don't know the effect you have on people. I've seen time and again how strangers come to love you right away, and the people we've met in Mazatlán are no different. Manuel brought it this morning. They didn't know about our financial situation, but when he told his family at the restaurant that we're stranded, they got together and shared what they could to help us. Because they care about you, Leonora. That's what makes you a better leader than Flemming. Not experience...or connections. You reflect God's love through the care you show in every interaction with people, and in turn, they care about you."

Hope that had been absent over the long night began to build in Leonora's heart again. Were his words true? She stopped that thought in its tracks. Hadn't she already learned that she could and should trust Marcus? It was time to listen to what he had to say. And believe it.

Marcus's brow wrinkled and he squeezed her hand. "Let's sit down for a minute. There's something else I need to say, and I don't want anything to remain between us."

Together, they claimed the chairs by the front door. Marcus pulled his seat close enough for his knee to press against hers. And even then, he leaned in as he spoke. "Overnight, I realized it's past time I tell you what happened to my family. I'll begin by saying that my mother begged me to keep it a secret. She was so ashamed and worried that if anyone in society knew, they would shun us, and everything she'd known her whole life would be gone. I never would have kept it from you if I hadn't made a stupid, youthful promise to her."

Leonora's stomach clenched. She'd been waiting for this moment, but now that it had arrived, nerves arose. Would he reveal that his family had no money as Alice had claimed? Or something far worse? What kind of terrible secret had he been keeping?

CHAPTER 21

*M*arcus could hardly believe the story was finally leaving his lips. It wasn't what he'd thought he would do last night when the reality of their full situation overwhelmed his thoughts. But he'd come to a point where his mind was clear of the emotions that had threatened to engulf him. After talking with his friends, he'd done something he had never managed to do before—speak God's truth to himself so he could make a wise decision.

For years, he'd been making choices based on the lie that God wouldn't help him, that God had let his family down and Marcus would have to fix things on his own. But the change in perspective that came with physical distance from his family helped Marcus see how wrong that was. God had never left him. Marcus had stopped looking for the reality of God's love and faithfulness in his life.

Now, he was finally ready to face his mistakes and reveal the last part of himself to Leonora. "My father's death was unexpected, but he had taken great care to leave us in a stable situation. We could have lived comfortably for the rest of Mother's life, at least. I'm sure everyone in Milwaukee knows that much."

Bolstered by his newfound determination to step away from the lies that had held him captive for all these years and encouraged by the sincere attention on Leonora's face, Marcus drew a breath and continued into the more difficult part. "But Mother didn't want a comfortable lifestyle. She wanted lavish. She wanted to keep spending as she had when Father was alive and like her friends did. While Father saw no problem with a man working to support his family, Eli claimed he was the heir to a fortune, and therefore, it wasn't acceptable to expect him to work. Mother supported Eli in that, driven by her fear of society's judgment."

"So you took that job at the bank to support them," Leonora stated as if she immediately understood where he was going with the story. If only he could stop there and let her believe he'd worked all those years to supplement what his father had left them. But that wouldn't help her understand his recent actions, and it wouldn't help him move forward.

"I did, but there's more that happened first." Marcus paused, rubbing one hand across the back of his neck as discomfort welled in his chest. "I've never told this part to anyone. I planned to discuss it with my mother when we returned home and warn her that I'm not going to keep her secret from you anymore, but, well, I don't want to hide anything from you ever again, from this moment forward."

He paused, pulling off his glasses and using his handkerchief to wipe them while gathering his thoughts. Leonora waited, giving him her undivided attention, which went a long way toward keeping him committed to this task. "My mother was at least wise enough to realize that she would spend Father's fortune in no time if she continued on how she wanted. Unfortunately, she was inclined to find a short cut, rather than to pursue legitimate means. So when a man came around talking about how he could grow our funds to double or triple what Father left us by making the right investments, she jumped at the chance. Without telling me or Eli."

"Oh, Marcus. I assume he did to her what Mr. Flemming did to us?"

"Of course. He disappeared the moment Mother gave him everything we had. That was the moment Eli should have assumed responsibility, but he and Mother both made up their minds that no one could know. Her pride and Eli's arrogance got in the way of making wise decisions. She wanted to go on living in a way that wouldn't reveal to anyone that we had nothing left, but she also wanted Eli to keep playing the part of the financially secure heir. So it fell to me to save them."

Hearing it out loud, Marcus couldn't quite believe he hadn't told Leonora in the first place, back when it happened. Yes, his mother did look gullible when the truth was told, and Eli had responded with typical laziness, which no one who had met him would ever have trouble believing. But that didn't make the truth less necessary. Attempting to save his family's reputation had only caused more trouble.

Her eyes softened in understanding, and she reached out to clutch his hand in hers. "You were only seventeen when you started working at the bank, Marcus. You shouldered their burden all these years without saying a word? You're a better son and brother than they deserve."

He shook his head at that. "Oh, no. I have plenty of faults. I helped them pretend for all that time. I should have refused to cover it up from the start. Instead, I allowed myself to be treated like a failure while they lived off my hard work. And I lied. They were small lies, but I lied so many times to so many people about our situation. I withheld so much, especially from you."

Feeling the need to impress upon Leonora the way she'd helped his faith grow, Marcus angled himself to face her and cradled her hand with both of his. "Last night, because of the situation we're in, I finally realized those little untruths and hidden details were sins I needed to be forgiven for. Both by God and by you. I'm sorry for hiding this from you and for the lies I told in the process. If I'd been honest with you from the start, you wouldn't have had any reason to doubt what I said about Mr. Flemming. I knew he was trouble because of all the signs I recognized in him that were the same as the man who swindled my mother. But I couldn't tell you that because of my cowardice over the last ten years. My choices caused you this pain, and I'm so sorry."

Marcus hadn't quite known what to expect from her reaction, but when she stood, pulling him up with her, his heart beat faster. Then she nestled herself against his chest, and Marcus gladly wrapped his arms tight around her. She squeezed his waist as she spoke words that were muffled but would never leave his memory. "I'm sorry too. You deserve far more trust than I gave you, Marcus. This isn't entirely your fault or entirely mine."

She tilted her head back to look up at him before continuing. "Do you think God can use this for something good, as the Bible says? I thought this expedition was God's way of finally giving me what I prayed for all these years, but now it's all crumbling. And I'm afraid my faith might be too."

Hearing her express doubts when her faith had always been so inspiring to him shook Marcus for a moment. But what an opportunity he had, to encourage Leonora to grow the way she always did for him. Unwinding one arm from around her, he gestured between them. "I don't know what God has planned, but this change between us has already come out of the expedition. There aren't any more secrets between us, and we can move forward in trust and honesty...and love."

Marcus held his breath while her eyes widened. Would saying the word out loud prove too much for her at that moment? But then her lips curved upward, and a glow settled on her face. "That's true, isn't it? We couldn't love each other well with secrets in the way, and we might have kept hiding them forever if not for this difficult situation. Maybe that's what God intended all along."

The relief at her confirmation of returning his feelings was even greater than that of sharing his family secret with her after so long. Marcus lowered his head and met her upturned lips with more passion than ever, mindful of the public location but unable to go on without kissing her again. Her arms raised to twist around his neck as she pulled up on her tiptoes to get closer to him. Marcus let himself run his hand over the length of her back one time before breaking the kiss.

The way her eyes shone as they pulled apart almost brought him back for another, but a cleared throat nearby stopped him. All four of their companions stood between them and the counter, each looking bemused in their own ways. A hot flush started working up his neck, but what did he have to be embarrassed about? He was in love. So he gripped Leonora's hand in his and turned his attention to supporting her while she led their group once again.

～

*T*alking with Marcus had erased all the guilt Leonora had felt overnight, all the building regret and doubt. She'd believed God's plan was for the expedition to be a success in the way she defined it. But the truth was, God didn't always work the way she wanted Him to. He did what was best. She might not understand how this was the best result, but God didn't have to explain Himself for her to trust Him. Her job was to be open to doing what He called her to do.

And right now, it was time for her to do her part, which, according to Marcus, was to call on the people who cared about her because she had been kind to them.

So Leonora straightened her shoulders, lifted her chin, and faced the group. "Here's the complete truth of what we're facing. Mr. Flemming had all our money with him, except the little bit I kept for our excursion. Thanks to Manuel, the wonderful local people gave us enough to pay our host for the rooms, but we still need to secure our passage home. Marcus said he and Mr. Brighton intend to see what they can learn about the ships that stop here and if anyone can help us arrange the trip, so they can get started on that. I'd like Mr. Howard to handle any money given to us by the locals here, so we can keep good records of it. Alice, Charlotte, and I will see if we can scrounge up something to eat. We'll meet back here at lunchtime. Do you all feel that will be effective?"

To her relief, everyone agreed, having a purpose and a part in fixing the problem an encouragement to their moods. It raised Leonora's spirits too. She stopped next to Mr. Howard to give him the money she'd meant to pay Juan with the night before, money she was now quite thankful he'd refused to take. Charlotte and Alice each handed him some bills they'd brought along, and Alice slid a gold chain from around her neck. When Leonora balked, Alice sent her a sweet smile and patted her hand. "I won't listen to a single argument. It's not precious, but it is valuable. I want to help."

And that summed up the entire day for Leonora. Everywhere they turned, someone was willing to help. Outside the hotel, Manuel caught up with Leonora and the sisters to tell them his mother wanted the whole group to eat at the restaurant for as long as they needed to and that she wouldn't take any money for the meals. Leonora tried to refuse and offer whatever they could afford, but Manuel shook his finger at her and said, "Do not try to argue with my mama. She always wins."

As he ran off to catch up with Marcus and Mr. Brighton, Charlotte turned to Leonora. "Now that our food problem has been solved so easily, we should visit the local authorities. Perhaps there's something they can do about Mr. Flemming."

Leonora shook her head. "I don't see what that would be. He's an American citizen. And the political situation here is unstable. I'm not certain involving ourselves in it would be wise."

But Charlotte dug in her heels, placing her fists on her hips. "Now Leonora, I know you like to handle things yourself. But it doesn't hurt to try. If nothing else, we can make it so he won't be welcome to stop here again. It's not much, but it might be a small bit of justice."

It felt futile, but Charlotte was so insistent that Leonora finally relented. With directions from the hotel owner, they made their way to the police station. By the time they entered the plain stone building, Leonora was more confident that this was the right move, after all. There was nothing wrong with seeking justice. After all, hadn't Mrs. Turner's choice to cover up a similar situation led to this entire thing happening in the first place? How different would Marcus's life have been if his mother had focused more on catching the man who hurt her family than on covering it up for the sake of her pride?

Determined to do the right thing for her friends, Leonora marched up to the first desk inside the humble building. An older man glanced up, took a double take when he saw they were American women, then asked, "*Qué quieres?*"

Leonora instantly deflated.

Leaning against Leonora's shoulder, Charlotte shook her head. "I forgot we wouldn't be able to communicate."

But then the man in front of them turned and called across the room toward one of the other two desks. A younger man in a matching uniform approached, stopping at his side. They spoke a few sentences in Spanish, and then the younger officer met Leonora's gaze. "How can we help you?"

His English was even better than Manuel's. With relief

spreading through her, Leonora explained the story to the young man, stopping every few sentences as he communicated her words to his coworker and a few times for Charlotte to interject.

Once they finished, the two policemen conferred quietly, although with the language barrier, they wouldn't have had to lower their voices at all. Leonora's certainty that this was the right thing to do melted into concern as the older man shook his head several times during the conversation.

Charlotte whispered, "I don't think this is going well."

Leonora bit the inside of her lip. "I don't think so either."

Finally, their interpreter turned his attention back to them. "I am very sorry, but there's nothing we can do. This man is not a citizen of our city, and even if he was, he is gone. You said yourself that you gave him your money, so he cannot be accused of stealing, only of leaving without you, which is not a crime."

Charlotte straightened, crossing her arms. "A crime *has* been committed here. He misled and abandoned us. You can't tell me that's not wrong."

Compassion softened the man's face, but he still shook his head. "Wrong and criminal are two different things. I wish it was different, but we cannot help you."

Pushing her chin high in the air, Charlotte whirled around on the toe of one dusty boot. "Fine. We'll go, then."

Arm in arm with Alice, Leonora followed Charlotte's lead back to the hotel with a mix of emotions roiling through her. She was tempted to give in to the same kind of devastation that had overwhelmed her the night before, but what purpose would that serve? She had resolved that morning to give her worries to God instead of trying to manage every situation herself, and now was the perfect time to practice that.

So she rested a hand on Charlotte's shoulder, pulling the sulking woman to a stop before they went inside the hotel.

"Charlotte, dear, I know it's difficult to hear that the authorities can't bring the kind of consequences we'd like to see for Mr. Flemming, but that doesn't mean there won't be any. When we get back to the United States, we'll pursue whatever avenues are available to us to make sure he can't do this to anyone else."

Charlotte turned and dropped back against the wall with a heavy sigh. "I know. It's so frustrating to watch him get away with this, though. Who's going to listen when we return, anyway? As that man said, he didn't steal the money from us. And he could claim any number of misunderstandings or mistakes to explain why he left us here."

For a while, the three of them stared out into the street, where locals were going about their business. Leonora spent the time praying, telling God how the situation was once again starting to feel like too much for her and asking Him to help all of them release the anger that came with this betrayal.

Suddenly, Charlotte bounced forward on her toes and snapped her fingers. "I've got it. The Explorers Club. We can enlist their help. He's a member there, right? That wasn't another lie?"

Leonora nodded, perking up a little herself. "Yes, I made sure to contact them before agreeing to any of this. That's a very good idea, Charlotte. Being removed from the club would at least put his character into question, which would hinder his ability to raise more money or gain the trust of anyone else he might try to trick. We'll contact them as soon as we get back."

Clinging to that tendril of hope, Leonora led the way to meet the others for lunch. Marcus and Mr. Brighton had heard of a ship expected to come into port the next day to deliver a shipment of equipment for the nearby gold and silver mines on its way to California. The dockmaster had agreed to send word to them when the ship arrived so they could try to arrange passage. Leonora and Charlotte shared their plan to keep Mr. Flemming from repeating his terrible deeds.

While their friends ate and talked, Marcus slid his chair close to Leonora's and lowered his voice so they could talk with some semblance of privacy. "I'm proud of you. I worried that you would be bitter about what Mr. Flemming did, but you seem to have worked out a way to find peace about it."

Leonora let all her love for Marcus come through in a smile. "That's because of your encouragement. This morning, I wouldn't have been able to do so. But you reminded me that God is bigger than this situation. I'm focusing on the fact that Mr. Flemming will ultimately have to answer to God for this, and that's far more frightening than answering to me, any day."

Marcus chuckled at that while he slid one arm around her waist. His fingers traced her side, and Leonora let herself relish the sensations his touch created. She also savored the lightness that came with letting go of the responsibility for everything that had happened. Giving her guilt, pride, and urge for vengeance over to God had allowed her to see that holding onto them would have only led her to bitterness.

Instead, she was now free to fill her life with the things she loved—like Marcus, and adventuring, and helping her friends explore the world. She intended to return home with a new perspective that would allow her to do what Papa had always done—follow God's lead, even if the path didn't make sense.

CHAPTER 22

*M*arcus stood aboard a hulking cargo ship, letting the ocean spray hit his face and marveling at the fact that they'd managed to get passage to return to America. God must have worked out all the details of their journey, after all, because it was close to miraculous.

Getting to this point had required a great deal of persuading since the captain of this vessel usually only dealt with cargo. He'd been hesitant to take on passengers until Leonora convinced him that they wouldn't need fine accommodations or be any trouble at all on the trip. It didn't hurt that she'd volunteered them to help with cooking and basic tasks around the ship as part of their payment. The agreement didn't make for an easy journey back, but at least it had worked.

During the entire process, Leonora had gone on and on about the way the locals of Mazatlán had come together to help them. Even after paying for the group's rooms, they'd brought more money to the hotel that went toward their passage, then sent them off with supplies to help entice the captain to allow them on board. She couldn't seem to grasp that her caring and curious nature often won her people's loyalty in an instant.

But Marcus intended to spend the rest of their lives helping her see it. He was looking forward to setting foot on dry land again, although not so much because of the trouble the trip had caused. While it had been unlike anything they'd expected, Marcus had found that he didn't hate traveling as much as he thought he would. Yes, it wasn't comfortable or easy, but it made Leonora happy. And it was more interesting than sitting in his office at the bank doing paperwork all day.

But he was ready to get back to Milwaukee because that moment would mark the beginning of Leonora being truly his. They had come through this trial together, and now he was confident nothing could stand in their way. Not his mother or Eli, not what anyone thought of their choices. As soon as he could, Marcus was going to talk to Leonora's mother and brother and then propose to her. He refused to wait any longer.

But for now, they still had a journey to complete. The ship was set to make port in San Francisco that afternoon. If all went well, they would get to the station in time to board the last train for the day and would be able to sleep while it carried them toward home.

The next few hours were a whirlwind of activity. The Exploration Society members helped cook one more lunch in the dark galley, then cleaned it from top to bottom while they waited for the ship to get to the dock. As they gathered their luggage, the captain half joked that they'd been such a help during that portion of the voyage, he should hire them on. When Leonora's face lit up at the idea, Marcus tugged her down the gangplank before she could agree.

As he'd hoped, they made it onto the late train, and Marcus slept like he never had before, despite the noise and constant motion. The morning dawned bright and clear. One more day, and they would be home.

Joining the others for breakfast, he had a feeling they all shared his excitement for the journey to be over. Miss Alice and

Mr. Brighton had their heads tipped close together in a corner, completely absorbed in each other's company. Miss Charlotte was reading a newspaper, and Mr. Howard was taking notes once again.

Marcus looked around. "Where is Leonora?"

Miss Charlotte and Mr. Howard also glanced around the buffet car. Mr. Howard shrugged while Miss Charlotte pursed her lips in thought before saying, "She left the sleeping berth with us earlier, but a bit ago, she excused herself. I thought she would have returned by now."

Panic washed over Marcus, but he forced it down. Leonora had proven she could handle herself. She was most likely talking with someone she'd just met or enjoying the scenery from a different car. He assured the others that he would find her and began walking through the train, one car at a time.

He finally found her in the last car, conversing with someone, as he'd thought. As he walked closer, Marcus's guard went up, hands clenching at his sides. It was the same man who had been following them on their first train ride, dressed in the same plain brown suit with the gold pin Miss Alice had mentioned on the lapel. But Leonora was listening with rapt attention and an easy smile on her face. So Marcus took a breath, prayed a quick prayer for their safety, and continued toward them.

Leonora saw him first and greeted him with a warm smile that dispelled all his concerns. "Good morning, Marcus. This is Mr. Jonathan Reade. Mr. Reade, Marcus Turner."

Marcus reached around Leonora to shake the man's hand, then she tugged on his sleeve before he could step back. "Please join us, Marcus. You'll be quite interested in what I've been learning this morning."

Marcus took a seat on the bench across from them, where he could see them both.

Mr. Reade rustled a stack of papers in his lap. "Miss

Thornton told me how I frightened the ladies on your trip out to California. I do apologize for that. I'm a private investigator, hired by a woman in New York who is engaged to Vernon Flemming. She suspects he's hiding a secret life from her. I've been following him around the country, gathering as much evidence as possible. But what Miss Thornton had told me about his actions in Mexico—well, that brings a whole new element to this case that will add to the list of crimes I intend to report to the authorities."

While that explanation sounded good, Marcus's suspicions were still raised. "How exactly did you know we would be returning on this train? We had expected to be gone for several more months."

Mr. Reade's mouth quirked in a smile. "A secret of my trade —always have a man on the inside. One of my colleagues is aboard the *Minden*. He was there to watch Mr. Flemming, but he reported your whereabouts to me before the ship left Mazatlán, guessing you'd try to return as soon as possible. From there, it wasn't difficult to watch the port for you and get on the same train."

The tension in Marcus's chest released, allowing him to take a good, deep breath for the first time in days. Not only were they almost home safely, not only had he and Leonora worked out problems that had been keeping a wall between them, but Mr. Flemming would be prosecuted, after all.

Marcus leaned back against the seat. How good it felt to know that this time, the con man would face consequences. With a light heart, he addressed the investigator. "And are you on your way home now that you have evidence of what Flemming is doing?"

Mr. Reade nodded. "I am. I've been on his trail since the fall while also working on several other cases. I'm ready to get home and rest for a bit. I'm sure you all must be relieved to have this troublesome journey almost at a close."

"You have no idea. My home isn't my favorite place, but I'll be appreciating it much more after this trial of a trip."

They both chuckled, and Marcus glanced at Leonora, hoping to see her eyes light up with amusement. But instead, she kept glancing his way, then immediately looking back at Mr. Reade when Marcus noticed. What more could be bothering her?

After a few more minutes spent exchanging details and pleasantries, Mr. Reade gathered his things and stood. "I appreciate your help, Miss Thornton, Mr. Turner. Thank you for sharing your story and helping me get this fraud the punishment he deserves. If you'll excuse me, I'm going to go have some breakfast."

Once the investigator exited the car, leaving Marcus and Leonora alone, Marcus shifted to the seat beside her and pressed his fingers under her chin, lifting it until she looked at him. "What's going on in that brain of yours? You're concerned about something. I can see it in your eyes."

She blinked a few times as if she was trying to clear away whatever he saw. But then one corner of her mouth lifted in a half smile. "It's unfair that you know me so well. If we were like other couples, you would still be figuring me out."

Marcus chuckled. "I doubt you'll ever stop surprising me, no matter how well I think I know you. Now, what's wrong?"

Drawing a deep breath, she squared her shoulders like a fighter getting ready for a match. "I can't help but remember that you weren't planning to come on this expedition in the first place. On your own, you would never have chosen this kind of travel. You even told me that you only came for me. It's not something you love or long to do, as it is for me."

Marcus straightened his glasses, then leaned closer so she had to look in his eyes. "What does that have to do with anything? I can't deny that I was motivated to go because I wanted to be there for you. But you knew that before we left. I don't see why that's upsetting you now."

As if rushing to get the words out before changing her mind, Leonora continued. "Because I could never ask you to keep traveling with me, not when I know your heart isn't in it. Marcus, I can't give up my love for exploration, and I can't bring myself to put any pressure on you to go with me. What if we resent each other years from now because we don't want the same things out of life? What if it's a problem we can't overcome?"

She paused only long enough to draw a quick breath, clearly intending to continue. But Marcus silenced her by rubbing his thumb over her lips. Sweet, beautiful, concerned Leonora. It was past time he proved to her that they were meant to be together. He only prayed she would listen.

~

*L*eonora gasped at Marcus's caress, but she certainly didn't mind it. His warm touch made her forget for a moment how worried she was about what their future would hold.

It didn't take long before reality returned, though, and she prepared to continue voicing the fears that had been stewing in her mind during the week on the cargo ship. Before she could start, Marcus shook his head, seeming to be aware of the wild directions her thoughts were going. "Leonora, take a breath and listen for a minute."

Lowering her head, Leonora tried to do as he asked while Marcus waited. When she was a little calmer, he met her gaze and continued. "We had different ideas about what our lives would look like for quite a long time. But I had to make most of my plans around providing for Mother and Eli. The moment Eli secured a fiancée who brings quite a lot of money into the marriage, he decided to take over the family estate as well. I'm free to do what I want for the first time in years."

He slid one arm around her, drawing her against his side as they sat next to each other on the bench seat. When his cheek rested on the top of her head, warm contentment filled Leonora, erasing much of the fear she'd been carrying around and allowing her to take his next words to heart.

"You know I quit my job at the bank before we left. My plan is to begin working as a surveyor. It may take some time for me to be secure enough to support us so we can marry, but it will give us the freedom to go wherever the Lord takes us. Leonora, it might not have started out being what I wanted, but I love traveling, as long as it's with you."

Leonora let his words wash away all the worries of the last few weeks. She'd been so worried that the mess she'd gotten them into might have ruined the beautiful relationship that had been in her grasp.

But then he stood, and before she could jump to the conclusion that he was upset, after all, he placed his hands on the back of the seat on each side of her. He leaned in close, his face filling every inch of her view when she looked up. To her endless amazement, there was still only love in his eyes.

"Leonora Thornton, you're a caring, compassionate, empathetic person who brings out the best in those around you. Any man would be lucky to have the chance to do even the smallest thing at your side, much less be there for the huge things you're going to accomplish. And I hope you're ready to hear that a lot because I'm going to work as long as it takes for you to believe it."

"So you're not ready to be done with me? After everything, you still want to be more than friends?" She was hardly aware of how desperate she was to hear him confirm those things until the words slipped from her mouth. But once they were out, she couldn't draw a full breath while waiting for his response.

Instead of speaking, Marcus lowered his lips to hers, a harder and more intense kiss than any they'd shared previously. The angle smashed his glasses against her cheekbones, but Leonora was too consumed with Marcus—with his touch and his words—to care. The train could have derailed, and she wouldn't have noticed one bit as long as Marcus kept kissing her that way.

Eventually, he pulled back, but he wouldn't let her look away. "Leonora, I love you. I've loved you since the moment I walked into your father's study and saw you poring over that map. I've loved you through every moment of growing up and thinking I would never have the freedom to tell you how I felt. A few challenges would never be enough to change my mind. It's you and me now. You're stuck with me."

Lightness filled Leonora, making her realize how much this had been weighing on her for the last few weeks. She reached up and ran her fingers over the layer of stubble he'd let grow on his cheeks. "No more secrets and no more doubts? Not for either of us?"

Marcus took her hand and pulled her up, immediately wrapping both arms around her and crushing her against his chest in the best way. "No more. Now that I know how it feels not to have secrets between us, I can't go back to keeping things from you."

The sincerity in his words was all the confirmation she needed. Together, they went to join the others and have breakfast. They sat side by side for the rest of the day, then again for the few hours the next morning. Outside the window, everything was greener than it had been when they'd left. There were even delicate flowers on the ash trees, a sure sign that spring had come in full. In Chicago, the group navigated changing trains again and before long, they were back in Milwaukee.

While they gathered their baggage and made sure everything was accounted for, Alice leaned against Mr. Brighton's shoulder. "It's strange to be back here, where the buildings and scenery and people are familiar, but to feel completely different inside."

The sentiment rang true for Leonora too. The expedition might not have gone the way they wanted, but it had incited change in all of them. It had forced them to face things that kept them apart from God and each other, things that made it hard to be fully themselves. So despite the apparent failure, God had taken them on that journey on purpose, after all. Maybe His way of working things out for their good in this situation hadn't involved their external circumstances, but instead was found in refining who they were and helping them grow.

Glancing at Marcus as the group said goodbye and went their separate ways to return to their homes, she had to admit that her circumstances had changed, too, just not in the way she'd thought they would. Now that they were back and facing their normal lives again, what would this new relationship look like? They'd been through so much together, and it was difficult to imagine how that would translate into their usual daily routine.

When she and Marcus arrived at her house, a mix of emotions washed over Leonora. Marcus must have felt something similar because he shuffled from one foot to the other as they stood on the front step, right outside the door. How did one say goodbye after being together almost all the time for such a long stretch? Should she invite him in? Or did he need some space, some time away from her?

Marcus opened his mouth and drew a breath to speak when the door flew open, startling them both. In a flurry of clothing, three small bodies flew out and tackled Leonora, almost knocking her to the ground. She laughed, wrapping her arms around as many of Cassia's boys as she could reach. "Oh, it's so good to see you all!"

The boys tripped over each other to tell her everything that had happened while she was gone, which apparently was a great deal. Cecil had caught a toad the size of his head in the garden. Eleanor had tried to chase the boys up a tree and fallen, spraining her ankle badly enough that she was still whining about it. The older boys had gone camping with their fathers and had endless tales of that adventure.

By the time she sorted through all the enthusiastic and highly embellished tales, Marcus had slipped away. A pang of regret brought a bit of sadness to the moment. She would have preferred to walk back through the door at his side. He was part of her family. If unofficially at the moment, it would be official soon enough.

Or had he left because he was unsure of what he wanted now that they were back in familiar surroundings?

No. Leonora mentally shook herself. If she'd learned one thing during the journey, it was that she could trust Marcus. He said he loved her and had insinuated he wanted to marry her. So she would rest in the certainty that he meant it. Letting the excited boys pull her into the house, Leonora prepared to tell her family all about the shortened journey and prayed that Marcus would have an easier time with his own explanations than he'd expected.

CHAPTER 23

*A*s Marcus walked into his house, the cold silence disheartened him as much as Leonora's absence did. He wasn't sure how he was going to explain to Mother and Eli that not only had the expedition failed, not only had they been duped as Mother had been years ago, but he'd also told Leonora all their family secrets without giving Mother so much as a warning.

As he crossed the foyer, the lack of connection to the place he'd always called home was clearer than ever. Home was Leonora. It was any moment she was by his side, no matter where they were. Since traveling with her, he now knew that it didn't matter if they lived in Mexico, Milwaukee, China—anywhere—as long as they were together.

Maybe the quiet, calculated life he'd once dreamed of wouldn't ever happen. Leonora was not a woman who preferred to stay in one place for long. But he didn't care about that as much as he once had. They would carve out a place for themselves wherever God took them.

It was that comforting awareness that gave Marcus the courage to walk through the door into the parlor, where he found both his mother and brother. He was ready to face this and deal with the consequences all at once.

The two of them looked up, startled. Mother even gasped.

Eli frowned at him over the top of an unfolded newspaper he'd been reading. "We didn't expect you back for another month, at least. Did you uncover all the treasures of the world that quickly, then?"

Bitterness rose in Marcus's throat, threatening to spill out in a sarcastic retort at the tone of his brother's words. But he thought of Leonora's sweetness in the face of Mr. Flemming's constant derision, the way she took setbacks with grace. He wanted to walk in his renewed faith the way she did. So he drew a deep breath and began with the truth, rather than anger. "Things didn't go as planned. As it turns out, Vernon Flemming is a con man."

Mother gasped, increasing the discomfort Marcus had felt from his first step back into the house. He'd never before dredged up the pain of the past on purpose. For years, every time something related to it came up in family conversation, she would burst into tears and hide away in her room for days. But no matter how painful, it had to be dealt with now. They'd all lived under the shadow of it for far too long.

So Marcus pulled a tufted chair close to his mother's seat and looked her straight in the eye. "Mother, there's something I need to confess to you. Leonora and I have loved each other for a long time, without knowing how the other felt. Before the trip, we discovered those shared feelings and have been moving toward what I hope will be marriage. While we were away, after we discovered Mr. Flemming's betrayal, I told her everything. All the details about Mr. Baptiste—what he did and our roles in covering it up for so long. She knows we don't have a fortune and that I've been working at the bank all these years to keep things running here for you and Eli."

Marcus finally paused. If only he could divulge the entire

story and then escape the room without facing the results of his confession. But that would be a coward's way out, the way he'd dealt with things for most of his life. It was time to change that pattern. So he squared his shoulders, ready to get all the pain of the last ten years into the open.

Before he could continue, Eli shrugged one shoulder. "As if it was so difficult for you, sitting in an office all day and controlling our finances as you saw fit."

Marcus had to take a moment and a few deep breaths before he could respond without letting his temper loose. "I think you mean holding the weight of responsibility for you and Mother, Eli. I didn't want to sit in that office—I had to. I didn't control the finances to limit you but because *someone* had to worry about making sure we had food and could keep the house."

Sniffling cut through the tension rising in the room. Marcus and Eli both turned to their mother, who had pulled out a handkerchief and pressed it against her mouth. Feeling worse than ever for making this moment necessary, Marcus slid off the chair to kneel in front of her. "Mother, I'm sorry. I wanted to wait and talk with you before telling Leonora. But I would have had to at some point—you must know that. Even Eli's fiancée will learn the truth sooner or later, despite his efforts not to tell her."

Looking at him through her tears, Mother reached out and rested one wrinkled hand on his cheek. "My dear boy, it's not that. You're right, of course. It couldn't remain a secret forever. For the last few years, I've been wondering how we would ever get out from under the weight of the mess I caused. I knew how wrong I was to let you take my mistakes on yourself for so long. But I don't know how to be as brave as you are. I don't think I can face the scandal if the truth is revealed to society."

Marcus took her free hand in his. "We don't have to be brave, just honest. You don't need to go out there and tell everyone all the details. We'll start with spending your money on things you need, not frivolities meant to impress society." He glanced over at his brother, who was watching them with a cautious expression. "And if Eli agrees, I can show him how to manage a budget that will allow you both to live comfortably enough on the money I've saved for you until he marries. But you will have to make changes."

Mother didn't seem convinced, but it was a moment of truth Marcus had never expected. It was a start toward them being a healthier family. Change might take time, but Mother and Eli could do it if they wanted to.

With a lighter heart, he sat down, and they talked about his trip, what had gone wrong and what had gone right. It was awkward at first, but even Eli participated with genuine interest after a bit.

Finally, Mother laced her fingers together in her lap and arched one eyebrow at Marcus. "And when will you bring Miss Thornton to have dinner with us? If you're going to propose to her, we should start spending time together."

He smiled, believing for the first time in years that such a meal would go well and not end with Mother or Eli belittling the woman he loved. "I'll arrange it soon. But it will be some time before I ask her to marry me. I quit my job at the bank before leaving on the expedition, so I have to work on being able to support her first."

His mother bit her lower lip for a moment, then her eyes widened, and she straightened in her chair. "I've got something to fix that. Wait here."

She jumped up with more energy than he'd seen from her outside of a society event in years. After she whisked out of the room with her skirts fluttering, Marcus glanced at Eli, who had dropped his newspaper into his lap and now stared at Marcus with a slack jaw and blank look.

It was a few minutes before footsteps pattered in the hall

and Mother entered the room with the same giddy energy as when she left. She rushed straight to Marcus and pulled her hand from behind her back, opening the inlaid wooden box she held to reveal a jumble of glittering jewelry. "Now that I've decided to embrace the reality of my life instead of destroying my sons trying to chase what I thought it should be, I'm ready to part with these."

Marcus looked up at her, warmth spreading through his chest. "Mother, I'm proud of you. I know wearing those has always been important to you."

"It was, but only because my friends envied them. That's not important anymore. I'm going to sell them, along with any other pieces I can find, to support us until Eli is married. That way, you can have the money you've been saving and use it to start your life with her sooner, without needing to worry about us. I won't keep you from your happiness a moment longer."

Speechless, Marcus stared at his mother. He gaped long enough that Eli took up his newspaper again with a huff. "Oh, thank her already, and get yourself to the jeweler tomorrow. That's the only way we're going to be rid of that moonstruck expression any time soon."

Marcus finally moved, rising to hug Mother and offering his brother an approving nod, which was returned with a surprising amount of respect.

With anticipation building in his heart, Marcus retired for the night. First thing in the morning, he would get to a moderately priced jeweler's shop he knew of. Mother and Eli were right. He'd loved Leonora since they were children, and she wouldn't balk at starting a frugal life with him while he built a new career. There was no reason to waste any more time before making their bond permanent.

∼

*S*unday morning dawned bright and clear, the first day of May bringing perfect spring-like weather. Leonora, however, couldn't seem to stay still.

After walking her home and then disappearing while her nephews distracted her, Marcus hadn't contacted Leonora once. Yes, it had only been two days. But it felt like a lifetime after they'd spent every waking hour together for close to a month. He'd quit his job at the bank before they left, so what could have been filling his days enough that he couldn't take time to see how she was settling back into normal life?

As she sat through the church service with her family, the root of her unrest struck her. She *wasn't* settling back in. She didn't want to, truth be told. The expedition, while unsuccessful in most ways, had still changed her. She knew now that she was capable of much more than leading a club and supporting her siblings' families, more than wishing she had the resources to go on adventures. She would never again presume to know what God had in store for her, but whatever it was, it would require her to step out of the comfortable, safe life she'd unintentionally built after Papa's death.

What she wanted more than anything right then was to talk to Marcus about all the questions that were in her heart and rolling around in her thoughts. He always pointed her in the right direction, and she could use a little of that clarity now.

Back at home after the service, Leonora headed toward the dining room, but Cassia gently grabbed her shoulder, stopping her in the hall. Her sister's expression was more serious than usual. Cassia pulled a thick parcel of papers and envelopes from behind her back and held it out. "Right after you left, I decided to do a little research of my own."

Leonora riffled through the pages—correspondence and official-looking reports. "What is all this about?"

"It's all the evidence that was gathered during the investigation of Papa's death. I contacted the Explorers Club, and they sent a man to bring us copies of everything they have and explain their conclusions. There are interviews with the crew, translations of the accounts from locals, even the report that was taken on the damage to the boat they were on when it happened. It's far more extensive and complete than we thought. And it's clear that it was indeed an accident."

Leonora stared at her sister. "I didn't think you had any interest in pursuing this."

Cassia's gaze softened, and her lips tilted upward. "I didn't. I was confident the Explorers Club did all they could. But I could see you wrestling with it before you left, and I wanted you to have the closure you needed in case you came home without answers."

Overcome, Leonora threw her arms around Cassia, enjoying the moment of camaraderie. When they pulled apart, Cassia went to check on the children while Leonora took the papers to her room to study later. Would Marcus want to review them with her? She couldn't imagine not including him in uncovering the answers to all her questions, but when would there be an opportunity?

The desire to see him again grew as they prepared for lunch, so when there was a knock on the door as she was overseeing Cornelius and Eleanor setting the table, Leonora's heart leaped into her throat. Only one person who needed to knock ever came to Sunday lunch.

Cassia beat her to answer it, though, leaving Leonora hovering in the dining room doorway while her sister greeted Marcus. But his gaze went straight past Cassia to lock on Leonora, stealing the breath right out of her lungs. He looked as handsome as ever in his brown suit, even while he twisted his felt hat in both hands. Had the trip changed him, too, making a meal with her family—which had been commonplace for so many years—into an event that made him uneasy?

That was unacceptable. Leonora marched straight to his side, took the hat, and dropped it onto the hall table. "I'm so glad you're here, Marcus. It wouldn't feel like Sunday lunch without you."

She wrapped her arm around his, pressing close to his side, and Marcus beamed a smile down at her. "I wouldn't miss it. You might like to know that things have gotten less uncomfortable at my house, though. Maybe next Sunday you'll join me for lunch there?"

Warm delight spread through her. It would have to wait until her family wasn't all peeking out of doorways along the hall to spy on them, but she looked forward to hearing what had transpired to improve the situation with his mother and brother.

A thump and shouting from the dining room set her into motion. Drawing Marcus with her down the hall, Leonora nodded. "I'd be honored. For now, though, will you help me make sure the children aren't throwing forks at each other instead of setting the table?"

The usual raucous behavior ensued once again, with Eleanor and the boys causing chaos while Felix and Paul pulled Marcus into their conversation about some stock or another. Once lunch was ready, all the family members took their usual seats at the table, with Marcus next to Leonora. Right where he belonged. Felix offered a prayer over the meal, and everyone started passing dishes and filling plates the moment he finished.

As they ate, Marcus seemed distracted. Felix had to repeat himself at least three times when he attempted to ask Marcus questions about the trip. Mother tried to start a conversation about what Marcus was hoping to do now that he was no longer working at the bank, but she gave up with an indulgent smile when he muttered short, almost nonsensical answers.

It went on long enough that Leonora began to worry. He'd

said things were improving with his family, so what could be wrong? Did he regret the decision to change careers? Was he doubting himself now that he was on the path to what he'd always dreamed of doing?

Once everyone finished lunch, they began spreading out around the house for a restful afternoon. Leonora's heart was still heavy over Marcus's mood. Could she encourage him somehow? He always did so for her, and now she could return the favor. So she drew him out into the garden, where Mother's flowers were beginning to open in a wild array of spring blooms. It was warm enough to bring out buzzing bees and set birds to chirping in the large maple tree that shaded one corner.

She hated to see him suffer a moment longer than necessary from whatever was making him anxious, so Leonora stopped a mere three feet past the door and turned to face him. "Marcus, something is on your mind. Will you tell me what it is? Are you worried about your future?" She rested her hand on his upper arm without pausing her words. "You're resourceful and smart and a hard worker. You don't have anything to worry about. You'll build the finest surveying career anyone ever saw and be so success—"

He cut off the flow of her words with a kiss that came so suddenly, it would have taken her breath away even if it wasn't the most delectable touch she'd ever experienced. The firm movement of his lips on hers chased away every word she'd been planning to say.

Leonora wrapped both arms around his neck, pressing herself against him from chest to knees. His hands rested on her back, holding her steady when the kiss threatened her balance.

After far too short a time, he pulled back. "I appreciate your concern for me, but I need you to let me speak for a moment."

She might have been embarrassed by her overzealous

babbling in any other situation, but with Marcus, she couldn't be. He looked at her with such fondness, with love brimming in his eyes, that she was able to smile in response while taking a step back and grasping her hands together in front of her. "I apologize. Go ahead."

Marcus pushed his glasses up into a more secure position, then paced a few steps in each direction while he spoke. "It's not my career that has my nerves on edge today. It's something far more important. And I didn't think I would be so nervous about it because...it's you, Leonora. It's always been you who remained by my side, who encouraged me, believed in me, *saw* me. I've loved you since the first day I met you, but I wasn't brave enough to admit it and risk looking like a fool if you didn't return those feelings. So I hid them for so many years. Too many."

When he stopped in front of her and took both of her hands in his, Leonora's nerves all stood at attention, waiting for what he would say next, hoping she was right about what she longed to hear him say. "I'm sorry I wasted so much time that we could have been together as more than friends. But I refuse to give up a single minute more. I spoke to your mother and Felix yesterday morning while you were out with Cassia, and they gave me permission to...well, I love you, Leonora. Will you marry me?"

Throwing herself at him, Leonora locked away every sensation of the moment in her memory. His hands catching her, his breath caressing her ear as he waited for a response, the way their hearts beat rapidly in unison. Unable to give up being in his arms for even a moment, she spoke against his shoulder. "Of course I will, Marcus. I love you, too, and I never want to even imagine a time when we aren't together."

He crushed her tight to him until she could barely draw a breath, and the relief she could feel in his movements fueled her joy. Finally, after all the years of pining for each other and believing things about themselves and each other that weren't true, there was nothing between her and Marcus but love and a bright, joyful future. While she couldn't—and wouldn't—begin to guess what that future would hold, Leonora could look toward it in complete confidence that God was holding them in His capable hands, and that in following Him, their relationship would grow into the adventure she'd always dreamed of.

EPILOGUE

September 20, 1911
Cairo, Egypt

*L*eonora used a small brush to remove sand from another few inches of ground with the utmost gentleness, thankful for the wide-brimmed hat that shaded her eyes from the endless Egyptian sun. It was intense even in the seven-foot-deep pit where she was working. Uncovering priceless historical artifacts was a slow, often tedious process, but it was one she'd fallen in love with over the month she'd been doing it.

The sound of feet clomping down the steps carved into the dirt wall broke the relative silence in the pit, but she didn't stop until brown boots appeared in her line of vision with a puff of dust. She squinted up into the sun, her heart jolting with a burst of love when she saw the dear face of her husband. How sparkling and new that word still felt, only three months after their marriage.

Holding out one roughened, tanned hand to help Leonora

stand up from the dirt, Marcus glanced around her assigned work area. "How's the digging going today, darling?"

Leonora rolled her stiff shoulders. "I found quite a few shards of pottery. It wasn't the most exciting day, though."

All around them, members of the archeology team and locals being trained to help on the dig site worked in similar pits dotting the vast ancient cemetery that was being excavated on the Giza plain. Behind them, the three towering pyramids dominated the sandy landscape. It was an awe-inspiring place to spend their time every day, without question. But even more delightful was the opportunity they had to participate in the lives of the local people they lived near and worked with. That had provided natural openings for them to share God's truth that they wouldn't have been able to create any other way.

Still holding her hand, Marcus tugged Leonora closer, and she giggled. "Have I told you today how proud I am of you? Getting to learn about archeology with such an impressive team is the opportunity of a lifetime. Even if you only ever find pottery."

"It was your surveying work that gave me the chance." A humble flush tinged his cheeks, but Leonora was prouder than she could express. After they'd returned from the ill-fated expedition, Marcus had managed to secure a position training with a very talented surveyor in Milwaukee. He'd learned quickly and started taking jobs on his own in no time. Not long after their wedding, his mentor had been invited to join the Harvard University team going to work on uncovering the cemetery at Giza. Uninterested in traveling for an extended time, he recommended Marcus for the job instead. "I know you'll point out that God opened the door, but your hard work helped."

Tweaking her nose in a fond gesture, he wiggled his eyebrows. "Thank you, my darling wife. But I didn't come over here to trade compliments. I have something you'll want to see."

He slid a battered envelope from his jacket pocket, and Leonora gasped. "Is that a letter from home?"

It was difficult to get consistent mail service across such a great distance and a significant language barrier, so receiving a missive, no matter how delayed it probably was, brightened Leonora's day every time.

After tearing the envelope open, Leonora skimmed the words in Cassia's familiar handwriting, giving Marcus the most important points as she went. "The Exploration Society has started working with the Milwaukee Public Museum to catalog all their new acquisitions, and this summer, they traveled to Colorado to study dinosaur bones that were found last year. Mr. Howard is doing a wonderful job as president, don't you think?"

Marcus nodded, his fingers tracing up and down her arm, which would have distracted her from anything less important. "Marcus, listen. There's news about Mr. Flemming."

Instantly, his hand paused on her waist. "Good or bad?"

"Good, I suppose. At the time Cassia wrote this, the trial was underway, and Mr. Reade was confident there was plenty of evidence to convince the jury that he's guilty of at least one of the counts of fraud."

It had taken some time before Leonora could forgive Mr. Flemming for his duplicity, but now she was able to feel mostly pity, mixed with a little relief that he wouldn't be able to deceive anyone else.

Thankful things at home were going so well while they lived their dream in Egypt, Leonora refolded the letter and slid it into her pocket. Then she put both hands on Marcus's chest and pushed up on her toes to steal a kiss. But before their lips met, he craned his neck to look at something behind her. "What is that?"

Leonora followed his gaze but didn't notice anything that should have caught his attention. "Where?"

Marcus walked to the far corner of the pit, to a spot she hadn't gotten to yet. He knelt and lightly brushed some sand back. Stretching forward to look over his shoulder, Leonora finally saw the darker, bluish stone. She grabbed a brush and joined him.

As they worked together to remove the dirt and sand as delicately as possible, a crisp stone corner came into view, clearly the work of human hands. Leonora rocked back on her heels and tried to calm her racing heart. "Marcus, we might have found a statue."

For a long moment, they both crouched in the dirt and stared at the smoothly carved stone. Then Marcus looked at Leonora. "You should go get Mr. Reisner. He'll be the one to lead the excavation."

The thought of approaching the lead archeologist, a Harvard University-trained expert, set Leonora's pulse racing. She'd had doubts about this venture, about whether or not God wanted them to travel so far from home again, this time indefinitely. But Marcus had reminded her time and again that they couldn't ruin God's plans. He had known every choice they would make before they even existed, and He would use them for His glory no matter where they were.

So she rose, smoothed her lightweight tan skirt, and drew a deep breath.

Marcus stood as well and tipped his head down to drop a kiss on her lips, something Leonora hoped she never got used to or took for granted. She stood on the cusp of the future she'd always dreamed of without knowing at the time that it would be as wonderful as this. Adventure awaited her, Marcus loved her, and God directed her steps. It was more than she could have imagined during those years of waiting. And the beautiful reality of it was worth every moment and every question.

Taking Marcus's hand, Leonora let him help her climb the

stairs, and together they walked confidently into whatever God's best meant for their future.

Did you enjoy this book? We hope so!
Would you take a quick minute to leave a review where you purchased the book?
It doesn't have to be long. Just a sentence or two telling what you liked about the story!

Love Christian Historical Romance?
Looking for your next favorite book?
Become a Wild Heart Books insider and receive a FREE ebook and get exclusive updates on new releases before anyone else.
Sign up for our newsletter now.
https://wildheartbooks.org/newsletter

AUTHOR'S NOTE

Unlike the first two books in the Adventurous Hearts series, *An Uncharted Dream* isn't directly inspired by one woman. Instead, it's based on a group of courageous, motivated women who pursued their passions despite never being allowed to join the males who did the same things.

The New York City-based Explorers Club has had members involved in a variety of famous discoveries and expeditions since being founded in 1904, including the first successful trips to the North and South Poles, the first moon landing, the top of Mount Everest, and the deepest point of the ocean. However, the Explorers Club didn't admit women until 1981. Many of us reading this were alive when they finally began recognizing the contributions of women! That's not because of a lack of interest on the ladies' part, though. Women were present on expeditions around the world for as long as men had been exploring. They were simply barred from joining this very influential men's club.

This story is loosely inspired by one particular group of ladies, who would have been highly qualified to join the club if not for their gender. In 1925, four women began meeting together out of frustration over being excluded—Marguerite Harrison, Blair Niles, Gertrude Shelby, and Gertrude Emerson. All of these women had done extraordinary things and traveled extensively. They were writers and photographers who tried to share the knowledge they gained from their experiences, but they were considered to be more of a novelty than serious explorers. They even had to watch as some of the men who were on the same trips with them were allowed to join the Explorers Club. In response, the four women ended up creating their own club, the Society of Woman Geographers, which was only open to women who had experience in exploration or various sciences. While this book differs from the real history in that it is set earlier and features a co-ed club, I'm sure alternatives like this existed around the country from the formation of the Explorers Club on.

An Uncharted Dream talks a lot about exploration in southern Peru. The real history that inspired the use of that location was the search for the last capital city of the Incan civilization. That hunt led to the rediscovery of Machu Picchu and the actual capital, Vitcos, both by Hiram Bingham in 1911.

Another important historic site I included in the story was Las Labradas, a beach north of Mazatlán, Mexico. It's a beautiful area on its own, but the presence of hundreds of ancient carved stones called petroglyphs scattered across the beach makes it a fascinating historical location. It's estimated that the carvings were created between 1000 B.C. and 300 A.D.

I also couldn't help including an Egyptian dig site. I can imagine many readers who would pick up this story share my interest in history, and I'm pretty sure a phase of fascination with Egyptian archeology goes right along with that love of the past.

The archeological project I included was one of several that happened at the pyramids in Giza around 1908-1911. Three different teams split up the massive cemetery that surrounds the pyramids and each excavated their sections simultaneously. The one I included in the book was run by Harvard archeologist (and fellow Hoosier) George Reisner. His team uncovered a series of large historically significant statues of the pharaoh Menkaure. You should definitely research Menkaure and the excavations around the pyramids more if you're as delighted by that information as I am.

While the history in *An Uncharted Dream* was fun to research, and I loved writing my first friends-to-more romance, it's the spiritual threads that I hope touch your heart. Leonora is plagued by doubts about God's will for her life, fearful that her decisions can somehow ruin His plan for her. I think it's a common worry for those of us who are raised in Christianity, and maybe for newer converts too. So I hope you'll see through her story that we place far too much emphasis on the role of our life decisions in God's plans. He's so much bigger than any mistakes or bad choices we could make. He's already given us His will in the Bible, with verses such as Micah 6:8, Romans 12:2, and Matthew 6:33. He wants the same thing from and for all believers. There's freedom for us to make our own choices in anything outside of that.

I hope you've enjoyed the Adventurous Hearts series. If you want to find out what's coming next from me, you can visit my website and sign up for my newsletter at www.abbeydowney. com/newsletter. You can also find me on Facebook and Instagram. Happy reading!

ABOUT THE AUTHOR

Abbey Downey started writing inspirational romance stories during naptime when her kids were babies and found she couldn't stop. She previously published two books with Love Inspired Historical under the pen name Mollie Campbell. She also works with Spark Flash Fiction producing a quarterly digital magazine that contains love stories under 1000 words.

A life-long Midwestern girl, Abbey lives in central Indiana with her husband, two kids, and one rather enthusiastic beagle. She loves watching her kids play sports and fixing up a 1900 farmhouse with her husband. Connect with Abbey at www.abbeydowney.com.

If you love historical romance, check out the other Wild Heart books!

Byway to Danger by Sandra Merville Hart

Everyone in Richmond has secrets. Especially the spies.

Meg Brooks, widow, didn't stop spying for the Union when her job at the Pinkerton National Detective Agency ended, especially now that she lives in the Confederate capital. Her job at the Yancey bakery provides many opportunities to discover vital information about the Confederacy to pass on to her Union contact. She prefers to work alone, yet the strong, silent baker earns her respect and tugs at her heart.

Cade Yancey knows the beautiful widow is a spy when he hires her only because his fellow Unionist spies know of her activities. Meg sure didn't tell him. He's glad she knows how to keep her mouth shut, for he has hidden his dangerous activities from even his closest friends. The more his feelings for the courageous woman grow, the greater his determination to protect her by guarding his secrets. Her own investigations place her in enough peril.

As danger escalates, Meg realizes her choice to work alone isn't a wise one. Can she trust Cade with details from her past not even her family knows?

∼

A Summer at Sagamore by Lisa M. Prysock

Can summer love survive amid mystery and mayhem?

When Abigail Greenwood and her cousins settle in for their annual summer retreat at the stunning and impressive Sagamore Resort in the Adirondacks, all she wants is to spend as much time as possible plunking out stories on her typewriter. But when her cousins insist she join them in the tradition of choosing a beau to adore from a distance during their stay, she reluctantly plays along, setting her sights on a mysteriously quiet and aloof guest. What started as harmless fun soon changes as Abby finds herself captivated by debonair—and handsome—Jackson Gable. Who is he, and why does his arrogant amused smile exasperate her so much?

When a series of events causing mayhem and mischief begin to occur at Sagamore, journalist Jackson Gable is determined to get to the bottom of it, since his father is an investor of the resort. Jack has a nose for mysteries, but he may have to use his recently earned law degree and some of his posh family connections to sleuth out the culprit. Are the events connected? Why are they happening? And why can't he get the beautiful Abby off his mind?

~

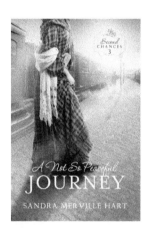

A Not So Peaceful Journey by Sandra Merville Hart

Dreams of adventure send him across the country. She prefers to keep her feet firmly planted in Ohio.

Rennie Hill has no illusions about the hardships in life, which is why it's so important her beau, John Welch, keeps his secure job with the newspaper. Though he hopes to write fiction, the unsteady pay would mean an end to their plans, wouldn't it?

John Welch dreams of adventure worthy of storybooks, like Mark Twain, and when two of his short stories are published, he sees it as a sign of future success. But while he's dreaming big with his head in the clouds, his girl has her feet firmly planted, and he can't help wondering if she really believes in him.

When Rennie must escort a little girl to her parents' home in San Francisco, John is forced to alter his plans to travel across the country with them. But the journey proves far more adventurous than either of them expect.